The Officer's Siren

Rain City Tales Book One

Brent Archer

*For Greg, Elle, Delilah, Luke, Maia, Tracy,
and the Roses with love and gratitude.*

Acknowledgements

Thanks to Annie Lou Pru for initial edits, Maia Strong and Gemma Juliana for keeping me motivated, and Delilah Devlin and Elle James for getting me started on this amazing adventure!

CHAPTER ONE

MIKE BRYANT STOOD bleary-eyed on Fourth Avenue in downtown Seattle after completing his overnight security shift at the Iceland Hotel. The damned truck should have been here. *Why does this shit always happen to me?* Trudging back into the lobby, he dragged his exhausted frame to the desk.

Isaac, the cheerful front desk manager, stepped around from the back of the counter and raised an eyebrow. "Thought you'd left."

"My truck's gone," Mike grumbled.

His dark-haired boss lay a hand on his shoulder. "Are you sure you remembered where you left it?"

Mike nodded. "I always park in the same spot, and I know the truck was there last night."

"Well, better call the cops," Isaac suggested. "I'm sure they'll find it." He returned to the desk.

Pulling out his cell phone, Mike's mind drifted back to the conversation he'd had with his cousin Alan two days ago. He'd gone out to start and warm up his pickup and then came running back in, chilled from the cold.

Alan stood at the door. "You know, Mike, if that truck gets stolen, the police will fine you for leaving it running and unattended."

"What?" Mike's eyes had widened while he drew his

arms around himself, breath floating in front of him.

Alan sighed. "This is the city, not rural Wisconsin. Even your rusted-out truck is a target. The thieves are usually opportunistic, and a warming truck with no driver is an easy grab."

Mike bristled. "My truck's in great shape."

With a frown, Alan glanced at the idling truck. "What's left of it, yes."

With a scowl, Mike hugged his arms closer. "It gets me to work and back."

Alan laughed. "So would the bus."

"Fine, Alan. I'll go back and freeze my ass off." He glared at his older cousin.

"Okay, have a good night." With a grin, Alan ducked back into the house and shut the front door.

"911, what's your emergency?" Mike came back to the present, focusing on the operator's voice.

"My truck's been stolen," he grumbled.

"All right, sir, let me get some details and I'll send an officer to you."

Mike gave the operator the make and model of the truck, and his location. After ending the call, he waited on a plush seat by the crackling gas fireplace.

His phone dinged as he fought to keep his eyes open, and Mike glanced at the screen showing an update to his news stories notifications. He nearly missed the cop's entrance, but he glanced up in time to see the tall officer, the weight of his exhaustion temporarily dispelling. Early thirties, the blond hair cropped on the sides but long on top framed a rugged face. His intense blue eyes scanned the room.

The crotch of Mike's slacks stirred as he took in the

handsome specimen in front of him. The officer's muscular arms bulged from his regulation blue shirt, a sturdy chest stretching the fabric. His classic V waist led to long legs.

The officer leaned on the front desk across from Isaac, his firm, round butt on full display. "I'm looking for Mike Bryant."

Mike stood up and approached the officer. "That's me." He tried to ignore Isaac's smirk.

Their gazes met, and the cop paused for he spoke again. "Officer Jason Lynch. You're missing a truck?"

Fumbling for words, Mike stuttered a response. "Yes, um, I left it parked out front last night, but, uh, now it's gone."

With half a grin, Officer Lynch took a blank report from the binder he carried. "Fill this out, please."

Mike took the paper and scribbled in the required information. He tried to keep his attention on the form but found himself more focused on the officer. He finished signing his name and glanced at the blond cop. Their gazes locked again, and a smile slid across Lynch's face. Heat rose into Mike's cheeks.

Nodding at the form, Officer Lynch maintained the grin. "All finished?"

Mike handed over the page. After glancing over the form, the cop took a business card from his wallet. "Here's how to contact me. We'll see if we can locate your truck."

Relief washed over Mike. He extended his hand. "Thank you."

Officer Lynch grasped it in a firm grip and shook. "My pleasure, Mr. Bryant." One of the officer's fingers rubbed along Mike's wrist, and he struggled not to let his gasp escape.

He returned the gesture, his pants suddenly too tight again. Trying to regain control, Mike released the officer's hand. "If you do find it, I'll come pick it up. You don't need to impound it."

Lynch nodded. "I'll be sure to call you." He smiled, winked, and strolled out the door.

With his knees nearly giving way, Mike stumbled back to the chair by the fire. He plopped down, trying to get his erection to subside.

Chuckling, Isaac came over from the desk and sat down next to him. "Quite a hunk."

"Yup," Mike nodded, a grin forming on his lips. "He's interested in me, too."

Isaac's lips formed a smirk. "Right. And how did you deduce that?"

"He did this." Mike took Isaac's hand and rubbed his finger along the wrist.

Isaac rolled his eyes. "To be young and full of pent up sexual energy."

Mike winked. "Who said it's pent up?"

JASON SAT IN his patrol car and adjusted his crotch. He hadn't intended to show his interest, but the gorgeous young man drew him to make a move. He liked tall lanky men in their twenties, and Mike fit the bill exactly. The long sandy hair and naturally tanned skin didn't hurt either.

Shaking his head, Jason stared into the rearview mirror at his own eyes. "What the hell were you thinking? You *know* how much trouble you'd be in if he reported you."

Should the Chief find out he'd made a pass, his career would break up on the rocks of unemployment. At least the guy returned his gesture.

He eased back in his seat and called in the information on the missing vehicle form, then climbed out of the cruiser to begin his final beat of his morning. Strolling up Fourth Avenue toward Blanchard Street, he paused and glanced down an alley.

A surge of apprehension shot up his spine. Two dumpsters sat overturned with garbage piled high across the tops about three hundred feet into the narrow alley. Jason quickly rounded the corner and cautiously eased his way down the cobbled roadway.

Once he cleared the dumpsters, he found a truck sat parked with its doors wide open. Approaching the abandoned vehicle, his hand slid to his holstered gun. He scanned the alley, and, once convinced no one waited to ambush him, he removed his hand from the sidearm and poked his head into the cab of the truck. A single key protruded from the ignition. Nothing else seemed broken or damaged on the inside. He noticed the ripped upholstery and the cracks on the dashboard. *Or at least, no new damage.*

Jason stood and examined the exterior of the vehicle. Rust had eaten away most of the metal around the wheel wells. A fresh dent adorned the front bumper, but otherwise, all the other nicks and scratches were covered in rust.

He checked the license plate on the front of the vehicle. *Wisconsin. Bingo.* Retrieving the young man's info from his pocket, he punched the number into his cell.

Two rings later, a tired voice answered. "Hello?"

Jason smiled. "This is Officer Jason Lynch. I think I found your truck."

"No way," the young man's voice perked up. "Already?"

"Dark grey, kind of rusted, and Wisconsin plates?" He omitted the word *junker*.

"Wow, yeah, that's it," Mike confirmed.

Jason smiled at the youthful enthusiasm. "It's in an alley off Blanchard and Fourth. Are you still downtown?"

"Yeah. I'll be there in about ten minutes. Thank you *very* much."

"Okay. See you soon." Jason ended the call and closed the doors of the truck. Checking his watch, he realized his shift had ended ten minutes ago. His stomach rumbled. Perhaps a breakfast date with the young man.

★　★　★

"ISAAC, HE'S ALREADY found my truck!" Mike bounded up to his bemused boss behind the desk.

His boss glanced up from the computer. "Where is it?"

"About five blocks away. I'm heading there now."

Isaac winked at him. "Have fun."

Heat rose into Mike's cheeks again, but he smiled. "I'm sure he has to get back on duty."

Leaning his arms on the counter, Isaac nodded toward the door. "You'd better go find out."

"See ya." Mike trotted out the door and down the street. The cool morning air helped his tired state. Both his frustration and anticipation mounted, waiting at each corner between the hotel and Blanchard Street for the lights to change.

Huffing and puffing, he turned the corner and hurried

down the alley past two overturned dumpsters. Officer Lynch stood leaning against his truck. Mike stopped in his tracks to take in the luscious man before him. He looked even sexier than before with the morning sun shining down the alley onto the metal buttons of his uniform. With his blond hair illuminated, he seemed to glow.

Mike's cock stirred and began to harden, pressing against the fabric of his slacks. Heat flushed his face, and he desperately tried to will his traitorous dick back down.

With a wave, Jason pushed himself upright. "Hey, found your truck. Did you leave a key in it last night?"

Furrowing his brow, Mike pulled a set of keys from his pocket and raised one above the others. "No, I have my key right here."

He tilted his head toward the cab. "There's a key in the ignition."

After a few moments of confusion, realization dawned, and he slapped his palm to his forehead. "*That's* what happened to my spare. I thought I'd lost it in Wisconsin."

"Must have fallen and got hidden under one of the mats. Thieves will find anything if they have the opportunity to search."

Mike approached the muscly SPD officer. "I'm grateful for all your help."

Jason arched an eyebrow. "Is that so? How grateful?"

Hesitating a moment, Mike searched the officer's face for the meaning of his words. He threw caution to the wind and took another step forward. "Very." He hoped he hadn't misunderstood the officer's hand signal at the hotel.

With a grin, Jason took a step back. "I'm off duty now. Let's get the paperwork done, maybe have some breakfast."

Embarrassment burned in Mike's face at the apparent rejection of his advance. Then the second part of the officer's words sunk in. "Wait, you want to grab a bite with me?"

Jason nodded. "You interested?"

Mike's cock throbbed with a vengeance, and nothing he could think of would make it subside.

Jason glanced down with a laugh. "I'll take that as a yes." He scanned each direction down the alley and took Mike's hand to guide him to the front of the truck. "Maybe after breakfast, I can take care of your problem."

Realizing he's read the signals correctly, Mike sighed in relief. "Are you sure?"

"Consider it the service part of *To Serve and Protect.*"

"I'd like that," Mike stammered out, pressing against the crotch of his work slacks.

Jason smiled. "Good. Let's get going. I know a great spot nearby." He glanced at Mike's hand, not quite suppressing a leer. "For breakfast, I mean."

CHAPTER TWO

THE SMALL CAFÉ on Westlake Avenue seemed the best spot to take Mike. Good food, fairly inexpensive for downtown Seattle, and a familiar place for Jason to get to know his date. He pulled Mike's chair away from the table and then pushed it forward as Mike sat down. He strode around the table and lowered himself into his own seat.

Mike picked up the menu. "I haven't been here before."

"This is my favorite breakfast stop. I like to come here after I finish work." Jason admired the young man across the table from him. Mike's angular face and full lips stirred his lust. "So, you work a night shift, too?"

"Yeah," Mike said, still scanning the menu. "My cousin helped me get the job. I'm saving up to go to school in the spring."

"Oh yeah?" A warning flag sprang up in Jason's mind. "How old are you?"

Mike smirked, lowering the menu enough for Jason to see his full face. "Don't worry, officer. I'm legal. I turned twenty-two last week."

With a sigh of relief, Jason opened his menu. "You decided to wait to start college?"

Mike's smile disappeared. "It's money."

"Sorry, didn't know it was a sore subject." Jason

scanned the offerings, unsure if he'd just blown his chances with Mike.

Mike puffed out a breath. "No, I'm sorry. I've had a lot of folks riding me about going to school lately. My cousin is really insistent, and in some ways, that's also kept me from going."

Jason placed the menu on the table, leveling his gaze at Mike. "Maybe we should change the subject."

"It's okay," Mike shrugged. "I had a rough childhood, or I guess you could say I didn't have a childhood. My mom didn't want me to go to school because she was afraid I'd turn into a gay liberal."

Jason shook his head. "Wow."

Mike chuckled. "Yeah. Anyway, since I've achieved both of her fears without setting foot on a college campus, I figured it was time to get my education."

The waitress approached their table. "Hi, Jason, how are you doing today?"

"Great, Sonja." Jason nodded across the table. "This is Mike."

Sonja grinned. "Pleased to meet ya. What do you boys want for breakfast?"

As he buried his face into the menu, Mike gestured to Jason. "After you. I'll know by the time you order."

Not sure why he bothered with the menu, Jason ordered his standard. "I'll have steak and eggs. Eggs over-easy, and the steak medium rare. Pink, but not raw."

"Gotcha." Sonja wrote the order on her pad. "And coffee?"

"Please."

She set her gaze on his companion. "Okay, hun. What can I bring ya?"

Mike returned his attention to her. "Double stack of pancakes, lots of butter and berry syrup if you have it."

"You got it. I have blueberry or strawberry."

Mike grinned. "Blueberry. Oh, and I'll have a hot chocolate with whipped cream."

Sonja finished jotting Mike's order. "Comin' right up." She collected the menus and strode to the bussing station to enter in their order.

Leaning forward, Mike locked his gaze on Jason. "You've heard about me. What's *your* story?"

Considering his answer, Jason sat back in his chair. His gaze didn't waver from Mike's green eyes. Something about this young man made him want to spill his entire story. "I just turned thirty-one, and it's weird not being in my twenties anymore. I went to college at eighteen and got a bachelor's in criminal justice. Three years ago, I left Spokane and came over here to join the SPD. I'm loving it."

Sonja returned with Mike's hot chocolate and Jason's coffee. "Your order's coming right up." She bustled to the next table.

Jason stirred creamer into his coffee, thinking about the rest of his story. The years at the Spokane Police Department, and the heartbreak that led him to Seattle.

Mike took a sip of his chocolate, giving himself a whipped cream moustache. "Why did you move from Spokane?"

With a smile, Jason took a swig of his coffee, then set the cup back on the table. "SPD had an opening, and I wanted out of Spokane." His mind drifted briefly to his prior partner. "Nothing to stay there for."

"I hear things are changing with the Seattle police."

Mike wiped the cream from his lip with his napkin. "And the new police chief seems to be cleaning house."

"That's for sure." Jason's thoughts shifted to his tough as nails boss. She'd fired four of her assistant chiefs and replaced them, not giving a damn what the union or the rest of the force thought about it.

Sonja brought their breakfast and the check. Jason snatched it before Mike could react. As Mike's eyes widened, Sonja laughed. "Don't bother trying to talk him out of paying, hun. It's a standing order from Officer Lynch that I only accept money from him."

Mike's eyebrow lifted, but he stayed quiet.

Fishing in his pocket, Jason pulled out his wallet and handed his credit card to the waitress. "Thanks, Sonja."

"I'll be back with more coffee." She strode away.

Narrowing his eyes, Mike sliced his knife into his stack of pancakes. "You didn't have to do that."

"Sure, I did," Jason grinned with a little feeling of triumph. "You're just starting out, and breakfast certainly won't break my bank. I'm glad you joined me."

Mike closed his eyes for a moment and then resumed cutting up his pancakes. "Thanks for breakfast."

"My pleasure."

With a grin, Mike poured some of the syrup onto his meal.

THEY STROLLED THE two blocks to Jason's cruiser. To Mike's relief, his truck was still parked behind the police car.

Leaning against his truck door, Mike yawned. "I'm exhausted." The weight of the large breakfast in his stomach left him feeling content and drowsy.

"Me, too." Jason tapped his foot against the curb before addressing Mike again. "Can I see you again? I'm off tonight, tomorrow, and Monday. I could cook dinner for you this evening or make breakfast for you in the morning."

Taken aback, Mike wondered what the officer had in mind. His initial behavior at the hotel seemed to indicate a quick fuck with no strings, but his offer to cook a meal felt more like a date. Not that he'd mind a date with the handsome cop. The surprise must have registered on his face.

Jason's mouth dropped into a frown. "Uh, that is, if you want to see me again."

Quick to allay Jason's fear, Mike nodded. "Yes, please."

"I know I promised to help out with our mutual problem in the alley," Jason said with a wink. "But you look pretty beat. When are you off next?"

Warmth spread through Mike's face. "Tonight's my Friday. I'm supposed to meet up with my cousin and his husband Monday evening, but otherwise, I'm free."

Jason wriggled his eyebrows. "So, what do you think? We could go for a hike around Mount Rainier or bicycle out on Vashon Island tomorrow afternoon."

Mike grinned. "Sure, breakfast in the morning and a hike in the afternoon sound great."

"Perfect," Jason said with a grin, his eyes drooping. "I'll look forward to it." He ran a hand through his hair. "I'm about to fall asleep. We'd both better get home and get some rest."

"Yeah, me, too." Mike hesitated, not really wanting to

walk away. "Mind if I give you a hug?"

Jason's smile widened. "I'd love a hug." He opened his arms, and Mike stepped into his embrace.

Wrapping his arms around Jason's muscled body shot a fresh shot of desire into his crotch. He gave a quick squeeze and stepped back from the embrace before he embarrassed himself.

With a chuckle, Jason also took a step back. "We'd better go before we end up skipping the second date and going to straight to bed."

"You say that like it would be a bad thing," Mike wriggled his eyebrows.

"Nah," Jason replied, his tired amusement lighting his face. "I just know I wouldn't be at my best, and I want the first time with you to be memorable in a good way."

More warmth spread through Mike's exhausted body. "I have no doubt it will be."

DRAGGING HIMSELF INTO his home in the Queen Anne neighborhood, Jason trudged up the wooden stairs, dropped his uniform to the floor, and fell onto the guest bed. Though he'd prefer his own bed, he'd done laundry before his shift and hadn't had time to fold and put away everything. The breakfast with Mike sapped the last of his energy. Closing his eyes, he let sleep wash over him.

When he woke, he realized he'd slept away the re-mainder of the morning and half of the afternoon. Though he'd reset his sleeping for the weekend with a full night's sleep later in the evening, he felt refreshed from his nap, and set about cleaning his house in anticipation of Mike's arrival in the next morning. Three weeks' worth of dust bunnies and mail needed attention, to say nothing of the state of his yard. The mountain of clean laundry stacked on his bed also beckoned.

Taking the night shift hadn't worked out as easy as he'd hoped. Though a night owl by nature, he could rarely sleep through the day, and it was only on the weekends that he even came close to catching up. Being exhausted all the time didn't lend itself to tidying up.

First things first, however. His stomach rumbled, and he set his thoughts to a late lunch. He grabbed a pair of snips from the kitchen counter and stepped outside through the back doorway, descending the steps from his deck to the small garden spot behind his house. Some kale remained, and a new crop of spinach dotted the bed. Three large pumpkins with a blush of orange on their skins pushed out from mildew-covered leaves.

He cut the majority of the kale and some of the spinach. An onion hidden under one of the kale plants joined his harvest. He returned to the house and washed off the greens, then cut up the kale. Next, he diced the onion and dumped the pieces into his smallest cast-iron skillet with a little bit of safflower oil. Turning the gas to low, he left the onions to simmer.

A pungent smell of rotting food assaulted his nose when he opened the refrigerator door. Wrinkling his nose, he dug through the crisper, finding a cucumber and a lone yellow carrot. A block of gorgonzola sat nestled in the back of the cheese drawer. Retrieving the vegetables, he shut the refrigerator door with a mental note to find the offending, rotten item and toss it into the compost. He sliced the cucumber then checked on the caramelizing onion.

The aroma made his stomach rumble again. With a

chuckle, he patted his belly. "Down, boy. Down." Glanced over his ingredients, he realized he'd have more salad than he could eat. As usual.

He stepped into the dining room and grabbed his cell from the sideboard, unlocking the phone and pulling up his contacts. He tapped the screen, and the face of his best friend, Emily Sanders, grinned at him as the call went through.

"Hey, Jason. What's up?" She sounded out of breath.

"Want to come over?" he asked, already knowing the answer. "I'm in the process of making enough food to feed the entire SPD."

She laughed. "So what else is new?"

"I met a guy," he stated, certain the news would have her banging down his door.

"WHAT?!" she yelled into the phone. "You bet I'm coming for dinner. Be there in half an hour. What should I bring?"

"Just yourself," he said. He considered having her bring a bottle of wine, but quickly thought better of it. "I still have that bottle of wine from the last party we threw. We'll crack it open over dinner."

Letting out a whistle, Emily's voice held a tinge of incredulity. "That was a year and a half ago. You haven't had it yet?"

Jason shrugged. "It's a good vintage. I wanted to wait for a special occasion."

She paused letting his words sink in. "Meeting this guy is a special occasion? Okay, I'll be there in fifteen minutes. I haven't finished my run yet today."

He returned to the kitchen to check the onions. "Well, okay, maybe it isn't *that* special of an occasion, but I think

I still have a couple steaks desperately needing cooking, and the wine will pair well."

"Alrighty, Sweets, I'll see you in a little bit." She ended the call, never one to say goodbye.

With another Jason, Jason ran a wooden spoon through the onions, surveying the golden color and turning down the flame. He rarely had trouble convincing his best friend to join him for dinner. Even in college, he did the majority of the cooking for the two of them. They'd toyed with the idea of getting married, but Emily knew he was gay. She'd let him down gently, telling him he'd be much happier with a guy, and promptly introduced him to Christoph.

Christoph.

A surge of sadness washed over him. He missed Christoph. His death was the main reason he'd left Spokane behind, though they were considering a move before Christoph had gotten sick. Even after four years, the loss stung, though he no longer had to excuse himself from the room when his former lover was brought up in conversation.

With a sigh, he returned his attention to preparing the salad. He pulled a glass bowl from the cabinet next to the refrigerator and dumped the kale, spinach, cucumber and carrot into it. After turning off the gas, he lifted the skillet from the stove and used a spatula to scoop out the caramelized onions onto the top of the salad. Foraging on top of the fridge, he found a ripe tomato and three avocados. Two of the avocados were brown, but the third was still green and perfectly soft. He sliced it and the tomato, adding them to the mix. Enduring another blast of acrid air, he retrieved the block of gorgonzola from the fridge.

He crumbled the cheese into another bowl and mixed it with olive oil, apple cider vinegar, and a sprinkling of thyme. Pouring the mixture over the kale, he tossed the greens and set the salad aside on the counter for the flavors to mix.

Holding his breath, he returned to the refrigerator and found the steaks he'd marinated four days ago in a glass pan. He let out his breath after closing the door to the fridge, vowing to give his kitchen a good scrub before Mike's arrival I the morning. Carrying them out the back door, he fired up the grill on the deck and started the steaks cooking, careful to note the time.

The doorbell rang, but he didn't bother to answer it. Moments later, Emily stepped through the back door, all smiles with her curly red hair tied back and wearing a teal and pink tube-top with black Lycra running tights.

Jason regarded her with a raised eyebrow and a be-mused smile. "What the hell are you wearing?"

"Oh, shut up," she spat. "I put on the first things I found."

Wrinkling his nose, he prodded the steaks and flipped them over. "Why do you even *own* that train wreck?" He swung his head to stare at her with narrow eyes. "Are you trying to make your boobs look bigger?"

She roared with laughter. "Honey, I'm half Italian." She cupped her voluptuous bosom. "I don't need to enhance my shelf, thank you very much."

"Then what's with the tube-top?"

She grinned. "Found it on sale."

He snorted. "Well, you'd better return it. The Eighties want it back."

Planting her hands on her hips, she shook her head. "You shit. This is back in fashion."

"And if you were twenty years younger, I'd say it works for you."

She rolled her eyes. "If I were twenty years younger, I'd be eleven."

With a smirk, he faced her fully. "Exactly."

"Moving on… First question—why don't you have the wine poured? And second—start at the beginning and tell me all about this guy."

GIDDY WITH EXCITEMENT, Mike checked his backpack to make sure he had everything he needed for hiking. Shoes, jeans, water bottle, sweater, lube, and condoms. He smirked at the last two items, barely able to wait to get Jason into the woods.

A knock on his bedroom door interrupted his thoughts. His cousin, Alan, poked his head into the room. "Hey, there's dinner if you want some."

"Thanks," he replied, still surveying the contents of his bag. "I'll be right there."

Alan left, closing the door behind him.

Tugging the zipper shut on his backpack, he turned and checked himself in the mirror. Hair styled, slacks clean, shirt pressed. Ready. He strode from his bedroom, slamming the door behind him. The hardwood creaked beneath his feet as he entered the living room through the archway and dumped his backpack by the front door.

Alan's husband Craig regarded him from the head of the dining room table. "Hey, there. Didn't hear from you this morning before I had to go to work. Everything go okay?"

Guilt hit him at not checking in with his cousins. They asked very little of him for staying there, but letting them know he got home safely from work was the cardinal rule.

"Yeah, sorry about that," Mike said, stepping into the dining room. "Work went fine, but my truck got stolen."

Alan carried a roast pan from the kitchen and set it on the table. "Stolen? That rust bucket?"

Rolling his eyes, Mike settled in at his spot at the table. The pork roast filled the room with a mouth-watering aroma, and Mike's stomach rumbled. He loved his cousins' cooking. Definitely one of the perks of living with them. That, and the fact that they never yelled, unlike most of his family in Wisconsin.

"Alan, behave," Craig tutted. He turned to Mike. "What happened?"

He stuck his tongue out at Alan then answered Craig. "Turned out thieves found the key I thought I'd lost two years ago and went for a joy ride."

Alan glanced out the window with a frown. "Obviously, you got it back."

"Yup," Mike replied triumphantly. "And I met a guy today."

Setting a carving knife and a two-pronged fork in front of the roast, Alan took his seat at the table. "A guy?"

Mike warmed as the image of Jason in his full uniform filled his thoughts. "The police officer was smokin' hot."

Craig cocked his head. "So, the cop found your truck. Who's the guy you met?"

With a lift of his eyebrows, Mike smirked. "The cop."

Alan sat back in his chair laughing. "You made a move

on an SPD officer? Daring."

"Actually, he made a move on me by inviting me to breakfast." His smirk softened into a smile.

Craig leaned in, elbows on the table. "And *after* breakfast?"

The smirk returned. "I came home. That's why I was late. He works nights, too."

Alan carved up the roast. "You didn't bring him home with you?"

Placing his napkin in his lap, Mike narrowed his eyes at his cousin. "Now, why would you assume that?"

Craig chuckled. "Because we *know* you."

The three of them laughed as Alan served up their plates. Mike's excitement grew at the mashed potatoes and pork gravy that accompanied the roast and grilled carrots.

"It's a good thing I'm going hiking tomorrow. Your cooking will make me fat." He took a bite, savoring the blending flavors on his tongue.

With a snort, Alan cut into his meat. "Cry to me when you're forty-three like we are, eh, Craig?"

"Definitely," Craig frowned. "You have such a high metabolism, we have to keep stuffing you just to keep you at a healthy weight." He took a sip of water. "So, tell us about Officer Friendly."

Closing his eyes for a moment, Mike visualized the sexy cop. "Blond, blue-eyed, and built like a brick house. In his early thirties."

Alan's eyes widened. "Early *thirties*?"

"What's the problem?" Mike leveled Alan with a withering stare.

Patting Mike's hand, Craig smiled. "There's no problem. It's just a bit of an age difference. I thought your usual type was late teen or early twenties."

"I do like them young," Mike admitted. "There's something about this guy, though. Besides, it's not like I'm going to get married." Mike checked his watch. Ten minutes until he needed to leave. He wolfed down his pork and potatoes and washed it all down with some water. "Thanks for dinner, guys. I need to get going."

As he got up from the table, he grabbed his plate and silverware. Passing Alan, he made for the kitchen.

Craig caught his arm before he crossed the threshold. "Hold on, you didn't even tell us his name."

"It's Jason. Jason Lynch."

CHAPTER THREE

AFTER REFILLING EMILY'S wine glass, Jason flipped on the gas fire and settled into his favorite rocking chair near the hearth. Emily took a sip of her wine and stretched her legs out on the sofa.

"So, this kid's in his early twenties?"

"Twenty-two last week," Jason replied, not sure he liked where this conversation was heading.

"Kinda young for you, isn't it?" she purred, teasing in her voice.

Jason took a sip of his wine, enjoying the tannins dancing across his tongue. Mike didn't seem like a kid to him, and the age difference didn't bother him in the slightest.

"I don't see a big deal. He's well into legal age," he said with a wink.

Grinning at him over her wine glass, she waggled a finger. "Naughty boy. Still, I'm glad you're finally getting some after all this time. I've been worried about you."

Jason leaned forward in the rocker. "Now don't get too excited. We haven't done anything yet, and even if we do, it'll just be a little fun. Maybe I'll get a friend with benefits out of it. I'm not looking for a relationship per se."

She shrugged. "I'm happy you're even willing to entertain the idea of someone sharing your bed. You've been celibate since Christoph died, and I *know* he wouldn't have wanted you to pine for him the rest of your life. It has been four years after all."

The mention of Christoph's name brought a pang of guilt to his thoughts. In some ways, the interest he had in Mike felt like cheating. Emily did have a point, though. Christoph told him shortly before he died to mourn for a little while but be sure to live his life.

Emily continued. "This little fling will be good for you. He likes to hike, you said?"

Pulling himself out of his memories, Jason nodded. "I'm going to take him out to Rainier tomorrow after we have breakfast and a nap. He works nights as well."

Her signature smirk appeared. "A nap, eh?"

"Yes, a nap, nosey Nellie. He'll need the rest so we can get in a good day's hike."

Raising an eyebrow, she grinned. "What happens if you exhaust him?"

Jason settled back in the chair and took another sip of his wine. "Well, he might just have to spend the night."

With an easy laugh, Emily pushed herself off the couch. "Oh, you men are all the same. Gay or straight, it's all about the sex."

He put on his best offended look. "Sex is *not* a bad thing."

"Never said it was." After taking the last sip of her wine, Emily headed for the kitchen. "Did you say you had dessert?"

"I didn't say, but I think there's some ice cream in the freezer, and some cookies left over from my Aunt Lydia's care package on the counter."

Placing his hands on the arms of the rocker, he began to stand.

She shook her head. "You stay and enjoy the fire. I'll dish up. Want some coffee?"

He shook his head, settling back onto the chair. "I'll be up all night if I do. Just water."

With a final glance at him, she entered the kitchen. Jason stared at the dancing flames over the ceramic logs. His gaze wandered up to the photo of him and Christoph on the mantle, and the feelings of guilt smashed into him again.

The picture screamed life. They'd been happy, even in Spokane. Sharing a little house in Brown's Addition, Christoph insisted they take a walk along the river every morning, rain or shine.

Jason missed those strolls, holding hands and daring anyone to say something about their public affection. No one ever did, and most folks smiled when they passed. After the EMTs took Christoph's body away the morning he died, Jason went for a walk by the river. Even though there was barely a cloud overhead, a brilliant rainbow arched across the sky over the falls. Taking it as a goodbye from Christoph, he'd been able to continue on. But not a day went by that he didn't stare at that picture and remember the man he loved.

I miss you.

Turning away from the photo, he finished his wine and set the glass on the floor beside him.

Emily strode through the kitchen doorway carrying a tray with two large bowls of chocolate ice cream. Aunt Lydia's oversized chocolate chip cookies perched precariously on top of each bowl.

"Here you go, Sweets." She handed him his bowl and set a pint of water down next to his empty wine glass. She took her bowl and cup of coffee over to the sofa.

As she resumed her perch, she sipped the coffee and set the cup and saucer onto the floor. "I'm guessing from the sad look on your face that you've been dwelling on Christoph again."

"You brought him up," he shot back. He took a bite of the cookie, the taste he remembered vividly from his childhood helping dispel some of his sadness.

"You know he wouldn't want you to give up your life."

"I know," he sighed. "Christoph told me as much. It's just hard."

Setting the ice cream onto the floor, she leaned toward him. "Jason, it's been four years. More than four years. You'll never forget Christoph. But really. It's time to get going on the business of living. You're not getting any younger."

He stared at her, arching an eyebrow. "My boyfriends are."

With a crack of a smile, she resumed eating her dessert. "So, what does one call a male cougar? Sugar daddy?"

He sipped his water. "Not at my salary. I believe the technical term is chicken hawk." He narrowed his gaze at her. "And if you call me that, I'll arrest you for inciting violence."

THE TRUCK RUMBLED to a halt in Jason's driveway and gave a lurch when Mike switched off the ignition. The police cruiser was nowhere to be seen, but a large midnight blue truck sat parked on the street in front of the house. Unsure if he had the right place, he checked his phone and the address Jason had texted to him. The house number matched, so he pushed his truck's door open and snagged his backpack. He slammed the door shut behind him and stood in the driveway, surveying the mostly white house with green gables. A wrap-around porch with square columns supporting the roof adorned the front, and a turret stood on the side of the two-story structure. Red and yellow leaves from a towering maple tree covered the small yard.

Somewhat refreshed from the three power naps that Veronica, his overnight manager, had allowed him, he marched to the front door with his backpack and rang the bell.

Footsteps inside the house neared, creaking across what Mike guessed were hardwood floors. The lock clicked, and the door flung open, revealing a smiling Jason.

Mike assumed his best door-to-door salesman persona. "Good morning, sir. Can I interest you in some lube? I have a large variety in my pack."

Struggling to keep a straight face, Jason crossed his arms and leaned against the doorframe. "How lucky. I'm fresh out. Do you give demonstrations?"

With a grin, Mike reached into his pocket and produced a condom. "With pleasure, sir. Where would you like me to set up?"

Unable to restrain his laughter, Jason reached out and gave Mike a quick hug. "I'm so glad you came."

Mike chuckled, savoring the embrace. "That's later in the demonstration."

"Well, then. Come right in." Stepping aside, Jason extended his arm toward the inside of his house. "I have breakfast if you're hungry."

A wonderful aroma greeted Mike. With a rumble of his stomach, he stepped into the house and shucked off his pack and jacket. The house was tidy, nothing flashy or overly pretentious. Hardwood floors and the basic, wooden furniture reminded him of his grandmother's farmhouse.

"Sorry about the messy yard," Jason said, leading Mike down a small hallway and into the living room. "I'm having trouble keeping up with the trees working the night shift."

A micro-suede couch and a rocking chair adorned the room, with a gas fire flickering silently behind the glass in the hearth. The window he faced opened out onto a view of Puget Sound and Bainbridge Island slightly obscured by trees and the neighbor's house below. Still, a view property in Seattle. The officer must be doing okay financially.

"You've got a really nice place." A house like this must've cost him a fortune.

Jason shrugged. "I came into a little money a few years ago. Nothing huge, but enough to buy my own piece of Seattle. I can afford living on Queen Anne with the house all paid for." He tugged on Mike's sleeve. "Want some breakfast?"

Mike's jaw dropped when they stepped into the dining room. Two plates waited on the wooden table with a pitcher of orange juice. Fresh bananas and blueberries adorned the edge of the platter holding a stack of pancakes. A variety of syrups and jellies, as well as a dish of creamed butter, accompanied the main course. Another tray of eggs completed the offering.

Clamping his mouth shut, he turned to Jason. "What army is joining us?"

With his face reddening, Jason ran a beefy hand through his straw-blond hair. "I get a little carried away cooking sometimes."

Mike's stomach gave another rumble. "I wouldn't want this amazing spread to get cold."

"Then let's eat." Jason ushered him around the table and pulled out his chair for him. "Allow me."

Lowering onto the seat, heat rose in Mike's cheeks. Jason's hands lingered on his shoulders before he stepped over to the chair beside Mike and took his seat.

He passed Mike the plate of eggs. "You don't mind delaying your presentation, Mr. Salesman?"

"Not at all," Mike replied, scooping eggs onto his plate. "It gives me time to perfect my pitch."

Laughing, Jason forked a couple of pancakes from the stack. "I have whipped cream if you want some."

Glancing between the pancakes and Jason, he wiggled his eyebrows. "For breakfast, or for my presentation?"

A grin graced Jason's lips. "Either or both."

With a chuckle, Mike helped himself to the pancakes. "We'll save it for next time." He took a bite and his eyes widened at the flavors. Cinnamon and apple, with maybe a hint of cloves, tickled his taste buds. He closed his eyes for a brief moment, savoring the delicious meal.

"Does it taste okay?"

With a nod, Mike cocked his head. "You made these from scratch, didn't you?"

Jason grinned. "I call them my harvest cakes."

"It's like an apple pie. My cousin Alan would *love*

these." He took another bite.

He passed over a small pitcher. "They're even better with maple syrup."

Mike blew through several pancakes until he couldn't eat any more. Sitting back in his chair, he downed a glass of orange juice.

Jason glanced around the table. "I guess that was a hit."

"I'll say. You're an amazing cook." Mike yawned. "Sorry, I was all raring to go hiking this morning, but your amazing breakfast has me ready for a nap."

"No worries. I assumed we wouldn't be leaving until early afternoon. Even though it would be nice to go out to Rainier, Vashon Island is quicker to get to. I also know a nice place in Tacoma for dinner."

Mike's eyes drooped. "I'm not sure I'm going to be able to give you that demonstration right away, mister."

"I'm a little tired myself." Jason stood and picked up their plates.

Mike helped clear the remaining pancakes and fruit. He watched Jason work in the kitchen and gained a new appreciation for him. Not only a nice cop, but a sexy man and a fabulous cook. This one might be boyfriend material.

Cocking his head to the side, he considered the implications of what he'd just thought. A boyfriend. He'd had several fuck buddies and flings in the five years he'd allowed himself to be out and active. None of those boys were even close to being dateable. So, what was different about Officer Jason Lynch?

After he placed the last dish in the dishwasher, Jason closed the door and started the wash cycle. He leaned against the counter, his muscular body stretched out before Mike. "I have a guest bedroom if you want to sleep in there."

Mike screwed up his courage. "Is that where you'll be?"

"Or you can share the bed in my room." Jason grinned sheepishly. "But I can't guarantee I'll be able to keep my hands off of you."

Stepping forward, Mike closed the distance between them. "I don't want you to."

The tension in the air thickened between them. Jason reached out his hand, brushing his fingers against Mike's cheek. "Shall we head upstairs?"

Tingles of pleasure radiated across his face at Jason's touch. "I thought you'd never ask."

Grabbing his hand, Jason led him up the wooden staircase and into his bedroom. The door closed with a click, and both men stripped down to their underwear. Mike took in the muscular bare-chested blond as Jason pulled him to the bed.

"You're stunning, Mike." Jason raked his gaze across Mike's body before laying him back. "Sure you're okay sleeping with me."

"No problem at all." Mike ran a hand down Jason's firm chest, savoring the soft skin against his fingertips.

"Damn, that feels nice." Jason hesitated then reached for the sheet. Once Mike was settled under the covers, Jason stood. "I'll be right back." He crossed to the windows and pulled the drapes closed, darkening the room. Returning to the bed, he slipped into the other side and covered them with the down comforter.

Sliding his arm under Mike's pillow, Jason pulled

Mike's body close. The warmth radiating from Jason's body lulled Mike closer to sleep.

"This okay?" Jason murmured, his fingers gently running over Mike's arm and further relaxing him.

"Feels good," Mike yawned. "Sorry, I'm falling asleep."

Jason kissed the top of his head. "Go to sleep. I'll still be here when you wake up."

JASON WOKE TO the pounding of rain against the window and an arm wrapped around his torso. Mike's head rested on his pec, the younger man's soft hair caressing his skin. Though reluctant to leave his companion alone, the pressure in his bladder necessitated leaving the warmth of the bed. He slipped quietly from under the covers and trotted to the bathroom.

After relieving himself, he washed his hands and crossed to the window. Tugging the drapes away from the sill, Jason assessed the severity of the storm. Rain lashed the windows with gusts of wind. The remaining leaves on the maple trees whipped through the air and covered the lawn and the street.

A rare flash of lightning lit up the dark clouds. Jason counted to three before the rumble lightly shook the window. *Well, that's the end of today's hike.* Letting the drapes fall back, he returned to bed. His feet brushed against Mike's warm leg, making the sleeping man sucking a deep breath.

"Oh, shit, sorry about that." Jason pulled his legs away from Mike. "I didn't mean to wake you."

Snuggling against Jason's body, Mike kissed his chest.

"It's okay. Just surprised me. Have you been awake long?"

"No, just enough to determine that the storm outside has cancelled our hiking plans." The warmth of Mike's leg pressing gently against the crotch of Jason's shorts made his cock stir.

Mike squeezed him in his embrace. "If it's raining cats and dogs outside, being under the covers with you sounds better than a hike."

Warmth spread through Jason, and he kissed the top of Mike's head. "That's sweet of you to say."

"I mean it." Mike's hand played across Jason's chest, sparks snapping across his skin in the wake of gentle fingers.

With his desire mounting, Jason's cock lengthened and tented his underwear. Mike had the same reaction, his erection pressing against Jason's thigh. Lacing his fingers into Mike's curly hair, he tilted Mike's head back and planted a kiss on his lips.

Moaning, Mike opened his mouth, and Jason probed inside with his tongue, exploring every inch. Their fervor increased, and Jason rolled Mike onto his back, hovering over him and breaking the lip-lock.

"I wanted to kiss you the minute I saw you in that hotel lobby." He pressed another kiss against Mike's lips. "And I wanted you bad in that alley."

"I wasn't sure. You stepped back when I made a move." Mike's emerald gaze bored into Jason. He traced the muscles of Jason's biceps.

Jason grinned. "I didn't want our first time being some quickie behind a dumpster."

Taking in the younger man beneath him, Jason marveled that he could feel this way again since he lost

Christoph. Desire swept through him, and he resumed their kiss, grinding his stiff cock into Mike's hardness. Mike stiffened beneath him, moaned, and clawed at Jason's back.

Afraid Mike would blow before they really got started, Jason backed off, kissing his way down Mike's neck and across his bare chest. A few dark hairs framed the nickel-sized nipples erect on his pecs.

He ran his hand lightly over Mike's smooth, firm chest and down his abs, eliciting a sigh from the young man. Mike's eyes rolled up before closing. Another sharp intake of breath came as Jason's fingers dipped under the waistband of Mike's underwear.

Jason avoided grasping Mike's hard shaft, but instead rubbed over his lower abdomen and traced a finger lightly where his legs met his balls. Mike shuddered, and a light moan escaped his lips. Encouraged, Jason continued to rub, his fingertips tickled by the short stubs of Mike's pubic hair. He leaned forward and kissed around one of Mike's nipples.

"Aaahhh…" Stiffening, Mike's body gave another shake.

Freeing his hand from the confines of the tight underwear, Jason grazed his thumb over the other nipple.

With a sharp intake of air, Mike's eyes flew open. "Oh, fuck."

Jason continued toying with the erect nub, lightly pinching with his fingertips. "A sensitive spot."

"Ah…yeah…oooh, it is…" Mike squirmed under Jason's teasing fingers.

Playing the young man like a violin, Jason elicited several more moans and whimpers from Mike before he lifted his hands away and caressed his way down across Mike's abs to the waistband of his underwear.

Mike's cock strained against the tight confines of the form-fitting shorts. A wet spot on the blue fabric fired Jason's lust. He lowered his lips to the throbbing shaft and kissed along its length.

Jason gave Mike's nipple a gentle pinch, and his shaft jumped against Jason's lips.

"So good…"

Grasping the elastic, Jason slipped Mike's blue underwear down his legs, freeing his thick erection. Jason tugged the soft underwear the rest of the way down Mike's body and flung them onto the floor.

Now fully naked, Mike spread his legs and gave his dick a couple of tugs. He moved to sit up, but Jason placed a hand on his chest and gently pushed him back onto the sheets. "Lie back. I want to pleasure you slowly."

Settling back, Mike whipped off the covers. Jason kept his gaze locked on Mike's while he lapped the length of Mike's cock with his tongue, savoring the salty flavor. Moaning and clutching at the sheet, Mike rolled his eyes back.

After two more slow licks up the shaft, Jason settled between Mike's spread legs and lapped at his large and tightening balls. The scent of sweat hit his nose, and Jason lightly grazed his teeth along the sack.

"Oh, wow, Jason." Mike squirmed beneath him, arching his back.

Jason kissed at the juncture of legs and pelvis, driving his tongue against the short stubble covering the skin. Mike laced the fingers of one hand into his hair. With gentle tug, Mike pulled him up.

Jason again locked his gaze on Mike. "Did I do something wrong?"

Panting, Mike shook his head. "Not at all. I'm just wondering if we should take a shower before the fun really gets going."

With another gentle tug on Jason's hair, Mike brought them together for a kiss. A mixture of emotions raged through Jason when their lips met. Lust and desire outweighed everything, but lurking under the surface, Jason realized he wanted to know more about this young man than just how well he fucked.

When the kiss ended, Jason smiled. "I still want to take you to dinner. Maybe the rain will subside tomorrow, and we can do our hike then."

"Dinner sounds great, but Tacoma is a long way to go."

Jason scooted back on the bed and placed his feet on the rug, shucking his briefs. Extending his hand, he laced his fingers in Mike's and pulled, helping him stand.

"Thanks," Mike grinned, give Jason's hand a squeeze.

They hurried over the cold floorboards of the bedroom and frigid ceramic tiles of the bathroom floor to the shower. Jason retrieved a couple of plush green towels from the linen closet and laid them over the rack on the door of the shower. His glance settled on the whirlpool tub under the window.

"If you want, we could sit in the jets of the tub."

Mike's eyebrow arched. "I'd be up for that."

"Let's do it, then." Stepping to the tub, Jason leaned over the step and turned the tap. As the water warmed, Mike's hand lightly grazed over the hair on his ass. Jason shook at the pleasure coursing through him.

"At some point, I'll need to be inside this." Mike continued down his legs and then gave Jason's ass cheeks a slap.

"We'll see. I haven't bottomed in a long time, and you have a formidable cock there." The thought of Mike pounding inside him made his dick, softened from the cold run, harden again. Christoph was the last to top him. Though he'd had some trysts in the last four years, none were serious, and he'd always insisted on topping. He chuckled to himself, remembering Emily's mistaken assumption of his celibacy. Not quite, but certainly no one was a repeat performance.

The water warmed, and Jason closed the drain. He programmed the jets while the tub filled. While they waited for the tub to fill, Mike kept his hand roving Jason's body. Each caress and brush of Mike's fingers fueled Jason's impatience to get his companion into the tub.

Jason turned off the tap once the water level rose just below the overflow and adjusted the jet controls. The motor started, and Jason felt a slight vibration on the edge of the tub as the water swirled.

Sweeping his hand toward the whirlpool, he turned to Mike. "I think we're ready." He glanced down Mike's body and settled his gaze onto the hard dick jutting from his between his legs.

Mike winked. "I've been ready for the last few minutes." He leaned forward and kissed Jason lightly on the lips then climbed over the edge and lowered himself into the frothy water.

When Jason stepped over the lip of the tub, Mike moved to him and wrapped his mouth around Jason's hardness. Standing in the warm, swirling water with Mike lashing his tongue over the head, Jason's knees buckled. He reached out and grabbed the edge of the tub, easing his butt to rest against it. Mike followed his movements and continued to suck, lightly caressing Jason's balls with his fingers.

Pleasure tingled through Jason's body, the sight of the dark-haired man working him over ramped up his excitement. Mike increased the pressure of his sucking, bringing Jason dangerously close to losing control and filling his mouth with come.

The light tingles spreading over his balls increased, and Jason fought the coming release. Pushing on Mike's shoulder, Jason shuddered. "You've got me close."

Mike brushed away his hand and bobbed his head faster, taking more of the shaft into his mouth on each descent. Jason closed his eyes and pressed his back against the tub. The rush of his orgasm swept over him.

"Gonna shoot," Jason warned, his legs stiffening and feet curling.

With a final swirl of his tongue, Mike snaked his finger beneath Jason's balls and found the pucker of his ass. He grazed his fingernail across the sensitive skin.

"Oh, fuck!" The sudden stimulation pushed Jason over the edge. He roared, shooting his load into Mike's still sucking mouth. Gasping for air and his whole body shaking, he pulled Mike off when the sensitivity of his cockhead became too much to bear. Mike settled back with a smirk as Jason's body sank into the warm water. His ass settled onto the seat, the water reaching the top of his chest. A jet pulsed into the small of his back, giving him a massage while he struggled to get his breathing under control.

"Fucking amazing." Jason closed his eyes, allowing the warmth of the water to continue to relax him after his release.

Mike settled onto his lap and wrapped his arms around Jason's body. "I find you incredibly sexy."

Opening his eyes, he held Mike in his gaze. "Definitely mutual." He folded his arms around Mike and held him close. Mike settled his head onto Jason's shoulder. He could have held Mike like this forever, their connection stronger than anything he'd felt since he lost Christoph.

The jets cycled off, and the water in the tub stilled. Rain continued to lash against the window, with the occasional leaf slapping against the glass. The romantic tenderness of this moment caught Jason off guard, and he resisted the swell of emotion threatening to turn him into a blubbering sap.

He gave Mike a squeeze and eased the sweet man off his lap before he completely lost it. "Let's wash off and decide what we want to do today." He waded through the water in a crouch, keeping his body mostly submerged, and grabbed the bar of soap in the large seashell next to the jet controls.

Returning to Mike, he patted the edge of the tub. "Hoist yourself up here and let me lather your legs." He rubbed his hands over the soap, building up a good froth. Mike lifted himself out of the warm water and sat on the edge.

After setting the bar back into the seashell, Jason raised one of Mike's legs and ran his hands over the hairy skin. He massaged Mike's substantial calves and dug his thumbs along his quads.

Mike sighed, resting his ankle on Jason's shoulder. "You've no idea how much I needed that. Standing all night takes a lot out of you."

Finished with the first leg, Jason repeated the treatment on the other, then spread them wide. Mike arched an eyebrow as Jason reached for the soap again. Without a word, Jason lathered up and resumed his position, eager to show Mike the same pleasure he'd just experienced. He caressed Mike's balls, gently rolling them in one hand while he ran his other over Mike's hardening cock.

Jason increased his pressure on the shaft, causing Mike to gasp.

"I thought we were just washing off," he choked in a strangled breath.

Still stroking, Jason trailed his fingers from Mike's balls to the insides of his legs, running back and forth between them. The shaft in his hands pulsed each time he grazed the tightening balls.

As Mike squirmed on the ledge, Jason jacked faster. "I wouldn't want to leave you hanging after such an excellent blow job." His speed increased, and Mike's legs flexed.

"I'm getting close," he cried.

Jason twirled his fingers around Mike's balls, causing the younger man to jerk. With a gasp, he threw his head back, and several spurts painted Jason's cheeks.

Sliding off the edge of the tub, Mike splashed back into the water. He bounced slightly as his ass reached the seat. Jason reached for the pile of washrags next to the seashell and grabbed one of the white cloths. He dipped it into the water and wiped off the copious load from his face.

Mike rested his head on the edge of the tub, sucking in

a couple of deep breaths. "Thanks. That was awesome."

With a chuckle, Jason sat beside him. "What are you hungry for?"

Winking, Mike ran his fingers over Jason's leg. "Round two. I still need to do my lube presentation."

"We should get some food," Jason chuckled. "I've got all night to wear you out."

CHAPTER FOUR

MIKE SLIPPED ON his jeans while Jason dug around in his dresser. His gaze settled on the naked cop, and he admired the firm ass and the V of his back.

Lifting a pair of bright green boxers from the drawer, Jason turned to face Mike. Even soft, the view of Jason's impressive cock and balls made Mike salivate. Round two couldn't come fast enough.

"You didn't say what you'd like for dinner." Lifting a muscular leg, Jason slipped on the underwear.

"Do you have any idea what kind of restraint it's taking for me not to ravage you?" Mike's dick stirred in his jeans. "I could easily skip dinner." His stomach took that moment to gurgle in protest.

Jason laughed. "I don't think the rest of your body agrees with your sexual appetite. How about I give you some choices if you're not coming up with anything that sounds good?"

Resigned to eating instead of playing, Mike nodded. "Shoot."

"Well, with the weather, we'd better drive," Jason said, pulling a pair of sock from the dresser. "I could take you anywhere in the city."

With a lick of his lips, Mike envisioned Jason driving him from place to place, ravaging each other throughout

Seattle. "I could take *you* anywhere."

Grinning, Jason shook his head. "Incorrigible. There's a great Chinese place in the International District, an awesome New Orleans-style place on Mercer, or a pub on 65th near Roosevelt that serves Australian style meat pies and delicious mac and cheese."

Cocking his head to the side, Mike pondered a meat pie. "You mean like a pot pie?"

"Not really. More like an Indian samosa, but not as spicy. Some have cheese in them." Jason bent over, lifting a leg and slipping on a sock. Mike watched, not taking his eyes off the muscular legs and the curve of Jason's ass. At the pause in the conversation, Jason peeked over his shoulder. "See something you like?" He slipped on the other sock.

Mike blinked. "I see a lot I like." His stomach rumbled again. "Okay, meat pies it is. You had me at the mac and cheese, actually."

Crossing to the closet, Jason peered inside and considered what to wear. Unable to resist, Mike stepped over to him and ran his hand along the soft skin of Jason's back. Goosebumps rose across his muscular shoulders.

"Mmm, that feels good." Jason closed his eyes for a moment, then snapped them open. "Naughty boy. Trying to distract me."

"Did it work?" Mike reached around to feel the crotch of Jason's boxers. A hardening shaft greeted his fingers when he slipped them inside the fly. "Ah, I see it did."

Jason spun around to face Mike. "Down, boy."

Wrapping his arms around Jason, Mike rested his head on the policeman's shoulder. "I'm so glad you came on to me in the hotel lobby."

"Me, too, though I took a risk."

With a final squeeze, Mike released his hold. "Okay, get some clothes on before you become too irresistible for me to contain myself."

"Yes, sir." Jason returned his attention to the closet and retrieved a pair of black jeans. After slipping them on, he grabbed an emerald green button-up shirt and slipped his arms into the sleeves.

Mike stepped closer to him and ran his hands under the shirt and along Jason's muscular chest. "Let me help you with those pesky buttons." With a flick of his thumbs on Jason's nipples, Mike pulled his hands from Jason's skin and slowly buttoned up the shirt. Jason had his eyes closed while Mike worked, letting out the occasional hum when Mike's fingers grazed his skin or strayed across the fabric to rub the hardened nipples pushing against the fabric.

After Mike finished, Jason sighed heavily and gave Mike a peck on the cheek. He tucked his shirt into his jeans and retrieved his belt from the crumpled pile of clothes on the floor.

"Okay, sexy man, let's get us some meaty pies." Jason led the way out of the bedroom and downstairs into the living room. "Can I get you some water before we go? I could use a glass."

Standing next to the rocking chair, Mike nodded. "Sure."

Jason left the room, and Mike glanced at the fireplace mantle to his right. He stood and examined the three pictures in metal frames. The first was of a group of five children and their parents. He presumed Jason was one of the kids. The next was an older couple, the man smiling big with his arm wrapped around the woman. She had her head on his shoulder and a grin for the photographer.

The final picture made his breath catch. A younger Jason, probably in his mid-twenties, stood with a guy in his early twenties riding him piggyback. He was kissing Jason's cheek and his arms were wrapped around the officer's chest.

"That's Christoph."

With a jolt of surprise, Mike swung to face Jason.

"Sorry, didn't mean to make you jump." He entered the room carrying two pint glasses of water. Joining Mike at the mantle, Jason handed him one and took a sip from the other.

Mike eyed the man next to him, unsure if he was in the middle of someone's relationship. "Is he your partner?"

"He was. He died four years ago from a rare cancer. Came on really fast and he was gone in two months."

"Wow. I'm sorry."

"We had three and a half years together." Jason continued to stare at the photo, pain etched on to his handsome features.

Mike sipped at his water, unsure if he should touch Jason or leave him be. "No one since?"

Turning to him with sad eyes, Jason gave a shake of his head. "I haven't found anyone I've clicked with. Normal and outdoorsy are my requirements." He frowned. "Going to the bar and picking up a guy lost its appeal years ago."

Mike's opinion of the officer shot even higher. "I love to go camping, and alcohol isn't my favorite."

The sadness in Jason's eyes faded, and he turned away from the fireplace. "Yeah? I'm looking forward to our hike."

After a final drink of the water, Mike set the empty glass on the mantle and faced Jason. "Me, too. But I'm looking even more forward to the mac and cheese. Ready to go?"

Chucking, Jason nodded and stepped away from the fireplace. Just as they reached the hall, a bright flash of lightning illuminated the room followed closely by the boom of thunder.

Mike jumped at the rumble. "Shit! That one struck close by."

The lights flickered and went out, plunging the room into darkness.

"Just as well we're going out for dinner," Jason said, moving through the dark house. "I'll get a flashlight."

Mike remained at the entrance to the hallway, thinking about Jason's past. The pain he'd seen when Jason stared that the picture gave Mike some pause at how ready the man was for a relationship. *Wait, a relationship?* Where had that idea come from?

A bright light came from the kitchen, and Jason returned. "Okay, we're good to go. Grab your jacket and we'll head out."

Following Jason down the hall to the front door, Mike retrieved his jacket from the hook. He slipped it on and zipped up. Jason handed him the flashlight and donned his own coat.

Jason opened the front door, and the wind and rain lashed through the entryway. "Let's make a run to my truck. If there's no power at the pub, we'll try something downtown."

Mike hurried out into the weather, running along the

path to the driveway and out to the sidewalk with Jason close behind him. They reached the passenger door at the same moment, and Jason thrust the key into the lock. He unlocked and opened the door.

Climbing inside, Mike took in the neighborhood. All the houses stood dark, as did the streetlights. Enough glow from other parts of the city illuminated the clouds and kept the street from complete blackness. The large maple waved in the wind, a ghostly image against the dark block.

Jason slammed the passenger door and ran around to the driver's side. He climbed in and started the engine. With a sigh, he reached across to Mike's leg and rubbed it.

"Quite a storm out here."

The large hand gliding across his thigh made Mike quiver.

Jason arched an eyebrow. "You okay?"

"Yeah," he hummed. "You have a nice touch."

Applying more pressure, Jason squeezed his leg a couple of times, then withdrew his hand and gripped the steering wheel. He shifted the truck into gear and flicked on the headlights.

As they drove along the dark streets, the prospect of Jason suddenly stopping under a bridge or at a park to take him brought a renewed stiffening of his dick.

Jason noticed him squirming on the seat. "What's up?"

Without a word, Mike took one of Jason's hands from the steering wheel and placed the palm on his crotch.

Squeezing the stiff shaft, Jason chuckled. "Ah, *that's* what's up."

Mike shrugged. "I had an image of being driven to some intimate spot and having you do something…disorderly to me."

The chuckle turned to an outright laugh. "I can't wait to take you hiking, though I doubt we'll get very far down the trail." Jason gave Mike's cock another squeeze, making the hardness confined in his jeans pulse.

Unable to contain himself any longer, Mike reached for Jason's jeans. A hard bulge met his fingertips. "I'm not the only one excited by this prospect."

"True," Jason acknowledged.

Mike's fingers fumbled with the zipper keeping the denim between him and his prize. With a tug it came down, and his hand slipped inside, fondling the rock-hard shaft within.

A gasp filled the truck, and Jason pulled onto a side street, still in the neighborhood affected by the power outage. The dark lane led to a small park at the end of the block. Jason drove the truck onto the service road and parked behind a brick restroom. Killing the headlights and shutting off the motor, he turned to Mike.

"You bad, bad boy," he scolded. "We shouldn't even be considering doing this in public."

Mike widened his eyes in feigned innocence, his body on fire and his patience waning. "But officer, I'm just trying to be a good citizen and help out a policeman in need."

Jason cocked his head to the side. "And how am I in need?"

With a grin, Mike squeezed Jason's pulsing shaft. "You seem to be restrained. Let me release you and give you some relief."

Reaching to his side, Jason reclined the seat and leaned back, the crotch of his jeans stretched. "That's mighty nice of you. I'd appreciate any and all assistance."

Certain the darkness shrouded their activities, Mike removed his hand from Jason's fly, unbuttoned the waist of his jeans, and worked the denim over the curve of Jason's ass. He fished inside tight briefs for the massive cock he'd sucked earlier, and pulled back the elastic band, gently moving it under Jason's large balls.

"How's that feel, officer?" he teased.

"Nice to be free." Jason stretched out his arms and placed his hands behind his head.

"I still have to give you your release." Leaning to his side, Mike turned his head and raked his tongue across Jason's ball sack. Jason gasped, but kept his hands locked behind his head. Encouraged, Mike continued to give each testicle a tongue bath until Jason slid down into the seat.

Mike lapped at the juncture of shaft and balls, then moved along the stiffness to the head and engulfed it. Jason's legs straightened, and his breathing became ragged. Moans and whimpers encouraged Mike to continue. He upped his rhythm and increased his suction, eliciting a loud *ah* from Jason while the cop's balls rose. Mike's hand rested on Jason's tightening thigh, and he hummed around the shaft.

Jason's leg began to shake. "I'm gonna blow," he choked out.

Not heeding the warning, Mike continued, swiping with his tongue under the head and bringing Jason over the edge. Jason's hands flew from behind his head and onto Mike's shoulders, holding him in place. Shot after shot of come flew into his mouth, and Mike swallowed as fast as he could.

Jason yelped after the sensations became too much for him and pushed Mike away. "Shit, you are amazing."

"All part of the friendly service." Mike wiped the saliva off his mouth with the sleeve of his coat and grinned.

"And what about you?" Jason panted.

On cue, Mike's stomach gurgled loudly. He shrugged. "Well, I guess the protein shake only made me hungrier."

Jason took a deep breath and straightened out his legs, then pulled the jeans back around his hips and zipped up the fly. Fumbling with the button, he winked at Mike. "Let's get you fed and then we'll satiate your *other* hunger."

JASON RECONSIDERED THE wisdom of bringing Mike to this particular pub. A popular hangout for several of his workmates, the pool table often hosted tournaments between the various police precincts in the city. Though he enjoyed the food, he rarely made an appearance, choosing to keep a healthy separation between his work life and his personal time – a painful lesson he'd learned in Spokane.

Sure enough, Jason spotted four of his colleagues as he held the door open for Mike. They waved from the pool table. Fred Collier, Jason's beat partner, left the group and approached. When he reached Jason and Mike, he stuck out his hand. "Hey there, Lynch. Good to see you out and about. Who's your friend?"

"Mike, this is Fred Collier. He's my partner when we go out on dual patrols." Jason did his best to suppress the tension in his stomach. Having Mike meet his workmates on what amounted to their second date felt strange, almost like a more formal relationship had already formed.

"Yup, every few days Jason and I cozy up in the patrol car and fight crime," Fred said with a grin.

Mike glanced at Jason and then addressed Fred. "Glad someone can keep him in line."

Fred laughed. "Well, sometimes anyway. I could tell you a few tales."

Nervous Collier would say something to embarrass him, Jason nodded toward the ornate wooden bar covering an entire wall of the pub. "We're gonna grab some grub at the bar. See you later."

"Say goodbye before you go." Collier stuck out his hand to Mike again. "Nice to meet you."

"You, too." Mike shook the offered hand.

Moving away from his workmate and the other gawking officers, Jason shepherded Mike to the bar. The bartender brought two menus and handed them off. "Howdy, gents. What can I get you to drink?"

Jason glanced at Mike. "Get anything you want."

Mike scanned the offerings on tap. "I'll have a ginger beer."

The bartender nodded. "Nice. And you, sir?"

"Hefeweizen with a lemon slice."

"Right you are," he nodded. "Want anything to eat?"

Jason quickly scanned the menu. "I'd take a steak and cheese meat pie, and a mound of tater tots."

"Oh, that sounds good," Mike beamed. "I'll have the same."

Arching his eyebrow, Jason glanced at his date. "I thought you wanted mac and cheese."

Mike seemed to waver for a moment but shook his head. "Nah, potatoes always win over macaroni, *especially* tater tots."

With a laugh, the bartender took their menus. "Amen, brother. I'll have your drinks right up." He moved to the taps and grabbed two glasses. "You guys doing anything tonight, or just come by for a pie and a pint?"

Jason gave Mike a quick glance and was met with a smirk. "The power went out, so we thought we'd come down to the pub for dinner."

After sliding the beer down the wooden bar to Jason, the bartender pulled the tap for the ginger beer. "Oh, yeah? What neighborhood?"

"Queen Anne. The power went out at my place just as we were deciding what to do for supper."

Placing the ginger beer in front of Mike, he leaned on the bar. "I'm pretty sure you're over twenty-one, but do you mind showing me your ID?"

Mike fished in his jeans pocket. "Oh, no problem." He produced his wallet and handed his driver's license over.

The bartender returned it. "Thanks. The State makes us check. Keeps us on the right side of the law, and that's where we like to stay." A cheer went up at the pool table, drawing the bartender's attention for a moment. "Especially since the law is in here most nights playing pool," he chuckled.

Jason smirked. "Wise."

"Well, gents, enjoy your drinks. Let me know if I can get you anything else before your food's up." He moved down the bar to another customer.

Mike sipped his glass. "This is good. I heard the Aussies like this stuff, so thought I'd give it a try."

"Ah, so you're adventurous," Jason replied, his mind drifting to the blowjob Mike had given him in the park, and the one he would have given Jason in the alley.

Mike shook his head. "I make an attempt but seem to always revert back to what I'm comfortable with."

"At least you're willing." Jason tasted the wheat beer and savored its flavor. A memory triggered – he and Christoph loved to get a pint after work. He shook his head. *Stop it, Jason. This is a date with Mike, not Christoph.*

Before he could dwell too long on his former lover, Jason turned to Mike. "So, tell me all about yourself. What do I need to know the most about who you are?"

Mike's eyes widened for a moment. "Uh, well...I'm planning to go to college in the fall, which I think I mentioned. My cousin and his husband took me in after I came out and my mom evicted me."

Jason frowned. "Wow."

"Oh, there's a lot more, but I don't want to burden you with it," Mike said with a frown. He stared at his drink.

Curiosity overrode Jason's propriety. "You can tell me anything. I'd like to hear."

Mike shrugged. "My brother tried to kill me several times during my childhood."

The warmth drained from Jason's face. "How do you mean? He was just careless with you?"

Eyeing him, then drinking more of his ginger beer, Mike hesitated. "No, he actively tried to make me dead. One time he was growing pot in our chimney and I found it. I climbed up on the roof and saw it sticking out. He came home and lost his mind. Pulled a gun and started shooting. I had to hide behind the chimney until Mom got home and got the gun away from him."

A pit formed in Jason's stomach. "Holy fuck."

"Mom always took his side. I was going to press charges another time when I called the cops because he threatened me and beat me up, but she begged me not to."

Mike spat the words. "She promised to get him under control, but as soon as I declined the charges, she went back on her word."

Shaking his head, Jason gulped down more of his beer. He returned his attention to Mike as he set the glass down. "So, not only did she not protect you from your brother, she discouraged you from going to school. Do you have any contact with her?"

"Very little. Coming out pretty much ended what remained of our relationship." Mike trailed a finger around the rim of his glass, staring into the amber liquid. "My cousin, Alan, has been around all my life. His mom and my mom are first cousins, but his mom is a lot older than mine. He took me in when he found out she'd kicked me to the curb."

"How long ago was that?"

"About four years. I know I've caused him a lot of grief, but for some reason he still wants me there. His husband Craig is great."

Jason whistled, not imagining ever taking in a distant relative. "He must really care about you to take in a second cousin."

"I know he does, but our relationship has really suffered since I moved in," Mike continued. "Being in the big city had me pretty wild. Alan's friend Isaac got me the job at the hotel, and that's helped, but I know Alan really wants me to go to college." Mike shifted on the barstool, and the frown returned to his lips.

A waiter brought their food, and Jason was grateful for the distraction. He had a million questions for Mike, but it was becoming clear that the young man had told him more than he meant to and was about to clam up.

The bartender came by as the waiter left. "You guys need anything else?"

His eyes wide staring at the mountain of tater tots, Mike nodded. "Some ketchup?"

"No problem." He addressed Jason. "How about for you?"

"Malt vinegar, please."

"Here you go." He reached under the counter and brought out the two bottles. "Enjoy."

Jason sprinkled the vinegar over his tater tots while Mike tapped his palm against the raised glass 57 on the side of the ketchup bottle. The taste of vinegar with salty fried potato danced across Jason's tongue. He chewed and swallowed, then cut into the pastry shell of the meat pie. Steam billowed out, as well as a wonderful smell of meat and gravy.

After he popped a morsel of the pie into his mouth, Mike briefly closed his eyes. Between bites, he met Jason's gaze. "Wow, these are good."

"I've been coming here off and on for a couple years. It's my go-to place if I'm craving some fried food." Jason took a bite of his own pie, the cheese and beef mixing with the savory pastry.

Mike set his fork on the bar and dipped a tater tot into the substantial mound of ketchup on his plate. "Your turn with the life story."

After dabbing his mouth with his napkin, Jason picked up the glass of beer and drained it. He signaled to the bartender for another. "Well, let's see. I graduated from the UW about eight years ago with a bachelor's in criminal justice. Went through the police academy in Spokane and lived there, then moved back after Christoph died."

"Family?" Mike asked, popping another tot into his mouth.

"All passed on. Cancer took my dad when I was four. Mom remarried and died in an airplane crash with her husband my first year of college. My sister died at three months."

Mike reached under the bar and rested his hand on Jason's leg. "That's pretty rough. I'm sorry."

"I've got my best friend from college Emily, and she keeps me balanced. She's as close as any family could be." Jason poked at his food as he pushed aside the old memories. "My dad's sister is still around, but she's getting quite elderly. She sends me care packages of cookies in the mail like she did when I was a kid."

"That's sweet," Mike grinned. "Who were all the kids in the picture on your mantle? I thought they might be your brothers."

With a shake of his head, Jason popped another tater tot into his mouth. "First cousins. It was taken at my grandparents' home in Wenatchee. I still hear from a few of them."

"That's cool. Mine are losers, and I'm glad they rejected me." Bitterness crept into Mike's voice again. "Not much of a loss."

"My life is pretty good these days," Jason continued, attempting to distract Mike. "I like my job, I've got a house and a truck, and I've done a bit of traveling."

Mike perked up. "Yeah? Where have you gone?"

The bartender switched out Jason's empty glass for another pint of Hefeweizen. "Thanks." He returned his attention to Mike. "I went to New Zealand last year, and Iceland in April. Both beautiful places."

"Interesting choices."

Jason chuckled. "I suppose. Iceland was a total whim. I wanted to see the volcano. Emily lived in New Zealand for a couple years, and when she realized it was time to come back, I decided I had better get over there before I lost the free room to stay in."

Mike sat back on the barstool. "I've always wanted to travel. Never had the money, and I've been working pretty hard the last couple of years. Now with school in the winter, I'm not going anywhere. Craig and Alan always seem to be traveling overseas. They promised to take me if I graduated college."

"Quite an incentive," Jason replied. "You can travel as a student dirt cheap, especially in Europe. Only need the money for the ticket and the room. Food can be relatively inexpensive if you're careful."

Jason grinned, impressed by the young man who'd been through so much during his childhood, managed to stay off the streets, and was actively making something of himself. He'd seen too many young people give up when hit with such adversity. Jason had almost been one of them, but Aunt Lydia had made his childhood bearable through his mother's parade of men before she remarried.

Mike finished up his meal and downed the last of his ginger beer. The bartender hurried over. "I can take your plate for you if you're finished. Want another ginger beer?"

"Nah, that's enough sugar," Mike replied. "Can I get a water with no ice?"

"Comin' right up."

Jason reached into his pocket and pulled out his credit card. "Here. We can close out the tab."

The bartender took the card and hurried away with

the plates.

Furrowing his brow, Mike crossed his arms and frowned. "Now look here. I need to pay for some of these meals."

With a chuckle, Jason raised an eyebrow. "Oh?"

"Seriously, Jason," Mike scowled. "It's really nice of you, but I'm going to feel bad if you don't let me pay next time."

Jason held up his hands, not wanting to offend Mike. "Okay, okay. I promise to give you a fair shot at the bill."

Mike rolled his eyes. "Don't make me pull out some of my tricks. I learned how to play this game from Alan and Craig."

As THEY MOVED toward the door of the bar, the cop who'd greeted them when they'd first come in hurried up to them. "Hey, guys. Paul got called away, and I need someone to play one more game of pool. Either of you in?"

Mike glanced at Jason who shrugged. He returned his attention to Fred Collier. "Sure, I can play a quick game, but I warn you, I'm not that good." He chuckled inwardly, eager to show the short, dark-haired officer just how experienced he really was.

Grabbing his arm, he pulled Mike over to the table. "No worries. You don't mind, do you Lynch?"

"Nope. I'll just sit and watch," Jason said, furrowing his brow. "I suck at this game."

The other officer, tall with short dark hair, and his wife, a stunning blonde with piercing ice-blue eyes, had their pool sticks ready, and the balls sat racked on the table. Fred handed Mike a pool cue and stepped back.

"You can break, Mike."

He glanced at Jason and winked, then bent over the table and lined up the cue-ball to just the side of the one-ball. With another glance and grin at Jason, he took his shot. Three of the balls careened into different pockets.

The couple stared at each other and then at Fred who shrugged. "Hey, what can I say?" He looked in the pockets where the balls rested. "Looks like we're solids."

Mike circled the table and lined up two more shots, perfectly executing them and dropping the balls into the pockets. He glanced over at Jason, who had crossed his arms over his chest. A smile crept across his lips.

Fred's jaw dropped when Mike hit the three-ball into the side pocket then sank the seven in the corner. "I thought you didn't play well."

Straight-faced, Mike shrugged at Fred. "Beginner's luck."

Letting out the holler of laughter, Jason slapped his knee. "Show these guys how it's done, Mike."

Happy to make Jason laugh, Mike bent over the table again, poking his butt toward his date. He lined up to drop the eight into the side pocket, calculating the angle of the bank shot like his aunt had taught him. Slowly sliding the stick between his index and ring fingers, he turned to Jason and licked his lips.

With his grin edging toward a leer, Jason looked like he was about to jump off his stool and take Mike right then and there.

Turning back to the table before Jason put him off his shot, he did one more calculation. "Okay, eight ball in the side pocket." He slid the stick back and executed the shot. The cue ball hit exactly where he wanted it to and smacked the eight ball into the side pocket.

Fred and the other officer stood and stared at the table with their mouths dropped open. They moved their gazes from the table to each other to Mike.

The officer's wife approached Mike shaking her head. "That was the most amazing game I've ever seen. Congratulations." She extended her hand to shake Mike's.

He returned her firm grip. "Thanks. I actually learned to play from my aunt. She and my uncle own a bowling alley in Wisconsin, and I spent summers with them. My aunt loved to play and taught me all about the game."

"Well anytime you want a game, I'll happily be on your team." She released his hand. "I'm Sarah Templeton, and that's my husband Alex."

Alex waved, still incredulous at Mike running the table. "Great job. I didn't see the fin rise up until it was too late."

All of them laughed as Fred patted Mike on the back. "Thanks for standing in. I'll tell Paul he needs to find a new pool partner. Come back for a game anytime you want."

"Thanks, Fred. Maybe Jason and I can come by sometime and play a few games." He turned to Jason and winked. "I can show him all my tricks."

Jason slid off the stool and stepped to his side. "How about we head off and leave these three to pick up the pieces?"

The desire and lust in Jason's eyes sent a thrill coursing through Mike. "Okay, I'm definitely ready." He turned to the other three. "It was great meeting you all. I'm sure I'll see you again."

They left the bar and headed for Jason's truck. Jason

took Mike's hand, holding it as they strolled down the sidewalk. "That was incredible. I'm so impressed."

Glowing from the praise and warm from the display of affection, Mike beamed. "I can usually get four balls on the break. I was a little off my shot." The firm grip surprised him. They'd already gotten to the hand-holding stage, and he found he didn't mind at all.

"I sure couldn't tell. Mind you, sticking that sweet ass of yours toward me would have put me off my shot." Jason squeezed Mike's hand. "I could easily have thrown you onto the table and ravaged you there and then."

Mike chuckled. "I'm not sure how the others would have reacted, but I'm certainly up for a little ravaging." He shivered, but it wasn't from the storm. "Let's hurry back to your place."

CHAPTER FIVE

J ASON AWOKE TO Mike spooned against his back. Sometime in the night he must've turned over since he remembered holding Mike when they'd fallen asleep. The stiffness of Mike's cock pressing against the crevice of his ass excited him, but he resisted the urge to let Mike fuck him.

He'd tear me apart.

Rolling over, he faced the sleeping man and pressed his lips to Mike's forehead.

Mike stirred and opened his eyes. "Good morning."

With a caress of Mike's face, Jason leaned forward and gently kissed Mike's soft lips. "How did you sleep?"

"Really well. You're awfully nice to wake up to." Mike turned onto his back and stretched.

Raking his gaze over his companion's lean chest, Jason pushed away the temptation to engage in some early morning play. "Should I run downstairs and make you some hot chocolate?"

With a grin, Mike nodded. "You're such a sweet guy."

"All part of the friendly service," Jason replied with a wink. He sat up and swung his legs over the edge of the bed. "Be back in a few minutes."

Mike also pushed himself out of bed while rubbing his eyes. "Maybe I'll jump in the shower." He padded across to the bathroom door with a yawn and entered.

Slipping on his robe, Jason watched Mike bend forward to test the temperature of the spray. He let out a whistle, admiring the curve of the younger man's ass. "I'll hurry back."

Mike laughed, shaking his butt. "Don't be long."

Before heading to the kitchen, Jason peeked out the window to find glorious sunshine. "Do you want to go hiking today?"

"Sure," Mike called over the noise of the shower.

Jason hurried downstairs to start Mike's hot chocolate and put on some coffee for himself. The dull ache of a developing caffeine headache pulled at his temple, and he didn't want to be cranky this morning. After setting his coffeemaker going, Jason lifted a small saucepan from the cabinet below the counter and set it on the stove. He pulled open the refrigerator door and retrieved the milk, pouring out about a cup into the pan. Turning on the pilot lighter, he waited while the stove clicked. Blue flame burst under the pan, and Jason decreased the heat to medium.

While he waited for the milk to warm, he put away the glass bottle and opened the spice cabinet next to the stove. His two jars of hot chocolate mix stood side by side, one chocolate and mint and the other plain dark chocolate. He chose the mint, thinking Mike would like it better.

Opening the fridge again, Jason found some whipped cream in a metal canister in the door.

When the milk began to show small bubbles on the surface and a whisper of steam rising, he flicked off the gas and poured in the mix. With a whisk he mixed the chocolate and then poured it into a cup.

As his coffee finished dripping into the pot, Jason heard the shower stop. He quickly poured himself a cup and squirted the whipped cream over the hot chocolate. Opening the fridge again, he spied a jar of chocolate sauce he'd bought at the farmers market last spring. Figuring it was as good a time as any to use it, he switched the sauce with the whipping cream canister and pulled a spoon from the drawer.

The lid popped as he twisted it open, and Jason dipped the spoon into the thick dark chocolate. He drizzled a spoonful onto the top of the whipped cream then grabbed both mugs and headed back upstairs.

Mike lay on the bed in his yellow briefs. Though Jason registered some disappointment at finding Mike partially dressed, he admired how well he filled out the tight-fitting underwear.

"Your chocolate is served." With a flourish, he presented the mug to the sexy young man.

Mike's eyes and grin widened in delight. "You even put chocolate on the whipped cream. I'm impressed."

"Glad you like it." He joined Mike on the bed, sipping his coffee. He winced at the bitter brew. *I should have ground fresh beans.*

Pulling the mug away from his mouth, Mike had a whipped cream moustache. Laughing, Jason took another drink of his coffee.

"Mmm, minty." He glanced at Jason, cocking his head to the side. "What?"

"You suddenly need a shave." Jason set his coffee on the bedside table and leaned toward Mike. "Let me get that for you."

Their lips met, and Jason licked along the top of

Mike's lip, tasting cream with a hint of peppermint mingling with the coffee on his own breath. Deepening the kiss, he thrust his tongue into Mike's mouth, mingling the cream on his tongue with the remnants of the chocolate on Mike's.

Breaking the kiss, Jason leaned back and surveyed his work. "There, got it."

"Very thorough," Mike chuckled. "I've got another problem."

Jason followed Mike's downward glance and found his cock straining against the yellow fabric. Jason's own dick began to fill out, but he willed himself not to dive down on the inviting bulge in front of him.

"I'd help you with that," Jason said, the strain in his voice evident. "But it might spoil what I have in mind for later."

Mike cocked an eyebrow. "Oh?"

With a twitch, Jason's cock pushed open his robe. He reached for his coffee and took another drink trying to will it back down. "It involves you and me naked and outside." He glanced again as Mike adjusted himself, the head of his cock peeking over the waistband of his shorts.

"Sounds intriguing." Mike rubbed his fingers over the cloth-covered shaft. "If you can wait that long."

Summoning up his last ounce of willpower, Jason finished the last gulp of bitter coffee and pushed himself off the bed. "I'll take a quick shower and we can go."

Mike took another sip from his mug. "I'll try not to jump you while you're naked."

"I'd better be fast then." Jason entered the bathroom and stepped into the shower. He turned the faucet on, and warm spray fell onto his chest.

Soaping up, he resisted the urge to stroke his aching hardness. He envisioned Mike naked, bent over a rock, and taking his dick. Concentrating on the shower instead of his aching erection, he rinsed off, then turned off the shower and stepped out. After quickly drying himself off, he hung the wet towel on the rack and returned to the bedroom.

Mike stood fully dressed, checking his phone. "I thought I'd better text my cousin and let him know where I'm at. They worry."

"It's good you have such a close relationship with them." Jason moved to his dresser and pulled out a pair of blue briefs.

"Would you like to meet them?"

Jason turned to face Mike, surprised at his suggestion. "You want me to?"

Mike nodded. "Sure. I already told them about you."

While considering Mike's suggestion, Jason slipped on his briefs and stepped to the closet for his jeans and a long-sleeved shirt. "Isn't that kind of like meeting your folks?"

"I suppose it is in a way," Mike confirmed. "I think the guys will like you."

Warmth flowed through Jason. Though surprised how fast the relationship with Mike seemed to be moving, he found he didn't mind. "Okay. When?"

"Maybe tomorrow for dinner?" Mike asked. "I can text and see if they're available."

The implications of Mike's request hit him. Not just a fuck buddy anymore. They'd moved into the dating stage. Glancing at Mike, Jason slipped on his jeans. *Smart, sexy, and going places with his life.*

Jason pulled his shirt over his head and took a breath,

suddenly nervous. A pang of guilt hit him as Christoph flashed into his mind. Emily was right, though. He did need to move on and live.

"Since I'm meeting your family, you should probably meet my best friend. I've already told *her* about *you*."

Mike looked up from his cell. "Yeah?"

"I can have her join us tonight after we get back from our hike." Jason moved toward the door. "Ready to go downstairs? My phone's down there."

"Sure." Mike hopped off the bed and joined him at the door. "Let's get our day started."

Leading the way down the stairs, Jason planned out their day. A hike around Mount Rainier would take too long if Emily was coming to dinner, so Tiger Mountain would have to do. The ferry to Vashon would also take too long, and he wanted to finish that hike with a dinner in Tacoma. Unless, of course, Emily wanted to drive that far.

They reached the living room, and Jason continued into the kitchen. He snatched his phone from the counter, touching the screen and entering his security code. After bringing up his contacts, he pressed to dial Emily.

She answered on the first ring. "Hey, Sweets, what's up?"

"Mike and I are going for a hike today." He hesitated, wondering at the wisdom of having his best friend meet his date. Still, he'd offered, so he'd better follow through. "We were wondering if you wanted to meet us for dinner afterwards."

She paused. "You sure you're ready for me to meet him? I've got so many stories I can tell…"

"I have just as many on you," he muttered. "Payback's a bitch."

She laughed. "Seriously, though. Big step for you."

"Yeah, well," Jason glanced at Mike. "You did encourage me."

"Indeed, I did," she chirped. "I'd love to meet him."

He nodded at Mike. "Great. Three options. You could come here after we get back, you could meet us in Issaquah for dinner, or meet up at our favorite waterfront pub in Tacoma. I'm thinking we'll be done around five."

"Okay, I'll meet you in Issaquah. I'm not wild about a drive to Tacoma today. Where for dinner?"

"A little Chinese and a chat over jasmine tea?" Jason lifted a brow at Mike.

Grinning, Mike nodded.

"Sounds like Shanghai to me," she replied, suggesting the second location of their favorite Chinese restaurant.

He gave a thumbs-up to Mike. "Done. See you at five."

"Sounds good." The phone beeped twice, and she was gone.

Jason returned his attention to Mike. "Ready?"

Grinning, Mike gave him a nod.

"Have you been up to Tiger Mountain State Park before?" Jason grabbed a couple of metal water bottles from his kitchen cabinet and filled one at the sink. After tossing the full one to Mike, he let the faucet run into his own.

"No, Alan doesn't hike, and Craig has been meaning to take me, but work's gotten in the way." Mike shrugged. "I'm still trying to get my friends to go camping, but none of them seem to want to rough it for a night."

"City slickers," Jason drawled and winked.

With a laugh, Mike turned toward the hallway and

moved to the door. "Most of them think camping is some kind of drag show."

Shaking his head, Jason followed and grabbed their coats from the pegs by the front door. "Just in case it gets chilly."

"Thanks."

Jason locked the door once they stepped into the cool October air. He unlocked his truck and held open Mike's door for him. Once he'd climbed inside, Jason hurried around to climb onto his own seat. Starting up his rig, Jason backed out onto the street and headed for Interstate Ninety.

THE MID-AFTERNOON SUN beat down on Mike, bringing a sheen of sweat to his brow. Though forecast to be warmer than usual, the heat of the day surprised him after the chill of the morning. A mile along the trail, according to the sign, he dragged his feet to a bench and plopped down.

Jason grinned, dropping his backpack to the ground and joining him. "Am I tiring you out?" The muscular cop slipped off his shirt and leaned back. The sweat dotting his defined chest glistened in the sunshine.

The image of licking the beads of moisture off the firm pecs beside him made the crotch of Mike's jeans tighten. "I just need a minute." He slid his hand along the jeans-covered leg of his shirtless companion. "You're making me horny."

Jason arched an eyebrow. "Is that so?" He glanced around. "There's the outline of a trail behind the bench. Looks like it winds up into the trees."

Twisting around, Mike spied the trail then returned

his attention back to Jason. "Do you want to explore?"

After slipping the straps of his pack over his shoulders, Jason stood and tucked his shirt into the back of his jeans. "Coming?"

Mike jumped up. "Hopefully." Winking at Jason, he hurried around the bench and picked his way up the faint trail and into the trees. Adjusting his fully erect dick, Mike continued through the woods. The path narrowed, flanked by Oregon grape, stinging nettles, and ferns.

Crunching along behind him, Jason tapped his shoulder. "Should we keep going?"

"Let's give it a few more minutes," Mike replied, not wild about getting naked around the botanical hazards. "Watch yourself on the nettles."

Jason paused and let the pack drop from his shoulders, catching one of the straps in his hand. "Thanks." He tugged his shirt from the waistline of his jeans and slid his arms into the sleeves. "Don't want our fun ending prematurely." Once he shouldered his pack, they resumed their trek through the underbrush.

The trail opened up again after passing through a stand of old trees and ended at a circular clearing. An ancient vine maple stood to one side, thick moss-covered limbs growing out from a central point. Ferns poked from the moss and blanketed the ground. The gentle rhythm of flowing water from a nearby creek trickled somewhere through the trees.

Jason came up behind Mike and laid an arm across his shoulder. "Beautiful."

Leaning against him, Mike scanned the clearing, half expecting a sprite to leap out from the undergrowth. "How about we get a little more comfortable?" He moved into the center of the clearing and unshouldered his pack.

Jason followed and tugged a small, fleece blanket from his backpack. "This should help."

With a grin, Mike unzipped a side pocket and produced a couple of condoms and a tube of lubricant. "Hiking makes me horny."

After spreading the blanket on the ground, Jason removed his shirt, and again Mike got an eyeful of the muscular officer. "I have a similar reaction to hiking." His hands ran down Jason's abs and framed the tenting bulge in his jeans.

Eager to get his date naked, Mike salivated while kneeling on the blanket. "Come here and let me take care of that."

With a nod, Jason unzipped his jeans and approached Mike. "Just remember, we can't get too tired out. We've got a mile hike to get back to the truck."

SWEATY AND TIRED from their hike and play, Jason eased his frame into the truck. Mike climbed in beside him and smiled, leaning back against the seat and headrest.

"Thanks for a great day." Mike took his hand and squeezed it.

With a gurgle of his stomach, Jason returned the squeeze then started the engine. "It's not over yet. You still have to meet Emily." His nerves flared at the thought of her questioning Mike, but he kept his cool in front of his date.

"I'm actually looking forward to it," Mike replied, turning his warm gaze onto Jason. "She sounds fun."

Jason chuckled as he backed the truck out and left the

trailhead parking lot. "Oh, she is. Just don't let her get anything on you."

Mike cocked his head. "Why not?"

He grimaced. "She never forgets a good story. I'm sure you'll hear at least a couple tonight."

Pulling his hand away, a mischievous grin spread across Mike's face. He rubbed his hands together. "Can't wait."

With a groan, Jason rolled his eyes. "This might be a mistake."

They arrived at the restaurant, and Jason parked his rig. He jumped out and jogged around the back, opening the door for Mike. Glancing around the parking lot, he spied a red Ford Mustang parked three stalls away beside a blue Element.

Mike spied the Mustang as well. "Cool car."

"That's Emily's. Her grandmother gave it to her when she turned sixteen. She's kept it in pristine condition all these years." He glanced at Mike with a wink. "Mostly."

"Oh?" Mike asked, arching an eyebrow.

Jason chuckled, remembering her fender bender. "Well, there was *one* incident…" He stopped himself, remembering this was his leverage story.

Jumping like a little kid impatient for a treat, Mike glanced at the car and back at Jason. "Come on, spill."

Jason just smiled, leading the way to the glass and metal double doors of the restaurant. They stepped into the foyer, and Jason rounded the large fish tank full of tropical fish. Mike paused to examine the fish while Jason scanned the restaurant for Emily. She jumped up from a booth in the corner and waved.

Waving back, Jason led Mike over to her.

"'Bout time you two got here," she pouted, holding out her watch.

Mike frowned. "Sorry. Have you been waiting long?"

She laughed. "Oh, the look on your face. Nah, I just got here a few minutes ago." She stuck out her hand. "I'm Emily."

Taking it, Mike shook. "Mike. I've heard a lot about you."

"Likewise," she nodded at the red, vinyl-covered booth. "Have a seat."

Mike sat on the bench seat and scooted in. Jason slid in beside him, and Emily took her place across the table. Jason took the opportunity to rest his hand on his date's thigh, enjoying the firm muscle beneath his fingers.

She glanced at Jason, a smug grin inching along her lips. "So, do I start the stories now, or should I wait until dinner's served?"

Laughing, Jason shook his head. "I'll remind you of the one fender-bender you had in your Mustang, and put it up against any story you have on me."

Emily considered, her face scrunched in concentration. "Hmm, you might actually have me there."

After passing a menu to Mike, Jason opened his and scanned the offerings.

Mike cleared his throat. "What do you two usually order?"

Peeking over the top of his menu at Emily, Jason nodded at his friend. "I love the Mu Shu duck and the pea vines."

"And I always get the garlic fried string beans," Emily piped up.

As Mike returned his attention to his menu, Jason

poured his tea. His attention wandered around the room. Several couples and families chatted as they ate. The table nearest to them had a family with two kids, mother, father, and two other men. One of the men and the dad had similar features including heads of thick, dark, wavy hair, so Jason assumed they were brothers.

The other of the two men, a blond-haired Brit, raised a glass, his voice rising above the din of the restaurant. "A toast to no more adventures."

The dark-haired one next to him clinked his water glass against the Brit's beer. "Hear, hear."

Jason refocused on his companions as his date returned his menu to the table. "So, did you decide on anything you'd like to try?"

"How about the chicken with snow peas?" Mike ran his finger down the menu, squinting at the offerings. "The other thing that looked interesting was the steamed dumplings."

Emily perked up. "I love the dumplings. Let's get an order."

Knowing they'd take a while, Jason flagged down the waitress.

She hurried over to their table. "You ready to order?"

"Just about, but we'd like an order of the Shanghai steamed dumplings."

"They take fifteen minutes," the waitress replied.

"That's fine." Jason glanced around the table. "You all ready to order, or should we wait a few minutes?"

Emily placed her menu on the table. "Let's do it now, but have the order come out after the dumplings. Or would you rather have them at the end?"

Shrugging, Mike turned to Jason. "Up to you."

"Let's have them whenever they come out." Jason focused on the waitress. "Chicken with snow peas, garlic fried string beans, and two orders of Mu Shu duck." He glanced at Emily. "Do you want the pea vines as well?"

Shaking her head, she grabbed her cup of tea. "Nah. We've got enough food unless you really want them."

"Okay. No pea vines." He handed the menus to the waitress after she finished writing their order onto her pad.

After she left, Mike leaned back in his chair. "So. Fender-bender in the Mustang?"

Emily rolled her eyes. "Not fair. I didn't get to tell any good stories about Jason."

Slinging his arm across Mike's shoulders, Jason grinned. "Do you want to tell it, or should I?" He enjoyed watching his friend squirm for a change.

With a frown, Emily took a sip of her tea. "Okay. So, Jason and I went skinny dipping at a lake way out in the woods in Southern Oregon."

Jason cleared his throat. "I feel it important to interject that *I* wasn't naked. I had the good sense to leave my boxers on."

"Okay, okay," she snorted. "*I* was naked. But you might as well have been. Honestly, I don't know how you intended to keep your modesty with white boxer shorts."

"It worked for me," Jason replied quickly, recognizing her stalling tactic. "Go on."

Her frown intensified. "Well, I'd hidden my purse and Jason's wallet in the shrubs, and we left our clothes on a large rock. We'd swum way out into the middle of the lake when Jason starts shouting."

Remembering like it was yesterday, Jason saw the faces of all three kids. "If I ever catch those punks, they'll be in for it. Three teenagers snatched our clothes and took off running."

"By the time we got back to the shore, they were long gone," Emily continued. "They'd left our shoes but took everything else."

Mike chuckled. "So, you were completely naked, and Jason had see-through underwear. What did you do?"

After giving him a squeeze, Jason grabbed his glass of water. "Recovered our valuables from their hiding place, slipped on our shoes, and hiked back to the car."

"*Anyway.*" Emily crossed her arms across her chest. "We get into the car and are backing out of the parking spot, when this patrol car appears out of nowhere behind me."

Mike leaned forward, wrapped up in the story. "No way."

"Yup. Crunch." Though her face was set in a frown, Jason could tell she was having a ball relating this story. "So, the cop gets out of his car and slowly strolls to the window. I figured there was no point in trying to cover up."

The waitress arrived with a steaming plate of Mu Shu duck and the chicken and snow peas. Jason watched the woman prepare the Mu Shu, depositing one wrap on each plate. "Rest of the order coming." She scurried back to the kitchen.

Mike lifted the wrap. "The officer is looking over your boobs…," Mike prompted. He took a bite, his eyes focused on Emily.

"I figured he'd be into at least one of us, though I think Jason tried to cover his see-through boxers. Of course, he asked me where my clothes were, and I explained while I leaned back in the seat how those punks had stolen our things."

Jason chuckled. "The cop leans in, cocks his head to the side, and grins with a little wave. *Heya, Jason.*"

"Oh, shit. You knew the guy?" Mike's eyes widened as he placed the rest of the wrap into his mouth.

With a nod, Jason sipped at his tea, then focused on Mike. "Turns out one of the guys on my team had gotten a job with the Oregon State Patrol a few weeks prior, and he just happened to be the one on duty in the park."

On the edge of his seat, Mike stared at Jason. "What did he do?"

"He started laughing and said he knew for a fact we weren't some couple fucking on the trail." Jason wriggled his eyebrows at Mike, loving the blush forming on his cheeks. "He gave us a couple of blankets and let us go. The damage to the cruiser was negligible, but the fender of the Mustang had a dent."

The server returned with a plate piled with string beans and a metal steamer filled with dumplings. Jason sat back while Mike loaded his plate. He watched his date, happy the young man was enjoying their dinner with Emily.

Once they'd dished up, Emily turned to Mike. "So, you've heard all about me and my naked road trips. Tell me about you. Brothers or sisters?"

Mike's face darkened for a moment. "One brother, but I don't like to talk about him too much. He spent a good part of our childhood trying to kill me."

Not letting it go, Emily frowned. "You mean being careless?"

Jason slipped his arm around Mike, furrowing his

brow. "We can change the subject if you want." Mike feeling uncomfortable or having to relive the memories just to satisfy Emily's curiosity was the last thing he wanted for their date.

"No, it's okay. My brother tried to shoot me several times. Once I had to hide under the house until mom got home and got the gun away from him. He'd joined a gang and didn't like it that I was a bookworm." He sighed. "I got out of there as soon as I turned eighteen, and I was lucky Alan and Craig let me move in with them."

Emily set her chopsticks on her plate. "Geez. Who are Alan and Craig?"

"My cousins." He considered his Mu Shu wrap and set it back on his plate. "I guess it made me a stronger person. I mean, I survived that stuff. My cousins took me in, and we've made a family of our own."

Giving him another squeeze, Jason kissed his forehead. "And now you've met me."

LEANING IN, MIKE laid his head on Jason's shoulder. "Thanks." Discussing his family always made him angry and sad, but he'd vowed to push past the difficult memories, trying to keep a positive outlook on his life.

Clearing her throat, Emily sat back in her chair and surveyed the empty plates in front of them. "How about some dessert?"

After a last bite of the Mu Shu, Mike nodded. "Sounds good to me. Where should we go?" He checked his watch. Only a quarter after six. "I don't have to be at work until ten tonight, so there's plenty of time for some sugary yumminess."

With a final squeeze to his shoulders, Jason moved his arm back to his side. "Do you need anything from West Seattle before work?"

Mike considered what he'd packed for their weekend and realized he didn't have a clean pair of slacks. "Yeah, I'd better stop at the house. Probably good to check in with the guys anyway. I'll drive in after that."

The waitress approached the table. "Anything else?"

Jason shook his head and turned his back toward Mike. "Here, put the bill on this." He handed the waitress his credit card.

Reaching into his pocket for his wallet, Mike frowned, realizing Jason had beat him to the punch again. "Jason, we talked about this. I need to pay for at least my part of the meal."

Emily chuckled. "Honey, don't bother. Once the card's out, it's over."

The waitress hurried away to the front, and Jason grinned triumphantly. "Hey, it's on me. Today was an amazing day, and I'm very appreciative you were willing to meet my best friend."

Emily placed her hand on her chest. "Why thank you, Sweets."

His smile curled. "Oh yeah, and Emily, too."

Sculpted eyebrows raising, Emily grabbed her paper napkin, balled it up, and threw it at him. "You are such a shit."

Jason burst out laughing. "She's more like the sister I always wanted, but she's my buddy as well."

Mike scowled but tried to be appreciative. The old family training that he had to pay for himself kicked in, and he suppressed his annoyance. "Okay, thanks." He pushed his wallet back into his pocket.

The server returned and handed Jason the black folder with the receipt. Jason scribbled his signature and handed it back to her.

"Thank you. Have a nice day." She strode back to the register.

Jason sprang up from the booth and held out his hand to Mike. "Shall we?"

Scooting along the seat, Mike accepted the offered help and pulled himself up after grasping Jason's hand. He didn't let go, even after standing, and savored their connection. "Thanks."

Emily stood and grabbed her purse. "Okay, where are we going?"

As they moved to the exit, Jason gave Mike's hand a squeeze. "How about the French bakery on California Avenue. It's just off Alaska, about mid-block. I think they're still open."

"Sounds great," she nodded.

Once outside the restaurant, they strolled to their respective vehicles. Jason held open the door of the truck for Mike, turning toward the Mustang. "You know where it is, right?"

She nodded and swung open her door. "Meet you in the parking lot behind."

Mike climbed in, and Jason shut the door. As he fastened his seatbelt, Mike reflected on the day. Hiking and some hot sex with the handsome guy he enjoyed spending time with. Then meeting Jason's best friend. The true test would be introducing Jason to his cousins. Alan had high standards and could be intimidating to those he didn't care for.

Sliding into the driver's seat, Jason grinned as he shut the door and started the engine. "Ready for something sweet?"

Visions of chocolate croissants danced in Mike's head. The bakery in West Seattle was world renowned for their pastries. "I sure am."

Jason leaned over and kissed him. Tingles spread through Mike while he pressed his lips against Jason's.

A beep interrupted their moment of affection. Emily's car sat behind them and she pointed to the watch on her wrist.

Laughing, Jason shifted into reverse as she drove out of the parking lot. "Sorry the something sweet was short."

Mike shrugged. "Hey, I don't mind short and sweet as long as it's chased with long and hot."

JASON DROPPED MIKE at his cousins' place after the stop at the bakery and arrived home tired but glowing. Opening the front door, he glanced back to assess the weather. The warm autumn day had given way to a chilly wet night. Raindrops splattered on the stones along the path he'd just hurried across.

Shutting the door to the gathering storm, Jason hung his jacket on one of the pegs on the wall and kicked off his shoes. He flipped on the light and strode into the living room, pausing to click on the gas fire. The blue flames leapt through the ceramic logs and danced merrily into yellow tipped fire. The hearth warmed quickly, and Jason stepped back.

It had been a wonderful weekend with Mike. Getting to know what a great guy he was made Jason optimistic about dating. The sexy young man captivated him, and he wanted to see Mike again and again.

His gaze wandered across the mantle and to the photo of Christoph kissing his cheek. Some of the glow of the fire lessened and his mood sank with it.

Damn it, Christoph. Why can't I move on from you?

He stared at the picture for a few moments, then turned away and sank into his rocking chair. Memories of their life together flooded his thoughts. The time they raced through the Dishman Hills to find a place to make out. They'd come upon a secluded spot only to have a bunch of hikers pass by.

The memory of their last day together pushed to the fore. Christoph lay on the bed slowly shutting down. Jason remembered stroking his hair while his lover stared up at him.

"Don't leave me, Christoph," he'd begged softly, pain and grief washing over him in a tidal wave.

Christoph's mouth parted in a sad smile. "I'm sorry, luv. You know I don't have a choice." He moved his hand to grasp Jason's. "Promise me you'll live your life and not pine for me."

The ping of Jason's cell brought him back to the present. He wiped away the tear slowly running down his cheek and read the message. It was from Mike:

Thanks for a great weekend. I can't wait to see you again.

Jason unlocked the phone and tapped against the screen.

Me, too. See you soon.

He sent the message and flicked the phone to silent. With a yawn, he stood and pocketed the cell. With one last look at the photo on his mantle, Jason clicked off the fire and moved to the staircase. After shutting off the light, he climbed the stairs and dragged his frame into his bedroom.

Suddenly quite tired, he stripped down to his briefs and slid into bed. Somehow, he needed to push past his feelings of guilt and sadness. After four years, he finally had a chance to date someone he liked. Yet, he was doing exactly what Christoph told him not to do: pining.

CHAPTER SIX

T HE MORNING SUN slipped through the window of the hotel as Mike headed for the lobby door. After twelve hours working and a full weekend, he was completely wiped out. Bed never sounded so good.

Isaac hurried over to him before he could get out the door. "Hey, Mike, hold on a minute."

Turning his tired eyes to his boss, Mike sighed. "Yes?"

"I just wanted to remind you that you have four days of vacation coming, and you need to use them before the end of the month. I can't authorize time off after this month because we'll start getting busy this fall."

Mike nodded. He'd thought about what to do with the time off. Visiting his family had crossed his mind, but he quickly thought better of it. The last person he wanted to see was his mother, and if he set foot in Wisconsin, she'd be there waiting to pounce. Even though she'd thrown him out at eighteen, she insisted on making him miserable with her presence and judgement even if he tried to sneak back to see the few friends still in his hometown.

His thoughts turned to Jason. Maybe they could go somewhere together. Was it too soon to consider something like that? After all, they'd only had two dates. Although, one of those dates spanned an entire weekend and involved meeting Jason's best friend.

Returning his attention to his boss, Mike nodded. "Okay, thanks, Isaac. I'll let you know." He turned away and resumed his exit of the building.

His truck was waiting for him in its usual parking spot. Mike experienced a twinge of disappointment. A missing vehicle would have been the perfect excuse to call Jason. Still, both of them needed their sleep after the long weekend.

Starting up the truck, he shifted into gear and waited a few minutes for it to warm up. His cell dinged, and he fished it out of his pocket. The text was from Jason.

Hey, thanks for a great weekend. Dinner tomorrow with your cousins, right?

Mike grinned at the screen. Instead of typing a message, he pressed the contact info button and called Jason.

"Good morning, handsome," Jason's baritone voice said.

"I got your text and thought I'd call while my truck warms up. What are you doing?" Mike closed his eyes, savoring the tones of Jason's voice.

"Just lying in bed," Jason replied. "How was work?"

The crotch of Mike's work pants tightened as his hardening dick pressed against it. "Good, but I'm exhausted." With a jolt, he opened his eyes. The last thing he needed was to fall asleep listening to Jason's voice with his truck idling.

"Well, you should get some rest. I'd offer to have you come over here, but sleep wouldn't necessarily be on the agenda."

With a laugh, Mike pressed his palm against his now throbbing cock. "I want to, believe me. I can just imagine you naked in bed."

"Why imagine when you can experience?" Jason teased.

The temptation of Jason's offer tore at him, and he weighed whether or not to go. With reluctance, he knew he needed to head back to West Seattle and his room. "Raincheck, I promise."

Jason sighed. "I understand. You probably need to check in with your cousins anyway."

"That's for sure," Mike replied. "They weren't home when I got my truck last night. I haven't seen them in several days now, and I know they'll be full of questions. I think we're still on for tomorrow night. I'll text you when I talk to them."

"Okay, well, get some good sleep and be careful on the way home."

With a smile, Mike revved his truck and checked his mirrors. "I will. Bye."

"Sleep well." The phone beeped twice, and Jason was gone.

Mike pocketed his cell. He maneuvered the truck onto the nearly empty streets of downtown and drove south. He briefly thought about turning around and heading to Jason's, but he knew he'd be in hot water with Alan if he didn't at least come home to prove he was still alive. The onramp to the Highway Ninety-Nine Viaduct made his decision, and he drove south and then west across the West Seattle Bridge.

He'd forgotten to mention to Jason the vacation days he had coming, but still wasn't sure if it was too soon for a getaway trip. He'd need to decide what he was doing quickly since he would have to beg Veronica to take his shifts while he was gone. He didn't want Isaac to have to work for him like the last time he had a couple of days off.

Turning into the alley behind the house, Mike rolled past the driveway and slipped the truck into reverse. He revved the engine and lifted his foot from the brake. The truck took the mini hill with reluctance but made it up the slope and rumbled to a halt.

Mike pushed the door open and stepped out then slammed it shut. He navigated around the garage and into the breezeway between the house and the garage. Just as he reached for the door, the bell Alan had attached to the back door jingled and the door opened.

Alan strode into the breezeway with his briefcase in hand and stopped when he saw Mike. "Well, hello stranger. Where have you been all weekend?"

"Having fun." He winked at his cousin and gave him a hug.

"I suspected no less," his cousin replied, a bemused grin on his lips.

Stepping back, Mike met Alan's gaze. "Are we still on for dinner with Jason tomorrow?"

"Sure. I wouldn't miss the unveiling," his cousin said with a chuckle.

Mike rolled his eyes. "Don't you have a bus to catch or something?"

Alan checked his watch. "Oh, shit. I'm going to be late. Craig's still here, so you can check in with him before you go to bed. We have a surprise for you."

"Oh?" he asked, curiosity battling with his drowsiness.

"Yup." With a grin, Alan trotted around the garage and into the driveway. Just as he turned into the alley, he waved. "Bye!"

Shaking his head, Mike watched him go. After Alan

disappeared into the alley, Mike reached for the screen door, his tired eyes trying to close.

Craig bustled up the stairs from the basement. "Good morning."

"Hey there." Mike pulled open the door and stepped inside after Craig passed. He climbed the four steps into the kitchen and trudged toward his room.

Craig stood at his bedroom door, blocking the entrance. "You'll notice there is no light coming from under your door."

A glance at the floor confirmed Craig's words, but his sleepy, fuzzy mind refused to analyze their significance. "Okaaay…"

With a flourish, Craig flung open the door and raised an arm toward the window. "That's because Alan installed blackout drapes under your regular curtains."

The room was considerably darker than the rest of the house, effectively blocking the sunshine outside. Mike smiled and leaned against the doorframe. "Wow, thanks. I really appreciate this."

"You're welcome," Craig said, grinning. "Are we meeting your new guy tomorrow?"

"As long as you still want to," he replied nervously.

Craig rested his hands on his hips. "Of course, we want to. Any diet restrictions?"

"Not that I know of." He considered the meals they'd already shared together, and Jason made no substitution requests at the restaurants or declined anything they'd been served.

"Great. I'll make pasta and sauce. Does he like shellfish?"

He shrugged. "I'll ask him after I get up."

Craig nodded. "Okay, just let me know so I can get all the stuff I'm thinking of."

With a frown, Mike imagined some weird gourmet concoction gracing the table. "You're not going to go too fancy, are you?"

Raising an eyebrow, Craig's lips quirked into a small grin. "Why? You haven't complained about my cooking before."

"Meeting Jason isn't that big of a deal." Who was he kidding? Introducing Jason to his family was a huge deal for him.

"So says you. I'm thinking of making mussels, scallops, and shrimp with fresh pasta and tomato sauce. Is that too weird for you?"

Mike sighed. "Should be fine." He really wasn't a fan of seafood and couldn't figure out why his cousins kept trying to get him to eat it.

"Don't worry," Craig said as he turned. "I'll make you a hotdog or some dinosaur-shaped chicken nuggets if you'd prefer something simple." He strode away through the hall and back into the kitchen.

Rolling his eyes, he flicked on the light and entered his room. He lifted one of the drapes from the window and checked out Alan and Craig's handiwork. The two white, plastic drapes had Velcro closing out the light. The curtains fell back against the panes as he kicked off his shoes.

He pulled his phone and wallet from his pocket and placed them on his dresser then dropped his pants to the floor and pulled off his shirt.

Another wave of exhaustion hit as he neared the door. With another flick of his wrist he turned off the lights.

The room was now almost pitch black save for the dim outline of the window. He stumbled toward the bed with his arms out trying to feel his way. After tripping over his abandoned shoes, he found the bed and sank down onto it.

Pulling the covers over his body and up to his head, he rolled onto his side and shut his eyes. As he drifted off to sleep, he imagined Jason's arms holding him. He liked the idea of sharing a bed with the hunky cop and hoped his cousins would like Jason as much as he did.

GIVING HIS HOUSE the cleaning overhaul it had been needing for several weeks, Jason hefted two large bags of old clothes out the front door. He flung both bulging sacks into the bed of his truck and pushed them against the cab.

It felt good to clean out his spare closet. Most of what was in there he wouldn't be caught dead in, and he was long overdue to get rid of the accumulation. He returned to the house and climbed the steps to his bedroom.

Just as he was reaching for another sack of clothes, his phone buzzed in his pocket. Standing upright again, he fished out his phone and found Emily's smiling face on the screen.

With a swipe, he accepted the call. "Hey there. What's up?"

"Heya, Sweets. I'm out for a jog and was wondering if you wanted a little company."

Jason stepped to the bed and sat down. "You're not wearing that Eighties tube top thing, are you?"

"No, I'm not. And I'm not going down that road with you again." Though tinged with irritation, he could hear the amused lilt to her tone. He wondered if she came up with those outfits just to get a rise out of him.

"Well, thank goodness for that," he chuckled. "Come on over."

"Are you sure?" she drawled. "I might not meet the dress code for Club Lynch."

Jason laughed. "Don't worry. Even if you're a fashion disaster, I know the bouncer and he'll let you in."

Now she laughed with him. "Have a glass of wine poured for me. I want to hear more about your weekend."

With a sigh, Jason stood and headed downstairs, the sack of clothes abandoned on the floor. "Okay. Where are you?"

"Just turning onto your street. Be there in a couple minutes." She ended the call.

Jason stepped across the kitchen and tugged open the door to the basement. He descended the narrow wooden stairs and turned right at the bottom into his small wine cellar. Several of the shelves stood empty.

He poked around the three full shelves and pulled out a couple of bottles to read the labels. Footsteps sounded across the hardwood above his head.

"Are you in the basement, Jason?" Emily called from the kitchen.

"Yeah, come on down." He wiped the dust off a bottle of Bordeaux.

The steps creaked, and Emily quickly joined him. "Where's my glass?"

"Sorry, I was just surveying the desolation of having you over so often." He swept his hand around the mostly empty shelves. "I need to take a trip over to Walla Walla and Yakima to restock."

She took a bottle of cabernet from the shelf. "This looks good."

Jason swept his gaze over the top row of shelves. Four bottles of prosecco and a bottle of champagne lay on their sides.

"We could have the red, or I could make a fizzy, fruity drink with the prosecco. I think I have some orange juice in the fridge."

Handing him the bottle of red, her eyes lit up. "That sounds great after a run. Would help me cool down."

He reached up and pulled one of the bottles off the top shelf. Returning his gaze to her, he took a moment to fully appraise her running outfit.

"For the love of God, what died to make your outfit?"

Scowling, Emily grabbed the bottle, spun on her heel, and made a beeline for the stairs. "Oh, boy, here we go."

The back made him cringe even more. Her tight-fitting t-shirt had a cheetah print, and the white running spandex made her butt look huge.

He followed her up the stairs. "Seriously, we need to plan a day out soon to get you some decent running attire."

When they reached the kitchen, she shoved the bottle of prosecco into his hands. "Just make the drinks. I get stuff on the sales rack, and it works for keeping my body covered while I'm running."

"Oh, but the glare…" Jason removed the foil cover from the bottle and popped the cork. Foam surged from the opening, and he quickly moved to the sink. "Did you shake the bottle?"

"Nope," she sulked. "Must have warmed from the hot air you're blowing about my clothes."

He chuckled and set the bottle in the sink, and then wiped off his hands with the dishrag. "Grab a couple of flutes from the china cabinet please."

While she moved to the fetch the glasses, Jason opened the refrigerator and retrieved the bottle of orange juice from the door. He spied a few leftover pancakes covered in plastic wrap on a plate, and briefly thought about the breakfast feast he'd prepared for Mike with a smile. Emily returned and handed him two crystal flutes, which he filled halfway with the juice. He then poured the prosecco to top off the glasses and handed one to his friend.

"You look flustered," she stated, her gazed narrowing. "Spill."

He cocked his head. "Flustered?"

"You never willingly go through your closets, and you seem to have this nervous energy today."

With her usual sixth sense about his state of mind, Emily had zeroed in on the anxiety he felt meeting Mike's family. The place had needed cleaning, but he'd jumped into long-standing projects instead of the deep clean he'd intended on.

"I'm meeting Mike's cousins for the first time, and I'm a little nervous." He leaned against the counter, eyeing his drink. Maybe he should have spiked it with vodka.

Her grin spread wide. "They're going to love you. Just like I do." She quirked her lips into an amused frown. "Just don't critique their outfits."

He laughed, lifting his glass and clinking it with hers. "To us."

She held him in her gaze. "And to new beginnings."

STANDING IN THE living room and waiting for Jason's arrival, Mike paced, his stomach twisted in knots. Though he'd told his cousins that this wasn't a big deal, having them meet his new boyfriend filled him with nerves. He really needed them to like Jason. Mike glanced out the window hoping to see Jason's truck pull up.

Craig buzzed around the small kitchen as he managed boiling pasta, steaming mussels, and bubbling tomato sauce. The house filled with the scent of the impending meal, and Mike had to admit how wonderful it smelled.

"Hey, Mike, would you mind setting the table?" Craig called out.

Turning away from the window, Mike nodded. "Plates or bowls?"

"Plates." Craig surveyed the pots on the stove. "On second thoughts, maybe bowls. I'm thinking the sauce might be a little runny."

"I'm sure it'll be great." Mike stepped into the kitchen and retrieved four bowls from the cupboard. He made to reach for the roll of paper napkins under the sink, but Craig shook his head.

He pointed to the linen closet. "Cloth napkins. We're having a guest."

The bell over the back door jangled, and Alan climbed the steps into the kitchen. "Hey, guys. Is he here yet?"

Craig moved to the sink with the steaming pot filled with water and pasta. "Not yet." He dumped the contents through the colander and set the pot back on the stove.

"Good. Still time for me to get my shotgun." Setting his briefcase on the floor, Alan approached Craig and wrapped his arms around his husband's waist. "Hi, handsome."

They leaned into each other, sharing a kiss.

Turning away, Mike rolled his eyes and stepped into the dining room. Leave it to his cousin to make him more nervous. He placed the bowls on the table, then retrieved the napkins from the linen closet as Craig had requested. He returned to the table as Alan rounded the corner into the dining room.

"Looks like Craig's made a real feast," Alan said, looking over the table. "It's one of my favorites, and he doesn't make it very often."

Mike sighed. "I told him not to go all out."

Alan laughed. "Fat chance of that when we're having guests for dinner." He patted Mike's shoulder. "Besides, he has to pass the cooking test."

Staring at his cousin, the knots in Mike's stomach constricted tighter. "The *cooking* test?"

Alan's face lit up. "Yeah. If he doesn't like the food, he's out."

Craig stormed into the dining room. "Alan, knock that off. He's nervous enough as it is." He turned to Mike. "It's okay if he doesn't like the meal."

Laughing, Alan left the room. "Of course, it is." He poked his head back into the room. "But it will count against him if he doesn't."

"Alan!" Craig stamped his foot, threatening his husband with the wooden pasta spoon.

Mike shook his head at Alan's echoing chuckle from the hallway.

Stepping back into the kitchen, Craig beckoned Mike to follow. "Don't pay any attention to him."

"Don't worry, I won't." Mike did care what Alan thought of his new guy. Quite a lot. But he knew his cousin was trying to get him riled up. "Alan really knows how to yank my chain."

"Well, you do make it pretty easy for him." Craig lifted the colander from the sink and gave it a shake. Water drained from the bottom of the metal strainer and into the sink.

Mike grinned. "I don't know how you put up with him."

Alan returned in a green pullover and jeans. "It's because I'm so sweet."

Dumping the pasta into a white bowl, Craig eyed his husband. "Yeah, that's the reason."

The doorbell rang, and the three men stared at each other.

Alan rubbed his hands together with a decidedly evil grin. "Showtime."

THOUGH HE'D FACED down some rough customers as a cop, Jason had to admit to himself that meeting Mike's family was more daunting than he'd originally anticipated.

He stood on the stoop of the white and green house after ringing the bell and waited while clutching a bottle of Bordeaux. Footsteps sounding from within approached. The wooden door opened, and Jason was relieved to see Mike greeting him.

"Hey there," Mike said, the smile on his face not hiding the stress tensing his body.

Jason gave him a quick hug and stepped into the warm house. A heavy scent of pasta and tomato sauce hung in the air, making his stomach rumble. Mike closed the door and stepped to Jason's side.

Two men stood in the living room. The taller had black hair and piercing blue eyes, while the other was about Jason's height with reddish-brown hair and green eyes. He could see the family resemblance to Mike in the shorter man and deduced that this was Cousin Alan.

"I'm Jason." He stepped forward and greeted the taller one first.

"Craig. Nice to meet you." His grip was firm and his smile genuine.

"A pleasure, sir," Jason replied with a nod.

Chuckling, Craig gave a shake of his head. "While I appreciate your politeness, there's no need to be formal with us."

"Thanks." Jason turned his attention to the other man. "You must be Alan."

"Correct." The man stood next to his husband, a neutral expression on his face. Jason shook Alan's hand and definitely felt more appraisal from Mike's cousin. The grip was firm like Craig's, and the man's gaze never wavered.

Presenting the bottle to Alan, Jason broke away from his piercing stare and turned to address Craig. "I know Mike said not to bring anything, but I thought I could at least contribute some wine to go with dinner."

With an approving nod, Craig took the bottle from Alan and read the label. "Thank you. You certainly didn't have to."

Jason shrugged. "I feel weird coming to dinner without bringing something."

"This should pair wonderfully with the sauce. Shall we open it up and try it? Mike, please get me four wine glasses." Craig carried the bottle into the kitchen.

With a smile at Jason, Mike made for the china cabinet against the wall in the dining room. "Sure thing."

Left alone with Alan, Jason met the appraising gaze of Mike's cousin.

"So, Jason. How did you meet Mike?"

"I helped him find his truck." He resisted the urge to call Alan *sir*. "Someone took it for a joyride and left it in an alley downtown."

Alan snorted. "Too bad you found it."

Chuckling, Jason relaxed. "I take it you're not too fond of Mike's vehicle."

"It has certainly seen better days." He glanced into the dining room and lowered his voice. "I'm not entirely sure it's safe for him to drive."

"As you say, it definitely isn't new." Trying to be diplomatic, he attempted to shift the conversation away from the condition of Mike's beloved junker. "Did he have it when he moved here?"

Alan rolled his eyes. "Unfortunately. Somehow, that clunker made it from Wisconsin to Seattle. Only broke down once just outside of Boise. One of the slowest drives of my life."

"Oh?" Jason's curiosity piqued.

"He'd loaded his truck with his stuff, and I followed in my car with a couple of his suitcases." Alan shook his head. "I don't think we did over fifty the entire trip."

He considered the route they likely took. "How did it do over the Rockies?"

"My truck did just fine, thank you very much." Mike strode into the room with two wine glasses. "Alan thinks I should sell it."

Taking the glass, Jason glanced at Alan. "Well, he

might have a point."

Alan grinned, but Mike frowned.

"I'm glad you two found something in common." Turning on his heel, Mike marched toward the kitchen.

Jason returned his attention to Alan. "Uh oh. I'm in trouble now."

"Don't worry about it. I give him shit about that clunker all the time. Cheers." He raised his glass.

Clinking his glass against Alan's, Jason took a sip of the red wine. Though dry, a smooth fruitiness greeted his taste buds.

Alan nodded. "Not bad. Should pair well with dinner."

As if on cue, Craig carried a white bowl full of pasta covered in tomato sauce into the dining room. "Dinner is served."

Mike followed Craig with two more glasses of wine and sat at the table.

Alan swept his hand toward the table. "Shall we?"

Attempting to put his best manners on display, Jason hesitated at the entrance to the dining room. "Where would you like me to sit?"

"Go ahead and grab the seat closest to you." Alan maneuvered around one of the chairs. "I'm usually at the head of the table, and Craig likes to sit next to me so he can have easy access to the kitchen."

Craig pulled the chair away from the table. "And because I like to sit next to you."

With a smile, Alan lowered himself onto the chair.

Turning to Jason, Craig winked. "And because I don't actually care where anyone sits at the table. It's more Alan's thing."

"Oh, no, I totally get it." Jason hesitated, unsure if he should really sit directly across from Alan. "My grandparents were very particular about where people sat at the table, especially when they had all the family over."

Mike took Jason's hand and brought him around to the seat next to his. Jason happily followed, enjoying Mike's touch.

Alan eyed Mike's glass as they sat down. "Wine, Mike?"

"I'm branching out," he said, scooting his chair in. "You and Craig really like it, and so does Jason. So, I'm trying it."

Once they were all seated, Craig passed the pasta bowl to Jason. "Guests first."

The steaming bowl held wide-noodle pasta covered with shellfish and a light covering of tomato sauce. The clams, mussels, and shrimp all looked fresh. Jason scooped a large helping onto his plate. "This looks great. Where do you get your seafood?"

With a dubious glance at the pasta, Mike accepted the bowl from Jason. "He gets it from some place on Beacon Hill."

"The fish is fresh, and the place is reputable, never fear," Craig said, lifting his wine glass.

After taking a small portion, Mike passed the bowl on to Alan. His cousin leaned over his plate and arched an eyebrow. "Eating light this evening?"

Mike placed his hands in his lap and sat up prim and proper. "I'm being polite and holding back so you and Craig can have plenty."

Craig laughed. "I have the chicken nuggets in reserve if you don't like it."

Rolling his eyes, Mike dug in and took a bite of the steaming noodles.

Alan held his fork against the serving spoon and heaped a large portion onto his own plate. "Well? Does it pass the test?"

Chewing, Mike nodded. He swallowed. "Once you get some, Craig, I'll take more."

Craig passed the salad to Jason. "First the wine and now the shellfish. Will wonders never cease?"

"So, Jason. Tell us a bit about yourself." Alan spun his fork in his pasta and lifted it to his mouth.

Mike's anxiety ratcheted up. Here came the questions from his critical cousin. He eyed Alan as he ate a forkful of salad.

"I'm from Spokane originally. My grandparents raised me after the rest of my family died. I joined the Spokane PD after I graduated from college." Jason paused to take a sip of wine.

"Where did you go to school?" Alan gave Mike his own pointed stare.

"UW," Jason said. "I was there four years."

The satisfied smirk on Alan's face irritated Mike to no end. "Points for the correct school."

Jason raised his glass. "Cheers."

Mike stared Alan down. The see-even-*he's*-attended-college glance was met with stubborn defiance. He knew damned well the point of Alan's comment, and it wasn't complimenting Jason on his choice of schools.

Shaking his head, Craig patted Jason's arm. "Don't pay any attention to him. You wouldn't have lost any points for being a Cougar." He lifted his own glass. "Well, not many."

With a swing of his glare to Craig, Mike placed his fork on the table. "Let's move on from the college conversation."

Jason glanced back and forth between the cousins. "Okay, then. Lost my partner to cancer about four years ago and moved back to Seattle to start over."

At the mention of his former boyfriend, Mike turned his full attention to Jason. Though his face stayed even, Mike could see the emotional scars Christoph's loss had left.

Craig sighed. "A lot of loss. Sounds like your grand-parents were huge in your life. Are they still living?"

"No, they passed away within about three hours of each other. She made ninety-seven, and he hit a hundred and two. They were married almost eighty years." More pain hiding behind Jason's pleasant expression. Mike made a mental note to comfort his boyfriend when they were alone again.

With a sideways glance, Mike's anxiety lessened as he watched Alan go from critical frown to satisfied admira-tion. Jason was the first man he'd brought home who even moderately impressed his cousin. Alan's opinion did mean a lot to him, though he was careful not to let his cousin know that *too* often.

He resumed eating his pasta, looking forward to head-ing out with Jason after dinner. Maybe they'd have time for a little snuggle before he had to head to work.

MIKE PLACED HIS fork on his empty plate. "That was really

good, Craig." Jason noted Mike had destroyed three helpings of the pasta. Mike seemed to like fish, or at least shellfish.

With a grin, Craig glanced at his husband. "He ate seafood and *liked* it."

Alan nodded. "Shellfish, no less. Definite progress."

Returning his hands to his lap, Mike leveled his gaze on his cousin. "I don't know what you mean. I love frozen fish sticks."

Craig rolled his eyes and sank back in his chair. "And we lost him again."

With a sympathetic smile, Alan patted Craig's hand. "Baby steps, dear."

Enjoying the family banter, Jason settled into his chair and sipped at his wine. He missed his own family. Watching Mike's interaction with his cousins reminded him of his parents and their playful poking at dinners. His grandparents had been less emotive but showed their love in little deeds and gestures. The obvious affection Mike's cousins showed gave Jason a fleeting connection to his absent family.

After scooting his chair back, Mike stood. "Can I help you guys clear up?"

Alan's eyes widened. "This is a nice change."

Craig swatted his husband's arm. "Behave," he scolded then turned to Mike. "Thanks, I'd be glad for your help."

Quickly standing, Jason picked up his own plate. "Here, I can help, too." He moved between Alan and Craig and lifted their plates and silverware from the table, stacking them on the one he already held.

Alan poured himself another glass of wine. "Thanks, Jason. That's mighty nice of you."

"No problem." Jason followed Mike into the kitchen and placed the dishes on the countertop by the sink. "Do we hand wash any of these, or can they go into the dishwasher?"

Mike opened a drawer to retrieve a box of plastic wrap. "I think everything there can go straight into the dishwasher." He transferred the remaining pasta and shellfish into one small bowl and covered it with the plastic. After smoothing the sides, he opened the refrigerator and placed it inside.

Pulling the dishwasher open, Jason placed the dishes inside in an orderly fashion, careful to leave as much room as possible for larger items. Mike left the kitchen and returned with another round of serving bowls and water glasses.

The two of them worked quickly, washing the wooden salad spoons in the sink and drying them with the dishtowel. With the dishwasher full, Mike reached under the sink for the detergent and filled the soap receptacle. He closed the dishwasher door and set the machine going, then replaced the box of soap.

Craig stepped into the kitchen carrying his empty wine glass. "Wow, guys. Nice job cleaning up."

Jason surveyed their work. All the pots and pans fit into the dishwasher, so the stove was clear. Mike wiped down the empty countertops with a dishrag.

Finishing the job, he wrung out the cloth and spread it over the arm of the faucet. "You made it easy for us. Not that much actually needed cleaning."

Alan joined them in the kitchen, standing next to Craig and wrapping his arm around his lover's waist. "Craig does a great job of cleaning while he goes. Even after twenty years I'm impressed with his efficiency in the kitchen."

With a shrug, Craig placed his wine glass on the counter. "I learned as a teenager working in the kitchen of a nursing home. There was always something to clean, and the night went faster if you kept ahead of the pile of dirty dishes."

Jason leaned against the counter. "Everything was delicious. Thanks for having me over."

Craig checked his watch. "Well, you're welcome to stay a while, Jason. I do have to get up early tomorrow, so I'll have to say goodnight."

Stepping forward, Jason extended his hand. "It was a pleasure to meet you."

With a shake of his head, Craig brushed away Jason's hand and gave him a quick hug. "We're delighted to have you over. Come back anytime." He turned to Mike. "You boys staying here tonight?"

Mike gave Craig a hug. "No, I have to work. I'll probably go to Jason's in the morning, so don't worry if I don't show up tomorrow."

Stepping back, Craig nodded. "Okay, have a good night then." He gave Alan a kiss on the cheek. "Don't be too long."

"Okay, see you in a few minutes." Alan swatted his butt.

Jason addressed Mike. "If you want, I could give you a ride to the hotel and then pick you up in the morning after I finish my shift."

"Really?" Mike's eyes lit up. "That'd be great."

"Grab your pack and we can get going."

Passing Alan, Mike stepped into the hallway. "I'll be

right back."

Alan watched him go, then turned his attention to Jason. "Glad you could come over and meet the family, so to speak."

"It was an honor." Treading carefully, he assumed his test wasn't over from the protective cousin. "I'm glad to see Mike has people who care about him as much as the two of you obviously do."

Leaning against the doorway of the kitchen, Alan nodded. "Mike's had some pretty hard times, especially since he came out. We've been around all his life, but we stepped in when the shit hit the fan. I'm none too popular with his mother."

"He's lucky to have you," Jason offered, his guard going up.

"Craig says I'm a bit overprotective of him, but I can't help it." Alan leveled a hard stare at Jason. "Just don't hurt him."

Something in Alan's stare gave Jason pause. It felt like he was staring at a father holding a shotgun on the front porch while the teenaged daughter got ready for a date.

"No need to worry," Jason said, meeting Alan's gaze head-on. "I have no intention of hurting your cousin."

Alan stepped forward and extended his hand. "Good. I'll hold you to that."

CHAPTER SEVEN

MIKE CLAMBERED INTO Jason's truck and fastened his seatbelt. Jason slammed the door shut and took a last look at Craig's and Alan's house. Alan stood in the living room clearly framed in the large picture window staring out. He waved with a grin.

Returning the gesture, Jason pulled open his door and climbed inside his truck. "How do you think it went?" He hoped the cousins got a good impression, and that he hadn't made any missteps with Mike.

Mike grinned. "I think they like you. Alan was all smiles by the end of the evening. The family story really impressed him. He's done a lot of genealogy on our side of the family."

Relief settled over Jason. "That's good. I enjoyed dinner. Craig is a great cook." Jason started up the truck and shifted into gear. Meeting the family wasn't nearly as difficult as he'd anticipated.

Mike's hand rested on his thigh. "Thanks for taking me to work." His fingers scratched against the fabric of Jason's pants and worked their way between his legs. Mike grazed the nail of his index finger across Jason's balls, leaving small quakes of pleasure in their wake.

Concentrating on the road, Jason spread his legs as much as he safely could. His cock stirred and strained against the confinement of his pants. Continuing to tease, Mike pressed his palm against Jason's lengthening hardness.

With a glance at Mike, Jason sighed. "I have to wait ten hours to get you into bed."

Ceasing his caressing of Jason's crotch, Mike returned his hands to his lap. "Sorry. You just get me all excited, and I'd like to celebrate after a successful dinner."

"Don't apologize. I love your touch." Jason glanced over for a moment. "Just frustrating I can't take you home after such a great evening."

"I'm sure the night will go by quickly," Mike replied. "We're booked solid, so I'll have lots to do."

Jason turned onto the West Seattle Bridge and drove toward downtown. The lights of the harbor glistened on Elliott Bay. Colored beams played across the water reflecting the Big Wheel as it cycled through its evening display.

They continued the journey in a comfortable silence. Jason took the exit for Highway Ninety-Nine. He considered all that had happened in such a short time. Meeting Mike had drawn him out of his shell and filled a space in his heart left vacant with the loss of Christoph. He was grateful to the fates for bringing them together.

"What are you thinking about?" Mike's question broke his reverie.

Jason turned his attention briefly onto Mike's handsome face. "Just thinking how lucky I am to have met you."

"That's sweet of you to say." Mike's cheeks pinked in the light of the streetlamps lining the highway. "I feel the same."

Screwing up his courage, Jason again glanced at Mike. "Say, I have some vacation time coming up. Would you like to go somewhere?"

With a grin, Mike nodded. "Funny you should mention a vacation. I have PTO days I have to use by the end of the month or I'll lose them."

"Perfect, then." Jason returned his attention to the road. "Maybe we can discuss where to go over breakfast." He exited into downtown and turned up Fourth Avenue.

Mike's hand returned to his leg. "Okay, sounds great. Are you cooking, or should I meet you somewhere?"

Waiting for a red light, Jason turned to Mike. "How about I meet you at the restaurant in the hotel?"

"That'll work." He nodded out the window. "The light's green."

"Oh, thanks." Jason shifted his attention back to the road and pulled up in front of the hotel. "Okay, see you around seven."

With a final squeeze, Mike let go of his leg. "Thanks for coming tonight. It meant a lot to me. Craig and Alan are my family."

Jason leaned into Mike and kissed his lips. He caressed Mike's face with his fingertips as their lip-lock intensified.

Remembering where they were, Jason pulled back, reluctant to separate from Mike but knowing his boyfriend needed to get to work. "I enjoyed this evening. See you tomorrow."

Mike gave him another peck on the lips and opened the door of the truck. "Thanks again for the ride." He slipped out of the seat and stood on the sidewalk. "Seven in the restaurant. See you then."

With a wave, Mike slammed the truck door closed and

trotted into the hotel. Jason watched him go, warmth and happiness firmly settled over him. *What a great guy.*

He shifted the truck into gear and pulled back into traffic. Heading home to grab his uniform, he contemplated where to take Mike on their vacation. So many options. Sun and sand, winter skiing, or maybe sailing. He'd have to see where Mike's interests lay.

THE SUN REFLECTED off the glass and steel buildings around the hotel, flashing warm beams through the windows. Mike surveyed the lobby and spied Jason parking his truck.

One of the hotel guests approached the counter. "Hi, I need to check out."

Mike smiled. "Of course. Your room number?"

"Four twenty-six." The tall, red-headed man fidgeted with the keycard in his hand.

Pulling up the information, Mike clicked the appropriate boxes indicating the customer was leaving. He glanced past the man to notice Jason coming into the lobby.

Warmth flooded through him as he returned his attention to the guest. "Looks like everything is in order, Mr. Martinson. Did you use anything from the minibar?"

The guest shook his head. "Nope."

Jason caught Mike's attention and waved. He pointed to the restaurant door and entered.

Mike nodded and then settled his gaze back on the guest. "Would you like to keep this on the same card as when you checked in?"

"Sure," he replied, checking the expensive watch on his

wrist. "Can you get me a cab to the airport? I don't think I have time to take the light rail."

"Absolutely, sir." He hit the print button and picked up the phone next to him.

"Robbie here."

Mike gathered the two pages from the printer and laid them on the counter. "I need a cab to take a guest to the airport."

"Be there in five minutes."

The phone clicked, and Mike replaced the receiver. He grabbed a pen from the container on the counter and handed it to the guest. "Take a look at the receipt and sign if it looks okay. The cab will be here in about five minutes. Robbie will get you to the airport much faster than the rail this time of the morning."

After signing, the man handed the receipt to Mike. "Thanks. Should I just wait over there?" He pointed to the chair by the fireplace.

"Sure. Head outside when you see the cab pull up." He closed out the room on the computer and smiled at the guest. "Have a great trip and thanks for staying with us."

"I'll definitely be back." The man gathered up his bag and suitcase and ambled to the chair.

Mike turned to Isaac. "Okay, I'm out. Jason just arrived."

The morning shift desk clerk, Carlo, stepped around the corner and approached the counter.

Isaac chuckled. "Perfect timing. Have a good breakfast."

Mike stepped away from the counter, and Carlo took his place. "Thanks, Isaac. I'll see you tomorrow." He hurried down the hall to the locker room and stripped out of his work clothes. Shoving them into a laundry bag, he took a ticket from the pile and wrote his name on it, attached the tag, and tossed the bag down the laundry chute. He opened his locker to retrieve his street clothes.

Once dressed, he slammed the locker shut and strode through the back hallway to the staff entrance of the restaurant. Stepping into the bustling room, Mike spied Jason seated at a booth by the window, typing on his cell.

Mike hurried to the table and slid onto the seat opposite Jason. "Good morning, handsome. Sleep well?"

Jason clicked his cell off and set it on the table. "I was on duty last night. Besides, I wanted to stay awake so we could nap together." He wriggled his eyebrows. "Among other things."

A surge of desire hit Mike. "Are you sure you want breakfast?" Mike's stomach gurgled, and he acknowledged his hunger pangs.

Chuckling, Jason handed him one of the menus. "Sounds like you need a meal, so let's go ahead and eat. We need to discuss our upcoming vacation."

Ariana, the morning shift waitress Mike liked most, carried a coffee pot to their table. "Hi Mike. Want your usual steak and eggs?"

He smiled at her. "Nah, I'm thinking blueberry pancakes and an over-easy egg."

"Coming right up." She turned to Jason. "How about for you?"

Jason closed the menu. "Actually, the steak and eggs sound good. Sunnyside up, and a biscuit, please."

Ariana nodded at Jason's cup. "Coffee?"

"Sure."

She poured his coffee. "You want something to drink,

Mike?"

"Hot chocolate, please."

"You got it." She moved away.

Mike returned his attention to his boyfriend, trying hard to contain his excitement. Time away from Seattle sounded like fun, especially with Jason. "So, where are we going on our trip?"

"Well, I need some parameters. We probably should keep it in the US. At least for the first trip."

Mike's ears perked up. "So, the second trip is overseas?"

"We'll see. Let's just stick with planning this one." Jason sipped his coffee and then held the cup in his hands, peering over the rim at Mike.

Ariana brought the steaming cup of hot chocolate and set it in front of him. "Here you are. Anything else you need for it?"

The mound of whipped cream on the top of the mug seemed higher than usual, and the chocolate sprinkles with a sprig of mint was a new touch.

"This is like artwork," Mike puzzled at the cup. "How am I going to drink it?"

The waitress produced a spoon. "Try this. You'll need it for the extra cream." She glanced at Jason. "Need more coffee?"

"Sure." Jason chuckled, placing the cup on the table. She poured him another cup. "Breakfast should be coming soon."

Mike dipped the spoon into the cream. "Thanks."

Jason took another sip of coffee, settling his gaze on Mike with a bemused grin.

Pondering the places on his list of must-do vacations,

Mike slid a spoonful of whipped cream and sprinkles into his mouth. The sweet milk and chocolate melted on his tongue with a delightful flavor.

Still watching him, Jason placed his cup on the table. "Do you want sun and warmth or snow and hot tubs?"

Mike licked the spoon and stuck it on his nose to hang.

Jason laughed. "Goofball." He plucked the spoon from Mike's face. "I'm partial to the beach myself."

Snatching back the spoon, Mike grinned. "A beach sounds amazing. I've never been to the ocean."

Jason's eyes widened. "What? Never?"

"Nope." Mike spooned another helping of the whipped cream into his mouth.

"We've gotta change that. The beach at Santa Monica is too cold to swim, especially now that summer is over. San Diego has some nice beaches."

With his excitement building, Mike pondered a sunny get-a-way with his muscular boyfriend. A few days basking nearly naked at the beach sounded perfect.

Ariana arrived with their breakfasts, and Mike salivated at the pile of pancakes covering his plate. Jason's eyes widened at the large steak covered in two eggs. The waitress placed a dish with a miniature jar of jam, a pat of butter, and a biscuit next to the steak.

"Can I bring anything else?"

Jason shook his head. "This looks great."

"Enjoy." She left them to their meal.

After buttering the pancakes and applying a liberal amount of syrup, Mike used his fork to cut a bite from the stack. He stabbed it and brought it to his mouth.

Jason cut into his steak. "This looks fantastic. You

usually get it?"

Mike swallowed the pancake, savoring the flavors. He took a quick sip of the chocolate and returned the cup to the table. "It's my favorite. I just felt more like pancakes today."

Jason took a bite of the steak and hummed his approval.

Using his knife, Mike cut up the remainder of the stack in front of him. He punctured the yolk of the egg and dipped a forkful of pancake into the bright yellow liquid before popping it into his mouth.

After swallowing, Jason nodded his approval. "Delicious. So, back to the beach."

Mike wrapped his hands around the cup of chocolate, enjoying the warmth on his fingers. "Let's do it. I'd like to see San Diego. Maybe I can get some information from Isaac about hotels and resorts."

"Sounds good. I suppose being in the hotel industry, he might have some useful contacts for us." Jason ate more of his steak.

They continued their meal, glancing occasionally at each other. Mike stiffened for a moment and shot Jason a glance when a sock-covered foot slid up his leg and along the sensitive inside of his thigh.

"Is that steak making you frisky?"

Jason grinned. "The sight of you sitting across from me is doing that. I thought I'd see if you were equally excited."

The crotch of Mike's jeans filled as the sensations of Jason's toes rubbing his thigh sent pleasure racing through him. The foot slowly moved between Mike's legs and across his balls.

Mike stifled a gasp as Ariana strode by their table. She paused at his eye contact. "Can I get you anything?"

Jason's foot continued its movement up to Mike's crotch and his toes gently drummed against Mike's stiffening dick.

Shaking his head, Mike leaned forward so she couldn't see what was going on.

Jason cleared his throat. "We're probably ready for the check."

Finding his voice, Mike reached into his lap and grabbed Jason's foot. With a temporary reprieve from the excitement Jason's playing had caused, he fished his staff ID card from his pocket.

"Put it on my account."

She took the plastic card from him. "I'll scan the barcode and be right back." She bustled toward the reception desk.

With a frown, Jason pulled his foot away and raised an eyebrow. "Now, you shouldn't have done that."

Mike caught the foot before Jason could fully return it to the floor. "Turnabout is fair play. Your money is no good at my favorite restaurant just like you wouldn't let me pay at the places you've taken me." He scratched his fingernails on the bottom of the sock-covered foot.

Jason snorted, squirming and biting his lip. Mike continued to tickle while Jason tugged his leg back trying to escape. He finally succeeded in freeing his foot, and Mike sat back laughing.

Before he could say anything, Ariana returned with Mike's card and the receipt. "Thanks for coming in, guys. Have a great day."

Mike signed the slip and added a tip. "You, too."

She cleared their plates and nodded at Jason's cup. "You want another round of coffee before you go?"

Narrowing his eyes at Mike with an eyebrow raised, Jason shook his head. "Nah, we'd better head out."

Mike pocketed his wallet and staff card. "Any time you're ready."

Jason pushed himself out of the booth and stood, offering his hand to Mike. Mike took it and hauled himself to standing. Slinging an arm around Mike's waist, Jason strolled with Mike out of the restaurant and toward his truck.

Enjoying the strength and warmth of Jason's embrace, Mike leaned his head in and rested it on the muscular cop's chest. It felt right to be in Jason's arms. He couldn't wait to take a trip with the man he was rapidly falling head over heels for, hoping it would be the first of many.

A WOMAN IN hot pink running shorts and a black halter top stood stretching on Jason's front porch as he turned into his driveway and parked the truck. Electric yellow basketball shoes rounded out the ensemble. With a start, he realized it was Emily.

Mike stared out the window. "Shouldn't she have those colors on the other way around?"

Shaking his head, Jason groaned. "She shouldn't have them on at all." He pushed open the truck door and stepped out of the truck.

Emily rose out of her stretch and waved at him. "Heya, Sweets. Thought you'd have been home a while ago."

"We stopped for breakfast." He took in her outfit.

"Oh, for the love of God…"

She held up her hand, her brow furrowing. "Stop. Don't even go there."

Mike opened the door and got out. "Hi, Emily. What the hell are you wearing?"

Throwing his head back, Jason roared with laughter.

Emily scowled. "Oh, so now he's got you doing it, eh?"

Mike cocked his head to the side. "What do you mean? I was only asking about your, um, choice in clothes."

She stabbed a finger at Jason. "He's been on me about my running clothes for years."

Rounding the front of the truck, Jason shook his head. "Maybe you should take up another sport."

Throwing up her hands, she shook her head. "Oh, for goodness sake. I don't know why I keep coming back for more."

Mike shrugged. "I sometimes wonder that, too, but then, he is kind of adorable."

"True, though he's unattainable for me." Emily moved her hands to her hips. "I've been trying since our first year of college."

Glancing from one to the other, Jason strode to the front door and stepped around Emily. "Now, you know that's not true. You had your chance. Besides, you gave up any romantic interest after that disastrous Thanksgiving dinner at your mom's."

She rolled her eyes. "Don't remind me. I thought my mother was going to clobber you with that turkey drumstick. The food fight was pretty funny, though. I think dad had been dying to hit mom with the mashed potatoes and gravy for years."

Now Mike laughed. "He caused a genuine food fight at Thanksgiving?"

Grinning, Emily trained her gaze on Jason. "Sure did. After it was all done, my mom served pumpkin pie at the kitchen table and acted like nothing had happened."

"She'd have been more convincing if she didn't have gravy all over her dress and potato caked in her hair." Jason unlocked the front door and pushed it open. "It's not like we could have returned to the dining room." Leading the way in, Jason kicked off his shoes. He padded down the hallway and into the living room. Emily and Mike followed, both plopping down on the sofa.

Standing by the fireplace, Jason snagged the remote from the mantle and clicked on the fire. "Looks like you've been running. Need some water?"

Emily nodded. "That sounds good."

"Okay." He said, lowering himself onto his rocking chair. "Okay. You know where it is."

Rolling her eyes, Emily pushed herself off the couch. "You're terrible."

He shrugged. "That's why you love me."

Mike chuckled as she stepped into the dining room. Before she was out of sight, Mike looked over the back of the sofa. "Can you get me one, too?"

"Sure." She glared at Jason. "I suppose you want one as well."

With a grin, he returned her gaze. "Since you're offering."

Sighing, she moved into the kitchen and out of sight.

Jason nodded at Mike. "Shouldn't you check in with Craig and Alan? Wouldn't want all that goodwill I just built up with your cousins to go to waste."

"Oh, yeah." Mike fished his cell from his jeans and typed on his screen.

Emily returned carrying two glasses of water in her hands with a third tucked in the crook of her elbow. She set one on the floor in front of Mike, took another from her arm and placed it on a coaster on the side table by the couch, and crossed the room to hand Jason the third.

"Thanks." Jason downed the water and held the glass as Emily returned to the couch and sat.

Mike read the screen of his cell and then pocketed it. "Craig says hi and hopes we have a pleasant day." He reached forward and retrieved the glass from the floor, taking a sip.

Crossing her legs, Emily locked her gaze on Jason. "So, what are you boys up to this morning?"

Jason rocked back in his chair. "We'll probably take a nap since neither of us has slept yet. We both work tonight."

"Nice. I won't keep you long." She took a swig of her water. "I was wondering if you have dinner plans."

Mike shrugged. "Not yet."

"Well, I got a recommendation for this hopping new restaurant in West Seattle I was thinking of trying and wondered if you wanted to come with me."

Mike sipped more water. "Which place?"

"Summerland Bistro. It's on Alki." She finished her water and returned the glass to the side table. "They serve British and Irish pub fare."

"I'd be up for that," Mike replied, shifting his gaze to Jason. "What do you think?"

Jason steepled his fingers. Emily's taste in restaurants

was about as good as her nose for choosing wine: well-intended, but often missing the mark. "Has it been reviewed yet?"

Furrowing her forehead, she crossed her arms. "Yes. Four and a half stars. And my friend Betsey Glover gave me the recommendation."

Betsey's opinion on the restaurant was enough for him. She was a gourmet chef and rarely approved of pubs. It must be good for Betsey to set foot in the place.

With a nod, Jason rocked back in the chair. "Okay, what time?"

Her demeanor brightened. "I'll be here at five. We can head over then."

Mike finished his glass. "That should work. I have to get my truck before heading to work anyway." He stood, and Jason noted the tired droop of his eyes. "Sorry, Emily, but I'm about to fall asleep. I'll see you later this afternoon."

She jumped off the couch. "No worries. I know you worked all night. See you at five."

Jason watched Mike move to the stairs. He turned and caught Jason's gaze, something other than weariness in his eyes. "Don't be long."

Emily laughed and stepped closer to Jason's chair. "Well, that was quite the sultry stare."

"We seem to be moving past the shy stage," Jason mused with a chuckle.

She reached down and poked at his ribs. "Like you were ever there. I'll head out so you can get upstairs."

Jason rose from the rocker. "Okay. Be here a little early. We should be up by four. Maybe we'll take a walk or something before dinner."

"Have a good rest, Sweets." She gave him a quick hug and strode to the door. After slipping on her running shoes, she waved.

Opening the door for her, he stared at her feet. "You know the pink and black is almost tolerable, but those shoes really need to go."

She sighed. "I'm not going to change my style of clothes. You'd never be satisfied anyway." She sprang from the doorway and jogged along the pathway to the sidewalk. With a final wave, she headed up the hill toward McGraw Street.

Jason shut the door and turned the lock, then hurried to the stairs. He had a boyfriend naked in his bed, and he didn't want to keep his man waiting.

AFTER A LOVELY dinner on Alki Beach, Emily bid them farewell. Mike waved after Jason's departing truck, then trudged up the steps of his cousins' house. Opening the front door, Mike salivated at the aroma of melted cheese and noodles. Craig and Alan sat at the dining room table eating dinner.

Craig glanced in his direction and grinned. "Hey, stranger. How was your day?"

Balancing on one foot, Mike untied his shoes and pulled them off one at a time. "Great. Jason and I spent the day together and met up with his friend Emily for dinner on Alki."

Alan scooped a hearty helping of macaroni and cheese onto his plate. "Too bad you're not hungry, then. Craig tried a new recipe, and it's even better than his usual."

"Aw, thanks, babe." Craig's grin spanned from ear to

ear. "You say the sweetest things when you're taunting Mike."

Mike laughed and joined them at the table. Conveniently, a plate and silverware rested in his usual place. He dove the serving spoon into the pond of melted cheddar, then frowned as he looked at his empty plate. "Were you expecting me for dinner?"

Lifting a glass of iced tea, Alan shook his head. "Nah, we knew you'd likely be out with Jason."

Craig shrugged. "I just set a place in case you were hungry when you came home." He eyed the pile of mac and cheese now adorning Mike's plate. "Apparently, he didn't feed you enough."

Mike used his spoon to clear the serving spoon of cheese and noodles. "We had plenty to eat. Even took a stroll along the beach." He placed a bite of macaroni into his mouth and savored the cheese on his tongue. Not finding the usual taste he expected of mac and cheese, he struggled to figure out what was different.

Watching him eat, Alan cocked an eyebrow. "Well, what do you think?"

"It's good." Mike bit his upper lip, struggling to identify the new taste. "What did you put into it?"

Craig leaned back against his chair. "Would you believe cloves and flat beer?"

With a swallow, Mike eyed the rest of his food. "Cloves? Doesn't that usually go into pumpkin pie?"

"Very good. Yes, it does." Craig nodded with approval. "This recipe called for it, and I think it adds an extra little zing."

Mike took another bite, the flavors dancing across his taste buds. "It's really good."

"Thanks." Craig sipped at his tea. "So, dinner on Alki?"

"The place was great. I had a steak and a mountain of garlic mashed potatoes." He sprang from his chair and stepped into the kitchen. "It's a beautiful evening by the water." Grabbing a glass from the cabinet, he pulled open the refrigerator and retrieved the filtered water pitcher from the door. After filling his glass, he returned the jug and nudged the refrigerator door shut.

Alan wiped his mouth with the green cloth napkin and eased his chair back from the table. "You're still hungry after a full steak and potato dinner?"

Returning to the table, Mike grinned. "Nah, I just wanted to try Craig's latest creation." He turned to his cousin's husband after he made short work of the helping he'd dished himself. "You can make that anytime."

Craig met his gaze. "Glad you approve. Do you work tonight?"

"Yeah. I have to be there at eleven." He checked his watch. "I've got about two and a half hours before I leave." After a yawn, he downed the glass of water and stood. "I'm going to take a quick nap and then head out."

As he left the table, Alan cleared his throat. "Forgetting something?"

Mike puzzled at his cousin, then noted the dirty plate and fork at his place. "Oh, yeah." He grabbed the dishes from the table and set them into the sink. Turning away from the sink, he stepped around Alan.

With a sigh, Alan lifted Mike's plate and opened the dishwasher. "One of these days, you'll figure out that dishes don't wash themselves."

"Oh, I know they don't." He nodded at Alan's hand

holding the plate. "You do."

He hurried out of the kitchen followed by Craig's laughter. The plates and silverware clattered into the dishwasher as Alan's voice carried down the hall. "You're not helping, honey."

Chuckling, Mike closed the door and shuffled to his bed. He found clean sheets and a freshly made bed. Craig must have been through his room while cleaning. He also noted no dirty clothes on the floor and a pile of fresh laundry neatly folded on top of his desk.

Grateful for the clean clothes, he pulled off his shirt and jeans and lay on top of the bedspread. Sleep quickly overtook him as he reviewed the day with Jason. The night couldn't go fast enough so he could be in those muscular arms again.

CHAPTER EIGHT

FRED COLLIER APPROACHED Jason as he changed into his uniform a week after his dinner with Mike and his cousins. "Hey, Lynch. Tomlinson can't make the pool tournament tomorrow night, so I'm out a partner. I don't suppose Mike would be interested in filling in?"

Jason raised an eyebrow. "I heard you two were bringing up the rear in the stats. Are you sure Paul can't make it, or did you sabotage him because you want Mike to run the table and improve your standing?"

Collier threw back his head and laughed. "No, he really can't make it." Tapping his chin, he stared at his partner. "Come to think of it, I *could* tell him that next week's match is cancelled if Mike can do that one as well."

Chucking, Jason shook his head. "I'll check with him later. He's asleep right now."

Opening his locker, Collier pulled out his shoes and shirt. "You're pretty sweet on him, aren't you?"

The warning bells in Jason's mind rang. "Yeah, I suppose I am."

"Glad to see you're pulling out of your loneliness."

With a glare, Jason swung around. He didn't need Collier or anyone else on the force up in his business. "What do you mean?"

"Dude, it's been clear to anyone even remotely paying

attention. When you joined the force, misery cascaded off you in waves." He laid a hand on Jason's shoulder. "As your friend as well as your partner, I'm just happy you've found someone."

Not sure how to respond, he simply nodded and turned back to his locker. He'd only let Emily in as he grieved through Christoph's loss. Several connections had fallen away, both family and friends. Collier had been there through thick and thin on their beat, but only at this moment did Jason realize the strong friendship he'd built with his fellow officer.

Collier opened his own locker and then tugged his sweatshirt over his head. "So, you'll check with Mike?"

Jason grinned. "Sure. What's your assignment tonight?"

Plucking a stick of deodorant from his locker, Collier raised his beefy arm. "I'm with you tonight. I think we get the privilege of patrolling The Blade."

With a frown, Jason pulled on his uniform slacks. Third Avenue in downtown Seattle had grown progressively worse over the last five years. The gang activity was bordering on out of control. Law enforcement had beefed up patrols, and none of the officers liked dealing with the constant problems and criminal activity on the section of Third Avenue between Blanchard and Pike Streets known as The Blade.

Once Collier finished dressing, both men emerged from the locker room to find the chief standing there. "Ah, Collier. I was looking for you. Change of plans tonight."

Collier's face fell into a frown. "Sure, Chief."

"I've been implementing random ride-alongs. Your turn tonight. We're patrolling Capitol Hill."

Now Jason frowned. "We're scheduled for The Blade this evening."

She shook her head. "Kirby and Emery are taking Third Avenue. I want you to patrol Pioneer Square. Should be a quiet evening for you, Lynch."

He nodded. "Yes, ma'am." He'd rather continue his conversation with Collier in the patrol car, but on the other hand, he could spend the time thinking about Mike and San Diego.

"Oh, and one more thing, Lynch."

A pit opened up in Jason's stomach, and he wondered what he'd done to incur the Chief's scrutiny.

"I heard your boyfriend cleaned Templeton's clock at pool a few nights ago." Her normally serious expression broke into a sly grin. "I hope I get to meet him."

Collier chuckled. "You should have seen the looks on their faces."

Relief washed over Jason, grateful he wasn't getting a ride-along or having to patrol the Blade on his own. "Yes, ma'am."

"Have a good night, Lynch. Let's go, Collier." She strode down the hallway with his partner lagging behind. He turned to give Jason a quick shrug before hurrying to catch up.

At least he wouldn't have a dangerous beat tonight. Pioneer Square was usually an easy assignment, and he was more than happy to avoid Third.

ISAAC APPROACHED MIKE as he closed his locker. "Colleen from the San Diego property sent me up a few brochures for the resort you asked about. I think you and Jason will really like it."

Setting his keys on the counter by the row of lockers, Mike took the offered pamphlets. *Sunland Ocean Resort.* He flipped through the colorful pages of happy people lounging by a large pool overlooking a sandy beach.

"Since you work for the hotel, you get a discount."

Mike's ears perked up. "Really?"

"Yup. One of the benefits of the job," Isaac confirmed. "Discounts start at fifteen percent, but I can pull some strings and get you a lot more."

"Thanks, Isaac. I really appreciate it. I'm hoping this trip will be especially romantic." He thought over the last few weeks, and about the steadily growing connection with Jason. "Jason seems ready to move forward with our relationship, and I certainly am."

With a chuckle, Isaac handed him the rest of the booklets and brochures he held. "That just means less sex."

Gasping, Mike snatched the pages. "Not going to happen. He's insatiable."

Isaac sighed. "So was mine. Until we got married."

Mike raised an eyebrow. "And when is the last time you did something romantic like a get-away?"

"I don't know." His boss shrugged. "Maybe a couple of years ago."

Opening his locker again, Mike placed the information on San Diego inside. "See, that's the problem. You have to keep the spice going. You can't just stop because you got the ring." He slammed the door. "Take him on a vacation, even if it's just a weekend away, and I bet you'll be clutching the sheets in no time."

With a laugh, Isaac shook his head. "Ah, youth. But I'll humor you and give it a try. Have a good night.

Veronica is waiting for you at the desk."

"Bye." Mike watched Isaac leave, and adjusted his uniform. The ill-fitting clothing was on its last legs. Stepping through the doorway, he rounded the corner and approached the back of the reception desk.

"Hey, Veronica."

The short woman with long, curly, and almost black hair grinned, her brown eyes reflecting her bubbly personality. "Hello, Mike. Looks like it's you and me tonight."

A smile brushed Mike's lips. This was her usual greeting when he came on shift, and it never got old. He loved her enthusiasm for her job.

"Isaac said you were planning a trip," she gushed, eyes wide with excitement.

"Yeah, Jason and I are going to San Diego in about three weeks. We're just starting to plan, and Isaac says I can get a discount because I work here."

She nodded her head. "I did a trip to Kansas City last year, and the hotel room was half off."

With a frown, he wrinkled his nose. "Why'd you pick Kansas City?"

"There's some cool stuff in KC," she retorted, crossing her arms and fixing him with a hard stare. "Don't knock it 'til you've been there. The Swiss bakery was particularly amazing."

Mike held up a hand. "Wait, don't talk about food. I didn't get enough dinner. I overslept, and my cousins were out."

Her hands flew to her hips. "Get your butt down to the grocery store on the corner right away. I'm not having you hungry and grumpy all night."

Mike lifted his eyebrows. "Are you sure?"

"I can handle things here. Just hurry up." She turned her attention to the computer screen in front of her.

He grinned. "Thanks, Veronica." Hurrying across the lobby, he shot out the front door and down the street. About halfway along the block, he nearly bumped into a couple of homeless guys, one tall and thin, the other heavy with crazed eyes.

Coming to a halt just before colliding with them, the tall one's heavily dilated eyes locked on his with a scowl. "How about a buck for some food?"

"Sorry, man. Can't spare anything tonight. Have a good one." Mike stepped around them and continued toward the grocery store.

The homeless guys stared after him. "Fuckin' kids," the shorter one slurred.

Mike shook his head as he crossed the street and stepped into the grocery store, remembering what Jason had called this neighborhood. *Another fun evening in the Blade.*

HOLDING HIS CELL to his ear, Jason heard the call connect. "Hey, Mike. This is Jason."

Mike chuckled on the other end of the call. "I know. I saw your handsome mug when I answered."

Jason cocked his head. "I don't remember you taking a picture with your phone."

"Well, you haven't been paying attention, then. I've got several." His voice lowered so that Jason had to strain to hear. "Some of which, I definitely don't show my co-workers."

His eyebrows shooting up, Jason gasped. "You naughty boy. I'll have to punish you."

"With your nightstick?" Mike taunted.

The swelling in his crotch made Jason squirm on the seat as he imagined slapping his cock on Mike's bare ass. "I think we'd better change the subject before I show up at your work and take you in the back room."

Another chuckle. "I doubt if Isaac would mind, though he'd probably want to watch."

"I bet he would," Jason mused. "Did you ask him about his recommendations for San Diego?"

"I'll bring over the stuff he gave me in the morning if we're still on," Mike replied, the excitement in his voice evident.

His cock pulsed harder in his uniform. "You bet. See you soon."

"Bye." The double beep of the call ending sounded in his ear.

Jason resumed his patrol through Pioneer Square, willing his erection to subside. Not an easy task with his mind running on what kind of pictures Mike had, and why Jason hadn't thought to take any of his boyfriend. He wished Collier hadn't gotten the ride-along tonight.

After parking the cruiser at First and James, he pushed open the car door and climbed out. Surveying the empty street, he closed up the car and locked it, satisfied things looked normal. He turned left and strolled along James toward the waterfront.

A ruckus caught his attention as he approached the cobbled alley. Several clangs sounded, and the crash of garbage hitting the street echoed into the night. He unclipped his flashlight from his belt and shone the light into the shadows. Two dumpsters lay overturned, their contents strewn over the cobblestones. Ahead, a lone figure ducked behind the furthest dumpster.

"Hold it right there." Jason stepped into the alley, drawing his gun. "Step back into the light where I can see you."

The wooden beam next to his head splintered as he heard the pop of a gun. Adrenaline kicking in, he dove for the cover of the nearest dumpster and flipped off his flashlight.

"Hey, copper. We gonna shoo' chyo ass," a taunting, high-pitched male voice echoed through the alley.

Jason realized he'd blundered into a trap. Checking his gun, he readied himself for the onslaught. He spoke quietly into the radio at this shoulder. "Officer pinned in alley at First and James. Request immediate backup."

Hoping his call had been heard, he switched off the volume to not further give himself away. Footsteps echoed through the alley. He considered running back the way he came, but knew he'd be mown down before reaching the entrance. He'd have to rely on his body armor and his wits.

Light suddenly shown from the windows above him and illuminated his attackers. Jason stole a glance and saw three Asian guys approaching slowly. They paused at the sudden illumination, and Jason took his chance. He leaned away from the dumpster and got a shot off. The guy in the middle of the group fell with a yell, clutching his knee. Clattering echoed down the alley as his gun fell to the ground.

The other two punks dove behind the second dumpster, leaving their comrade on the ground.

"Fuck-ah got my leg," the thug screamed. "Kill him!"

A pair of headlights and flashing lights from a police car appeared at the far end of the alley, and another cruiser swerved into the narrow roadway. Four officers flew out of the cars.

The punk on the ground immediately threw up his arms in surrender, and the other two dropped their guns and stood with their hands on their heads.

"Up against the wall." The familiar voice of Officer Mark Emery was music to Jason's ears.

Another of his buddies, Pamela Kirby rushed up to him. "Lynch, you okay?"

He sank back against the dumpster, the rush of his near-death experience receding. "The fucker missed, but it was close. Thanks for getting here so fast."

"We got worried when we couldn't raise you on the radio. Glad you're okay." Pamela stood and worked with the other officers to arrest the three punks.

Jason took a few moments to calm his breath and settle his mind before he stood and approached the officers. "Who are they?"

Slapping his cuffs onto the guy on the ground, Emery turned to Jason. "Some of the Asian Bloods by the colors they're wearing. Strange they're so far north."

Grabbing the punk's shirt, Jason pulled him forward. "This isn't your territory. What are you doing here?"

The spikey-haired gang member flashed a broken-toothed grin. "Gunnin' for coppahs."

Jason shoved him back on the ground, and the man yelped.

"Fuckin' pig cop shot my knee," the gang member crowed.

Turning the switch on his radio, he spoke into the microphone. "Need a medic in alley at First and James. Three gang members in custody."

The radio crackled, the operator's voice dripping with concern. "Lynch, report your status."

"Unharmed."

"Aid car on its way."

Officer Angela Preston approached. "Jason, glad you're all right. Why don't you head back to the station and get started on the paperwork? We can finish up here."

"Thanks." He turned to go, but she placed her hand on his shoulder.

"Once you're finished, head home. You've just survived an assassination attempt. I think that's enough for one night."

He nodded, then left the alley and returned to his patrol car. The full force of her words slammed into him as he shut the door. He'd almost been killed.

The same feelings he had the day Christoph died hit him like a semi-truck, and all the warmth in his body drained away. Mike would've had the same experience if that thug's bullet had been just a few inches closer to his head. Despite Collier's observation about his happiness, he cared too deeply to let Mike ever have to go through the pain of his sudden death.

Clearing his mind, he knew what had to happen. With a heavy heart, he headed to the station, already hurting for what he had to do.

MIKE PUSHED OPEN the front door to Jason's house, tired but excited to see his boyfriend. "Hello?"

"Come in, Mike."

As he strode through the hallway, he pulled out the information Isaac had given him about San Diego. "My boss gave me some ideas for our vacation." He entered the living room to find Jason in the rocking chair, his gaze fixed firmly on the photo of Christoph.

"Have a seat." His voice seemed flat and distant, almost as if he didn't really register Mike's presence.

Mike approached Jason and wrapped his arms around him. "Hey, what's going on?"

Lifting his arms, Jason shrugged off Mike's embrace. "Please sit over there." He pointed to the sofa.

Confusion at the sudden rejection left Mike cold. After he settled on the cushion, he furrowed his brow. "Jason, what is it? Has something happened?"

Jason's gaze locked onto Mike. "In a way. Look, Mike. The last month has been nice, but I think it's time you moved on."

A hole opened in the pit of Mike's stomach. "What?"

"We're not the right match," Jason continued in the same monotone. "You need to find someone else." His stare hardened.

With a gasp, Mike sank against the back of the couch, the pamphlets and papers Isaac had given him falling to the floor. "But why?" Mike racked his mind for what might have changed in just a few hours. Earlier that morning, they'd spoken on the phone, playful and wanting to see each other.

"My job is too risky to have a boyfriend, and clearly that's the relationship you want." His gaze didn't waver. "I can't give you what you need."

Mike shook his head, trying to dispel the rising

numbness. He searched Jason's face for some sign he didn't mean it, but Jason kept his stare level and his voice even.

After placing his head in his hands, Mike wiped his tearing eyes then slid his hands along his cheeks. He stared hard at Jason. "I don't understand. I just don't understand."

Jason stood, his face betraying no emotion and his voice holding the same flat tone. "I think you should go."

In a daze, Mike rose from the couch. He moved toward the door with Jason following. This couldn't be happening. Things were going so well, their California vacation just a couple of weeks off.

Rounding on Jason, he stared hard into his eyes. "You're sure this is what you really want?"

"This is the way it has to be." He reached across Mike and pulled open the front door. "Goodbye."

Mike stumbled through the doorway, then turned back. "But Jason…"

Jason stepped behind the door. "Goodbye, Mike." The door slammed shut and the lock clicked. Jason's footsteps receded down the hallway.

After staring at the closed door in numb shock, Mike left the porch and trudged to his truck. Turning the key, the truck rumbled to life, and he waited for the engine to warm up. The wave of emotions burst through his wall of shock and numbness. Tears rolled down his cheek, and he shouted and slammed his fists against the steering wheel.

With a crack, part of the plastic broke off. He smashed his fists down on the dashboard with another scream, then brought his hurting hands to his face. Choking back sobs, he got himself under some semblance of control and put the truck in gear, needing to get away from the two-story Queen Anne house he'd associated with someone he thought cared about him.

The early morning sun shone through the windshield as he climbed the hill away from Jason's home. All he could think about was the empty bed waiting for him in the sanctuary of his bedroom.

"JASON FRANCIS LYNCH, what the fuck were you *thinking*?"

Jason jumped straight out of his rocking chair as Hurricane Emily roared through his front door and stormed into his living room. He'd not seen this level of fury on her face since that dumbass boyfriend of hers dumped her about five years ago, and she *never* invoked Jason's middle name.

Stalking right up to him, she plowed her finger into his chest. "How could you rip that poor boy's heart out like that? I'm ashamed of you!"

Already feeling shitty, Emily's words tore deep into him. "You have no idea how hard that was for me to do."

She leaned back, slamming her hands onto her hips. "Oh, let me get out my violin. You had *no* reason to break off the relationship. NONE!" she roared.

He held up his hands, wincing from her shrill yelling. "Okay, Emily. You need to cool it. How did you find out anyway?"

"He called me in tears to say goodbye. You've devastated him." Her angry glare burned into him, and she seemed on the verge of violence.

He grabbed her arms and maneuvered her onto the

couch. "Now hold the phone here. You need to calm down and take a few deep breaths."

Staring at his hands, her face reddened, and she made to stand up. He continued to hold her back, keeping her on the couch and kneeling in front of her. "Look, I feel horrible, but I can't put Mike through losing a lover the way I lost Christoph."

Fire burned in the glare she shot him. "What makes you think that's going to happen?"

"I almost died last night." He held her gaze. "At least with Christoph I got to say goodbye. If that bullet had been three inches to the left, I'd be dead."

The red drained from her face as her eyes widened. "What bullet?"

"Promise you won't deck me if I let go of your arms?" Finally breaking through her anger, he relaxed his arms but still held onto her.

Her eyes narrowed. "I can't promise, but I'll hold off until you explain yourself."

Carefully, he released her arms and quickly retreated backward to his rocking chair. She still glared at him from the couch, but she said nothing.

He took a moment to get his thoughts together. "Last night, I had the misfortune to stumble into a gang assassination attempt. Lucky for me the punk was a lousy shot." He ran a hand through his hair as he fought down the emotions of both the prior evening's attack and the loss of Mike. "I realized that my job's too dangerous for a relationship. I don't want him to worry about whether I'm going to make it home each day."

"So, you're going to be a celibate monk?" Throwing her hands wide, she furrowed her brow and dropped her jaw. "You broke it off with the most wonderful guy to come along in your life in over four years."

"You've never lost your lover," Jason shot back, fighting his irritation and grief to keep his tone level. "Yes, you were there for me, but you haven't actually had to experience that kind of emotional trauma firsthand." With a heavy sigh, he sank back in the rocker. "Mike shouldn't have that kind of stress just as he's starting out in his life."

Considering his words, Emily paused, the fury etched on her face subsiding. "You're a fucking idiot."

Anger burned its way through his grief, and his hands tightened on the arms of the rocker. "And that's your learned opinion, is it?"

"Damned right," she snapped, then closed her eyes and took a breath before returning her gaze to him. "You have a dangerous job. I get it. But you have no idea when your number's going to be up. Did you even give Mike a choice? That kid's seen some real shit in his life, you know."

The stories of Mike's growing up flooded his memory. "Yes, but he's not suffered that kind of loss."

She crossed her arms over her chest. "So, you think you're protecting him?"

"Yes."

She shook her head. "Sooner or later, he'll have to deal with loss. He may have already. Death is part of life. You can't shield him from it."

"I can protect him from having to deal with me being killed," he replied, the excuse sounding weak even to his ears.

"Jason." Her gaze intensified. "Do you love him?"

Turning away from her, he stared into the fireplace.

The flames danced and intertwined. Did he love Mike? Could he remember what love felt like?

They'd certainly grown close in the month or so they'd spent together. All the hikes where they screwed themselves silly in the mountains. The glasses of wine and snuggling by his fireplace. Cooking together, and most importantly, waking up in each other's arms.

"Well?" Emily persisted.

His gaze locked with hers. Her silence demanded an answer.

In that moment, he knew the answer, and his heart ached for what he'd done. Protecting Mike only resulted in hurting him. "Yes, I love him."

She crossed her arms. "Then you'd better go and fix this monumental blunder. I recommend roses and some serious groveling."

CHAPTER NINE

M IKE'S MISERY, HAVING lasted an entire week, showed no sign of abating. He still didn't understand what had happened to make Jason end the relationship. Things seemed like they were going great. He'd even rearranged his schedule for their planned trip to California to coincide with Jason's vacation from work.

Sauntering into the hotel, Mike prepared for his shift. Veronica took one look at him and brought her hands to her hips. "Mike, how long are you going to mope? Take it from me, baby. If that louse is too dumb to realize the good thing you two had, you should be glad to be rid of him."

Her words made him feel worse. "Thanks, Veronica, but I don't think he really thought through what he was doing."

Tone softening, she brought her hands up to the desk. "Still no idea why he broke it off?"

"Not a clue. One day we were planning a trip to San Diego, and the next, we were done." He took a deep breath, stifling the welling sadness. "I gotta change."

With a forced smile, he trudged to the locker room and donned his work uniform. When he returned to the desk, Veronica was just finishing a check-in.

"Here is your room key. Take the elevator to the

fourth floor, and it'll be the third door on your right." She handed the key to the guest.

As the guest departed with the valet close behind her, Veronica turned to Mike and gave him a big hug.

"It'll be okay. You'll find someone else."

He sighed. "I suppose so. I just wish I knew exactly what I did wrong." He didn't want any one else. Jason seemed the perfect fit. Funny, sexy, a great sense of humor. Men like Jason didn't come along every day.

Shrugging, she returned to the computer. "I doubt you did anything. Something rattled him. You can't blame yourself for that. Maybe he has commitment issues."

He stared at her while she worked, racking his brain again for a reason. "He only said he had a dangerous job. No real explanation."

She returned her gaze to him. "He *is* right that he doesn't have the safest occupation on the planet, but to end a good thing just because he thinks something could happen? He's a fool, and you don't need that crap."

Mike's head dropped to look at his feet. "Yeah, I suppose so." He knew she was right, but her words didn't make him feel any better.

"Well, if you want a distraction, we've had several vehicle check-ins this evening." She typed something in to the computer. "I'm about fifteen minutes away from being finished with my part of the audit."

Checking his watch, he was impressed Veronica had finished so fast. "You're an hour early."

She shrugged with a grin. "I'm that good."

"And modest." Mike chuckled, moving to the key box. The usual pile of slips accompanied car keys. "Let me know when the printout is ready. I'll do my first random floor walk-through of the evening and then head over to the garage."

JASON'S STOMACH FLIP-FLOPPED as he pulled the patrol car up to a vacant parking spot in front of the Iceland Hotel. Checking his watch, he noted the time at one in the morning. Mike didn't usually do the vehicle audit until two, so hopefully he'd have some time to talk.

Peering across the passenger side of his cruiser and into the hotel, he saw Veronica standing at the desk, but no sign of Mike. He pushed open the car door and grabbed the dozen roses from the seat next to him. With a deep breath, he slammed the door and strode into the lobby of the hotel. Unsure of his reception with Mike's manager, Jason cautiously approached the desk.

Veronica's eyes narrowed. "Well, if it isn't Officer Heartbreaker. Back for another round?"

Meeting her glare head on, he shook his head. "No, I'm here to explain myself."

"How nice," she sneered at him. "Maybe you should have done that *before* you shattered his heart."

Her words stabbed right at his guilt. "Wow, you women know exactly where to hit."

A further narrowing of her eyes made him regret his words. "And what do you mean by that?"

He held up a hand. "Look, I've already had a round of this from my best friend."

"Did she tell you that you're an idiot?"

With a sigh, he shifted from one foot to the other. This interaction was even more uncomfortable than the tongue lashing he'd gotten from Emily. "As a matter of fact, she did. It took a week for her words to sink in and for me to get up my courage to face my mistake."

"You *bet* it was a mistake." She stabbed a long, painted fingernail at him. "Mike is a great guy and he deserves better. What the hell, Jason? Why did you do that to him?"

"Look, Veronica. You gotta understand. I almost took a bullet a week ago." He paused, gauging her reaction. Though her eyes softened slightly from angry, narrow slits, she didn't respond. He hoped that was a good sign and continued. "I thought if I'd died, Mike would be destroyed. I wanted to save him from that."

Veronica's anger subsided, her tone more controlled and quiet. "You can't protect him from life."

"I know that now." He glanced around the lobby. "He'll probably tell me to fuck off, but I'm hoping I can at least explain to him what happened. Is he around?"

Eyeing him closely, she reached under the desk and grabbed a plastic keycard. Hesitantly, she passed it to him. "He's in the garage kitty corner from the hotel. Go out the door, cross the street and cross again. The door is the first on the right as you head toward Westlake."

He clutched the key and the roses. "Thanks, Veronica."

With a sigh, she turned to the computer and began typing. "I hope things work out." She returned her glare to him. "For his sake."

MIKE ENTERED THE garage and pressed the button for the elevator. His mind wandered to Jason, and sadness washed over him. Not understanding was the worst part of the break-up. The door clattered open and he stepped inside.

Slowly, the carriage rose. *This fucking thing takes forever.* He tried to focus on his work, but his former boyfriend continued to pull his attention. Sadness swelled to the fore of his emotions, and he fought for control. Crying at work was *not* and option, even if he stood alone in a deserted parking garage.

The doors finally opened after the elevator shuddered to a halt. With a shake of his head, he stepped into the garage and forced his attention to the task at hand. Checking the print-off with the tickets attached to the keys, he made sure each car matched the description in the log and all the keys were accounted for.

Stepping away from the last car, he checked his watch. *One o'clock. Not bad. Finished it in half an hour.*

After gathering the keys, he pushed them into his pockets and turned toward the elevator. Thinking better of it, he trudged toward the staircase. Jason returned to his mind, and his mood soured.

He'd been so excited about their trip, exploring a new place and seeing whether they traveled well together. Alan had told him several times that the reason he and Craig worked out so well was because they could travel together.

With a sigh, he entered the stairwell and began his descent. Rounding the corner, he found two guys spread out on the steps with a bag of dirty syringes and a glass jar full of liquid. He recognized the bottle as the typical container his brother sold filled with heroin to the pathetic addicts in his hometown. The larger guy had his pants down and a needle in his hand. The other's face resembled a rat: narrow nose, small mouth, and a pointy chin.

The two guys shook with a start, staring wide-eyed at

him. He figured they were harmless. Just getting their hit. Someone must have left one of the doors ajar earlier, and these guys had gotten inside and camped out.

The big guy pulled the needle away from his leg. "Shit, man. What the fuck are you doin' in here?"

"Just my job." Mike stepped by the first of the junkies and continued down the staircase. "Come on, guys. You know you can't be in here."

When he passed the rat-faced guy, a hand clamped around his ankle. He lost his footing and tumbled down the steps. Arms flailing, he managed to catch the rail just before he reached the bottom stair. Several of the keys in his pockets fell out and clattered on the cement landing. Pain flew up his arm, and he released the metal rail. He slumped onto the landing.

The big guy plunged another needle into the side of his own leg. "Dude, wha' the fuck you do that for?"

His attacker descended the stairs with narrowed eyes and a venomous smirk on his lips. "The little shit was disrespectin' me. It's the same kid that didn't give us no money for dinner." Hovering over Mike, the guy's rank breath made his stomach turn while more pain crashed through his arm. "You hear me, bitch? You gonna pay up now."

Mike didn't have time to react, taking the druggie's boot to his face. His head smacked against the concrete floor, and everything went black.

JASON USED THE card Veronica had loaned him to enter the parking structure. He considered the elevator but figured it would be faster to take the stairs. Clutching the roses, he opened the internal door and entered the concrete stairwell. Solid walls rose up between the steps. Voices echoed from above.

"Fuckin' hell, dude!" a deep voice bellowed. "You knocked him out."

"Damn right I did. Now, I'm gonna shoot him up with our stuff. Gettin' me another customer."

Fear jolted through Jason. Dropping the flowers, he drew his service revolver and took the stairs two at a time.

"You hear dat, man?" the first voice floated over the echo of Jason's footsteps.

"It's jus' that busy businessman comin' for his fix," the other replied.

After a couple of flights, Jason rounded the corner to see Mike spread out on the landing. A strung-out thug lifted Mike's arm and readied a needle with his other hand.

Cold fear slammed into Jason's gut. He aimed his gun at the addict and screamed at the top of his lungs. "Drop the fucking needle and put your hands in the air!"

The man jumped back, the syringe flying out of his hand and rolling down the steps to rest at Jason's feet. Keeping the guy covered, he slowly ascended the steps to the landing where the man he loved lay still. On the next flight, a large man struggled to pull up his soiled jeans.

"Both of you. Hands up and don't move." He pressed the button on the radio resting on his shoulder. "This is Officer Lynch. I need backup, Third and Virginia, parking structure. Holding two drug addicts. Send an ambulance for an assault victim."

The radio crackled. "On the way."

Still training his gun on the two men, he shifted his glance to the prone man. "Mike? Mike, can you hear me?"

He didn't stir.

Keeping an eye on his captives, Jason pressed two fingers against Mike's neck. A strong pulse beat against his fingertips, and relief washed over him, though the blood coming from the young man's nose and the swelling on his face gave Jason cause for concern.

Returning his full attention to the addicts, he addressed the one who was about to inject Mike. "Did you shoot him up?"

The disheveled man just stared back.

"Answer me!" Jason roared, his voice echoing up and down the cement stairwell.

The rat-faced addict's eyes widened. "Fuckin' shit, man. Chill da fuck out. I didn't do nuffin' to him."

Jason narrowed his glare. "And that's why he's unconscious?"

A grin missing several teeth parted his thin lips. "His face ran into my boot."

Fury burned through Jason, and he fought the urge to shoot the pair of them. His finger tightened against the trigger.

The other guy at the top of the stairs shrank back, pointing his finger at his buddy. "He tripped the security guy and kicked his face when he hit the bottom of the stairs. He was gonna shoot him up with China White."

"You fuckin' snitch!" The attacking druggie rounded on the bigger guy on the stairs.

"Hold still!" Jason yelled, and the rat-faced addict froze. Sirens sounded in the distance and rapidly drew nearer. "You're lucky I'm a rational person. You." He pointed his gun at the larger guy at the top of the stairs. "Stand up slowly and put your hands against the wall." He trained his gun on the other. "You, too."

Both men complied as Jason glanced down the stairs behind him. Officers Thoma, Downes, and Kawaguchi with guns drawn, ran up the steps.

Kawaguchi reached him first. "You okay, Lynch?"

"Yeah," Jason breathed. "But Mike's not." With the arrival of backup, Jason allowed a measure of relief to stem the adrenaline pumping through his system.

"Thoma and Downes, cuff these bastards and read them their rights."

The other two officers eased past Jason and arrested the addicts. Lowering his gun, Jason crouched down beside Mike and turned to Kawaguchi. "Is the aid car here?"

"They're downstairs. We wanted to be sure you were safe before the medics came up." He turned to his radio. "Kawaguchi to medics, bring a stretcher."

Thoma and Downes marched their prisoners up to the next level and into the parking structure out of Jason's sight. Kawaguchi followed them when he saw the two medics carrying a stretcher and their gear up the stairwell.

Jason addressed them. "Head trauma. He fell down the steps, and the assailant kicked him in the face."

"Okay, stand back," the EMT said, moving past Jason. "We'll take care of him."

Helpless to do anything further, Jason ascended three steps and watched, his adrenalin-high waning. He'd broken off their relationship because of his dangerous profession. Yet, Mike was the one unconscious and bleeding. Emily was right. Every job had its dangers, and it was stupid to walk away from love because of a hypothetical situation. He'd be sure to thank her if Mike was willing to take him back.

A BRIGHT LIGHT shone behind Mike's eyelids. Too bright for his or Jason's bedroom. His head throbbed, but he opened his eyes, unsure where he was. His blurry vision righted itself after a few blinks, and he found Alan and Craig sitting next to him.

The white ceiling above him glowed bright. He noticed a pouch of fluid on a metal hanger sitting next to his bed. His mind felt muddy, and he couldn't bring his thoughts together enough to figure out his surroundings. "Where am I?"

Standing, worry lines creased Craig's face. "Harborview Medical Center. One of those addicts kicked your head and knocked you out."

Alan scooted his chair closer. "We've been so worried about you. Veronica called us after Jason found you."

"Jason found me? I don't remember." A haze of confusion clouded his thoughts. Memories crowded his mind, some blurry. He remembered tripping down the staircase, but nothing after that. He tried to move, but pain flew up his right arm and he cringed.

Standing, Alan's face also creased in concern. "What's wrong? Are you hurting?" he asked, his words coming out in a rush.

"My arm," Mike responded, surveying his wrist. "Something happened to it when I fell down the stairs."

"Alan, why don't you grab the nurse?" Craig suggested. "Maybe they can give him something for the pain."

"Be right back." Alan left the room.

Craig settled in the chair next to Mike's bed and took

his good hand. "What do you remember?"

Scrunching his forehead, Mike tried to recall the events in the garage. "I finished the car audit for the overnight shift. I decided on the stairs because the elevator takes too long." The misty vail over his memory lifted, and the attack came flooding back. He shivered. "There were two guys doing heroin in the stairwell. One of them grabbed my ankle as I went by, and I tumbled down the stairs. I caught the railing about halfway down, but it wrenched my wrist and I let go when I hit the landing."

"Why did they attack you?" Craig asked.

"The one said I was disrespecting him." The memory of the rancid breath of the rat-faced druggy made his stomach twist. "I wouldn't give them money when I almost crashed into them a few days ago. He came down the stairs and stomped on my face. I don't remember anything after that." Another surge of pain jolted his arm and Mike sucked in a sharp breath.

The door opened, and a middle-aged nurse with curly, dark hair and blue scrubs followed a worried Alan into the room. "You doing okay, hun?"

"My arm is really hurting," he hissed through clenched teeth, enduring another wave.

"Okay, I'll be right back." She stepped from the room and returned a few moments later with a syringe and a bottle. She logged into the computer station next to his bed and scanned the bottle and the side of the syringe. "I'm going to give you some painkillers through the IV mix. It should take effect pretty quickly." She prepared the medicine and injected it into the cannula near his wrist.

Almost immediately, the pain subsided.

"That better?" she asked, disposing of the needle.

"Yes, thanks."

She took his vitals and checked the machine behind him. "Now that you're awake, we can see what Doctor Adler thinks about releasing you to your family, or if she'd prefer you stay overnight." The nurse left the room.

Alan stood next to Craig. "So, we were talking. We think it's time you leave this job. You only have two more months until school starts."

"But what about rent?" Mike's pride flared. He couldn't see how he'd manage financially without a job.

Glancing at Craig, Alan continued. "We'll forgo the rent until your student aid kicks in." His brow furrowed, and Mike swore he detected a slight tremor in Alan's voice. "Look, Mike. You could've been killed. The overnight shift isn't safe downtown. You were going to quit when school started anyway. I doubt Isaac will begrudge you leaving two months early."

Not convinced, he glanced between the two men. "And medical insurance?" This situation proved he needed to stay working until school started.

Craig sighed. "We'll figure it out. I know we can't put you on our plan, but if something comes up, we'll do what we can."

Closing his eyes, Mike considered their offer. He needed to work to at least feel like he was contributing. They'd been so kind to him, and he didn't want to take further advantage of his cousins.

He opened his lids and looked from one man to the other. "Guys, I really appreciate your offer, but can I think about it?"

Alan was about to say something, but Craig set his hand on Alan's shoulder. "Sure. Take all the time you want."

"But…" Alan stuttered.

Craig whipped his head to glare at his partner. "Alan."

With a laugh, Mike raised his good arm and grabbed Craig's hand. "You two are like an old married couple."

Alan raised an eyebrow. "We're not old."

A knock at the door drew their attention. Expecting the doctor, Mike sucked in a sharp breath at the surprise of seeing his visitor.

Jason poked his head inside the room. "Hi. May I come in?"

"I GUESS YOU can." Mike's tone held no invitation or pleasure at seeing him.

Jason clutched the dozen replacement roses he'd picked up from the florist downstairs, plucked up his courage, and entered the room. The original bouquet had ended up trampled by the three officers and the EMTs when they'd responded to his call to rescue Mike.

With a slight frown, Craig nudged Alan. "Let's go get a cup of coffee."

Narrowing his eyes, Alan glared at Jason. "I don't need any."

Letting go of Mike's hand, Craig linked his arm in Alan's and gave his husband a glare of his own. "Alan. Coffee. Now."

Jason endured Alan's angry gaze as Craig dragged him from the room. All the goodwill he'd garnered with the cousins very clearly had gone, though Craig seemed to acknowledge his saving Mike from the druggies. At least he had when Jason called Craig to tell him what had happened.

Once the cousins left the room, he turned, offering the red roses to Mike. "I brought these for you."

Seeing Mike laid out on the hospital bed, his nose taped and purple and white bandages circling his head, made Jason catch his breath. He wanted to wrap his arms around his former boyfriend, but the neutral stare Mike leveled on him kept him in his place by the door.

"Thank you. You can set them on the table," Mike said warily. His face remained neutral, but anger flickered in his gaze.

Jason stepped farther into the room and placed the bouquet on the small wooden table. He approached the bed before his courage failed him. Needing to clear the air between them, he took a deep breath.

"I came to apologize to you," Jason blurted, trying to find the words not to screw up his chance to reconcile.

Furrowing his brow, Mike regarded him with a cool gaze. "For what?"

"Everything. For being an idiot. For hurting you. For letting you go." He stopped, not wanting the welling emotions inside him to spill over. "When I found you unconscious, I nearly lost it and blew those druggies away, especially the one who was about to shoot you up with heroin."

Mike's gaze didn't waver. "What were you doing there anyway?"

"I came to talk to you." Holding nothing back, Jason laid all his cards on the table. "To ask your forgiveness, explain what happened between us, and beg you to take another chance on me."

Mike's mouth opened slightly. "You want to get back

together?"

"Yes. Please, Mike. Let's give it another try." He grabbed Mike's hand and brought it to his lips.

Though Mike didn't pull away from him, he didn't offer any hint of forgiveness. "What about your dangerous job?" No malice in the question. A good sign.

"Emily told me I was an idiot, and so did Veronica. Look what my fear got me. You in the hospital." He kissed Mike's hand again and held it against his cheek. "I need you, Mike. I've been miserable since I fucked up and broke off our relationship."

"But why did you do it?" Pain filled Mike's voice. "I don't understand what I did to make you want to leave me."

"You didn't do anything." Jason choked down the sob threatening to overtake him, his heart aching that Mike thought their breakup was his fault. "You know I lost someone I deeply cared about. Last week, I almost died in a gang shootout. I didn't want someone I love to go through that kind of pain."

"Wait." Mike's eyebrows shot up. "You...*love* me?"

"Yes, Mike." Jason nodded and kissed his hand again. "I love you."

Mike's features softened, and his thumb caressed Jason's cheek. "I love you, too."

Hope rose within Jason. "I promise I'll never intentionally hurt you again, and I'll do anything to make it up to you."

Mike paused, clearly considering. A gentle smile graced his lips, sliding his hand across Jason's hair. "Okay, we'll give it a try."

With an explosion of joy, Jason smiled. "Thank you."

He bent forward and tenderly pressed his lips to Mike's. He placed a hand on Mike's chest as the kiss intensified until Mike gave a yelp.

Jason snapped his head back. "You okay?"

"My nose," Mike chuckled. "It's pretty tender."

Squeezing his hand, Jason placed a kiss on his cheek. "Sorry."

A dark-haired woman in a white physician's coat marched into the room followed closely by Alan and Craig. Alan's gaze narrowed again as he took in the scene before him, but Craig smiled from ear to ear.

"Hello, Mike. I'm Rachel Adler. Nice to see you awake." She approached the bed, looking down with kindness in her eyes. "You've had quite a time, I gather."

Jason gave Mike's hand a final squeeze before he stepped back and let go. Even Alan's glare couldn't squash the elation surging through him.

With a grin, Mike addressed the doctor. "You could certainly say that."

"YOUR COUSINS TELL me you're having pain in your right arm." She gently lifted his hand, and he winced from the pain stabbing his wrist. "We'll need to take an x-ray and see what's going on. If it's not too bad, I'll send you home. The concussion has subsided, and we can probably take the bandages off your head." Gently returning his hand to the sheet, she moved around to the footboard of his bed.

"What about my nose?" He touched his nose with his good hand and winced from a sharp pain.

She stood at the computer station, typing in a few notes. "We've taped it, and that's about the best we can do. It'll heal on its own. Not too much damage." After clicking the mouse a couple of times, she returned her full attention to him. "We did have to shave part of your head to put in stitches, though. I recommend a hat until they come out. Probably not a good idea to get your hair cut until after they're removed. Light duties at work until you've fully recovered. I'll provide you with a note to take to your boss."

"Oh, no. I have a customer service job." He grimaced. "I'm not sure I can wear a hat."

"We can get the stitches out in about a week and a half. Do you have vacation time, or perhaps your employer will let you take sick time?"

Mike's mind flashed to the owner of the hotel. The cheap bastard would probably make him take the days with no pay. "Doubt it."

Stepping forward, Alan patted his good hand. "We'll figure it out. At least Labor and Industries should pay for your medical bills."

She smiled at Mike. "Give me a few minutes, and we'll get you into X-ray for your wrist and arm." Nodding at the others in the room, she strode out the door.

Mike reached for Jason, who was keeping to the back to the room. "Come join us." He noted Alan's scowl. "And you can wipe that sourpuss frown off your face, mister."

With his eyes wide, Alan took a step back. "You must be feeling better."

Taking Jason's hand, Mike nodded. "We're going to give it another go."

Before Alan could say anything, Craig stepped forward. "I think that's great." He glared at Alan. "Isn't that wonderful news?"

"That remains to be seen," Alan murmured with a glower at Jason.

"Alan!" Craig snapped.

Before Mike could admonish his cousin, Jason released his hand and addressed the two men. "It's okay, Craig. I totally deserve Alan's distrust. All I can say is I'm sorry, and I'll do whatever I can to restore your faith in me."

Alan kept a stern gaze locked on Jason. "I guess we do owe you some thanks for saving him."

Attempting to placate the situation, Mike cleared his throat, catching the three men's attention. "Why don't the four of us go grab some dinner when I get out of here?"

Jason nodded. "That would be nice. I'm off tonight."

Surprised, Mike stared at him. "How can you be? It's Wednesday."

The three men glanced at each other before Jason smiled. "Mike, it's Friday afternoon."

"What?" He sat up straight, realizing he'd missed two shifts at work. He might get fired and not have to quit. A wave of dizziness pounded into his head, and he quickly lay back.

Taking his hand, Jason moved back to his side. "You've been out for over two days."

He gaped at the three men he loved most. "Two *days?*"

Jason interlaced his fingers with Mike's. "The bastard kicked you really hard."

"But who covered my shifts?" he spluttered. "Isaac—"

"Better not say a fucking word about it," Alan interrupted, barking out the words. "Or I'll be sure we sue that hotel for every penny they have."

Doctor Adler returned before Mike could respond. "Are you ready for your photo shoot?"

"Yes, let's get this over with. I'm hungry."

CHAPTER TEN

DINNER WAS A tense affair, but Jason made the most of it. He explained what happened with Christoph, and his near assassination with the gang ambush. Alan calmed down at Craig's insistence, and Jason was grateful they were willing to listen.

Alan picked at his food. "Okay, I sort of get where you were coming from, but I'm not impressed with how you handled it."

Nodding, Jason set his fork down. "Neither am I."

With his arm in a sling, Mike struggled to chase a blueberry across his plate. "I'm never going to make it three weeks with this sling. It just had to be my right arm."

Grateful for the distraction, Jason stabbed the offending berry with his fork and handed it to Mike. "Allow me."

Mike took the fork. "Thanks."

"I might have to help you with lots of things if the guys are willing to let me take care of you." He glanced at Alan who seemed to be doing his best not to disapprove.

Craig patted Alan's hand. "I think that's a great idea. You could camp out at our place if you want."

With a raise of his eyebrow, Alan's restraint failed, and a frown formed on his lips.

Careful to not antagonize Mike's cousin further, he

shook his head. "Maybe we're not ready for that yet. How about you come stay with me for a few days. I can help you convalesce."

A smirk spread across Mike's face. "You just want to play doctor."

Jason shrugged. "I like to leave my patients satisfied."

Mike wriggled his eyebrows. "I know."

With a laugh, Craig rose from the table. "I have to run to the bathroom." He eyed his husband. "Be nice." He dodged chairs as he wove his way through the restaurant.

Alan returned his attention to Jason. "Okay, but when you're at work, he should come home."

"Oh, come on, Alan. I can handle being by myself overnight. Besides, I have to go to work as well."

Alan's nostrils flared. "You mean you're actually going back to that job?"

"For now." Jason recognized Mike's stubbornness.

Noting the tension beginning to build between the two cousins, Jason cleared his throat. "Maybe we could go for a drive in the country or hike an easy trail around Mt. Rainier. Whatever you feel up for."

Grinning, Mike returned his gaze to Jason. "That would be fun if you don't mind me going slow."

"We'll take it at your speed," Jason assured.

Craig returned to the table. "Okay, Alan, I think we should head off. I want to actually get some chores done today."

Reaching for his wallet, Jason scanned the table for the bill. "How about I get breakfast?"

"Too late." Craig held up the receipt. "I took care of it on my way back from the bathroom."

Mike winced as he sat up straighter. "Craig, I thought

our rule was the bill hits the table so we all have a fair chance at it."

With a shake of his head, Craig inserted the receipt into his own wallet. "Not today. You're injured, and I didn't want you to be embarrassed when I easily snatched the check away from you."

Jason bit his lip, stifling a laugh.

"Oh, come on. I could have gotten it," Mike whined.

Placing his hand on the table, Craig leaned toward Mike, fixing him in his gaze and raising his eyebrows. "Okay, how about this. I didn't want you lunging over the table playing slapjack with Alan and making your injured arm worse."

Rising from the chair, Jason stood behind Mike and patted his good shoulder. "Thank you for breakfast, Craig. If you like, maybe I can return the favor tomorrow morning and have you two over for a meal at my place." He paused, thinking about the state of his house. "Actually, maybe day after tomorrow? I'm probably not quite ready for breakfast guests."

Alan nodded. "That works. I wouldn't mind seeing your place."

"Great." Jason smiled, hoping breakfast would be progress with Mike's cousin. "How about nine o'clock? I'll text you the address."

Both Alan and Craig stood and pushed in their chairs. Craig knelt and gave Mike a hug. "Have fun today."

Alan also embraced him. "Be careful with your arm."

With a sigh, Mike returned the hug with one arm. "Yes, Dad."

The two men weaved their way to the door, Alan glancing back but not pausing.

Jason pushed his own chair under the table. He waved at Alan and Craig as they looked back, then helped Mike out of the chair. Grabbing Mike's coat, he held it open.

"I'm okay, Jason." Mike attempted to grab the coat from him. "Don't fuss."

"Sorry. I'm just grateful you're here with me." He draped the coat over the sling. "What do you want to do today?"

Without missing a beat, Mike stared at him. "I want to go back to your place and snuggle."

Warmth spread through Jason's body. "Really?"

"Yup."

Jason swung his arm toward the door. "Your chariot awaits."

MIKE STRUGGLED INTO Jason's truck. It wasn't as easy as he thought it would be without his right hand to pull himself in. Jason gave him a push up and helped maneuver him into the seat.

As he fumbled with the seatbelt, Jason swung into his own seat and reached over. "Let me help you with that." He clicked the buckle into place, lingering his hand on Mike's thigh.

Mike savored the tender touch. "Hurry and get me home. I've missed being beside you."

"I've missed you, too." Jason leaned over and gave him a gentle kiss. The truck hummed, and he pushed the gear shift into reverse. After backing out of the parking lot, he drove them through town and onto Queen Anne Hill.

During the trip to Jason's place, Mike's mind turned over the events of the last few days, even though he'd been asleep for nearly two of them. Though Jason had pushed him out of his life, he'd come charging back like a knight in armor when Mike needed him the most. He found it easy to forgive the man who'd saved his life, especially now that he understood where Jason was coming from.

While they waited at the last light before the turn onto Jason's street, Mike turned to his boyfriend. "I'm so glad you want me."

The light turned green, and Jason continued driving. "I never stopped wanting you. I was just an idiot for thinking I was protecting you by pushing you away." He took Mike's hand and squeezed it. "I'm so sorry."

Mike brought the hand to his lips and kissed the knuckles. "I know. Let's promise each other we'll talk about stuff like this when it comes up instead of running away."

"Agreed."

Jason parked the truck in his driveway and hurried out and around to the passenger door. Mike felt like a small child being helped out of a car seat when Jason leaned in and unbuckled the seatbelt. Jason eased his arm around Mike's body and pulled him from the seat.

A shot of pain sliced up Mike's arm when he stepped onto the pavement, and he winced. "You need a lower truck."

Jason pulled his keys from his pocket. "Sorry about that. I think we may need to use the cruiser while you're injured."

The thought of taking the police car everywhere didn't appeal to him. "I doubt that's a good idea. We'll make the truck work."

Holding hands, Mike and Jason sauntered along the

path to the front porch. The last time Mike stood in front of the house, Jason had pushed him away. He shook off the memory of his despair.

"Anything wrong?" Jason's forehead wrinkled.

"I haven't been here since we broke things off." He stared at the door, remembering the sound of it slamming in his face.

With a frown, Jason halted and glanced back at his truck. "Should we have gone to Alan and Craig's?"

Mike shook his head. "I think Alan's head would have exploded." Though he'd been patient at the restaurant, Mike could tell his cousin thought his getting back with Jason was a mistake. Best to let Craig work on him before having Jason stay over.

Jason laughed nervously. "Yeah, I think you're right. I hope he can handle being here tomorrow." He squeezed Mike's hand. "Seriously, though. Are you okay staying with me?"

"Yeah, I'm fine." Glad to return to Jason's home, he gave his partner a reassuring glance. "Especially since you want me here."

"Very much so." Jason nodded, guiding him along the path. When they reached the front door, Jason inserted the key into the lock. He swung the door open and let Mike go in first. He kicked off his shoes and moved into the living room. He stopped short, staring at the messy state of the usually tidy house. A dirty fast food container sat on the side table next to the rocking chair as well as a fork and a couple of soiled napkins. The pamphlets he'd dropped that terrible morning still lay untouched on the floor.

Jason shuffled into the room. "I'm sorry about the mess. I haven't felt like doing much of anything since…uh, I broke up with you."

Mike crossed to him and wrapped his good arm around Jason's body. "It's okay."

Jason returned the hug and held him close. "I've missed holding you."

Resting his cheek on Jason's firm chest, Mike closed his eyes and savored the intimacy of their embrace. All the tension in his body melted away.

Jason rubbed Mike's back. "How about we go upstairs?"

"I'd like that," Mike replied, the suggestion both exciting him and filling him with warmth.

They broke the embrace and ascended the stairs still holding hands. When they reached the bedroom, Mike stood at the door and surveyed the carnage. Piles of dirty clothes lined the walls with more take-out containers on the night stand. The break-up must have been as horrible for Jason as it had for Mike. Jason's place had never been in this bad of shape when they'd been together.

"Oh, jeez. I didn't realize it was this bad." Jason blushed furiously. "Let's go to the guest bedroom. I haven't been in there for a while, so it should be clean."

Mike turned and moved down the hallway. He opened the door to the guest room, unsure of what he'd see. With a sigh of relief, he found a clean room with the double bed ready and waiting.

Jason hurried down the hallway behind him, carrying lube and condoms with a sheepish grin. "Just in case, but I have no expectations you'll be up for any play."

A smile pulled at Mike's lips. "I'm sure we can make use of those."

Following him into the room, Jason shut the door and

stepped to the bed. He deposited the rubbers and lube on the comforter and turned to face Mike.

Mike went to remove his shirt, but a surge of pain wracked his arm. "Ow, that hurt."

Jason rushed forward to stand in front of him. "Let me help you." He carefully unsnapped the sling and lowered it from Mike's arm. "That okay?"

Instead of the sharp jolt he'd received when he made the attempt, only a dull ache remained now. "Yes, thanks."

Frowning in concern, Jason touched his shoulder. "Do you need one of the pain pills?"

Mike shook his head. "I'm okay. There's still four hours until the next one. I don't want to go off schedule."

With a frown, Jason stepped closer. "Doctor Adler said to take them as needed. If you're hurting, you shouldn't wait."

"I'll feel better when you get me undressed and into bed," Mike said, leaning forward and kissing Jason's neck. Standing in front of his lover, he longed to be wrapped in the warmth of Jason's naked embrace.

Trailing his fingers down Mike's chest, Jason reached the button of Mike's jeans. Little surges of pleasure radiated from Jason's touch, and Mike reached his left arm to his boyfriend's face. He rubbed his thumb along Jason's cheek, the stubble scratching against his skin.

Jason pulled open the fly of Mike's jeans and sank to his knees. He tugged the denim down to his partner's ankles and used a finger to pull the boxer briefs away from Mike's stirring cock.

When their gazes locked together, Jason opened his mouth, engulfing the head of Mike's dick in a delicious warmth. He swirled his tongue around the tip before sucking in the rapidly lengthening shaft.

Mike moaned, surrendering to Jason's pleasuring of his cock. His legs shook as the intensity of the moment washed over him. With his shaft throbbing, Mike laced his fingers into Jason's hair.

With the familiar tingle already beginning in his balls, Mike took a shaky step back, releasing his cock from his lover's mouth. He lost his balance because of the jeans wrapped around his ankles, but Jason caught him before he fell.

Catching his breath and regaining his balance, Mike steadied himself with his left hand on Jason's shoulder. "You're overdressed for this party."

"I can quickly take care of that." He wriggled his eyebrow and pulled off his shirt, then nearly ripped open his pants. With a quick tug, his briefs came down, letting his thick cock slap against his body while his clothes pooled at his feet.

Admiring the sexy man before him, Mike nearly tripped again on his jeans. Jason hurried forward and helped Mike to sit on the bed. He pulled the jeans away and tossed them and his boxer briefs onto the floor.

His voice gentle, Jason trailed his fingernails up Mike's sides, giving him goosebumps. "Can you lift your arms?"

Mike slowly raised both hands above his head, careful not to agitate his injury. Taking his time, Jason raised Mike's t-shirt over his head and eased it above his wrists. Small painful jolts flew down Mike's arm, making him wince.

"Sorry," Jason murmured and flung the shirt onto the pile of their clothes on the floor. "Are you okay?"

Mike brought his arms back down to his sides with a

nod. "I'm fine."

A wicked grin formed on Jason's lips. "Now that I've got you naked, I'm going to make love to you." He placed one hand on Mike's chest and the other on his back, lowering Mike to lay on the bed. "Over and over again."

Jason resumed sucking on Mike's cock, bringing him back to full hardness. He swirled his tongue around the head and shaft, then bobbed up and down while stroking with his hand.

Thrashing both from the pleasure surging through his body and the intense connection between them, Mike trembled when his balls rose and the build-up to his release intensified.

Jason suddenly stopped sucking and rose above Mike. He grabbed a condom and broke open the package. Mike pulled his legs back, but Jason stopped him without a word. Taking the rubber from the package, Jason pinched the tip and squirted some lube onto the condom. He rolled it down Mike's shaft.

Realizing what Jason was about to do, Mike gasped. "Are you sure?"

With a grin, Jason released Mike's now sheathed dick and lifted his leg to rub some of the lube onto his hole.

"Want? Absolutely. Able?" He eyed Mike's pulsing erection, and a small, worried frown pulled at his lips. "We'll see. No sudden thrusts or you'll break me in two."

Jason swung his body to straddle over Mike's hips. He guided the tip of Mike's cock to rest against his pucker. Not believing Jason wanted to bottom, Mike gasped when the head of Mike's cock punched through his lover's defenses.

Groaning loudly, Jason closed his eyes, and his mouth

tightened into a grimace. "Holy shit, you're big."

Concern flooded Mike's thoughts. "Do you want to stop?"

"Hell, no. I want you completely inside me." Pressing back, Jason took more of the shaft and stopped with a wince. "It'll just take me a minute."

The tightness and warmth of Jason's ass tested all of Mike's restraint not to thrust forward and impale his lover. Jason eased himself inch by inch down Mike's cock until his ass rested on Mike's pelvis. Holding still, Jason closed his eyes again and took a couple of breaths while he got used to the length and girth.

Mike's concern heightened, worried he'd rip Jason apart. "Are you okay?"

"Yes," Jason wheezed. His eyes still closed and mouth taut, Jason eased himself up a bit then descended. After a couple more cycles, he increased his rhythm, and soon he rode Mike's cock hard. On each downward thrust, Jason squeezed his ass muscles, bringing Mike quickly to the edge of orgasm.

"Baby, you better stop that, or I'm going to come," Mike warned. Small shocks of pain radiated through his bad arm, but his other hand gripped the bedcovers firmly. Their lovemaking and the sensations coursing through him cancelled out most of the hurt all the shaking caused.

Jason squeezed again, making Mike gasp. "Do it, sweet man. Come for me. I can't take too much more of your thick cock my first time." He squeezed again, and the tingling in Mike's balls intensified.

Taking the lead, Mike gripped Jason's hip with his good hand and thrust hard. Jason gasped again. Mike established a quick driving rhythm until perched on the edge of orgasm.

"I'm so close!" Mike hollered, his strokes became more erratic. Jason took Mike's shaft completely inside him and clenched his muscles. With a roar, Mike unloaded inside the condom, his body spasming from the intensity of his release. His body continued to shake with tremors of pleasure while Jason stroked his own cock.

"I'm there." Jason tugged a couple more times, then fully impaled himself on the still erect shaft. He shot several spurts of come onto Mike's chest with a loud cry. Each blast accompanied an exquisite squeeze on his cock. The warm release splashed across his pecs and up to his chin.

After grabbing a few deep breaths and pressing his hands into the mattress above Mike's shoulders, Jason eased himself off Mike's softening dick and lowered himself onto his side. He placed his head on Mike's shoulder and sighed.

Mike slipped his good arm under Jason's head and around his muscular shoulder. In the afterglow of their coupling, Mike mused on the resumption of their relationship. This time their sex wasn't just fucking. It was lovemaking, and it felt right.

After kissing the top of Jason's head, Mike squeezed Jason closer to his side. "I'm a mess."

Jason lifted his head to survey the damage. "You sure are. Did someone spray you down with a come hose?"

"Looks like it," Mike replied with a grin. "Wanna get a washcloth and clean me up?"

"Be right back." Jason jumped up and ran for the bathroom. He returned shortly with the cloth and joined Mike on the bed.

The warmth of the damp washcloth soothed Mike's body. Jason carefully cleaned away the mess, removed the condom, and tied it off. He tossed the washcloth and condom onto the pile of clothes on the floor and snuggled close against Mike's uninjured left side, resting his head on the now clean chest.

Mike considered bring his right arm up to trail his fingers along Jason's side, but thought better of it when a stab of pain made him wince.

"You okay?" Jason asked, concern heavy in his voice.

"Fine," Mike replied. "I can't believe you let me top you."

Tilting his head back, Jason kissed his neck. "I've wanted to give myself to you for a while. Now seemed like the right time."

"Thank you." Mike gripped his shoulder, savoring the warm, soft skin under his fingers. "I'm kinda thick, so I bet it hurt."

"Kinda?" Jason chuckled. "You're the size of a beer can. You felt amazing. Next time, I'll last longer."

"I'll definitely look forward to that." Mike kissed the top of his lover's head then yawned, rapidly losing the battle to stay awake. "Rest up, because I want you inside me."

CHAPTER ELEVEN

"**H**EY, EMILY, IT'S Jason."

"So?" She demanded, her voice impatient. "What happened? Is Mike okay?"

Jason glanced at Mike sleeping peacefully next to him. The afternoon sun shining through the window gave his lover a glow like an angel.

"The bridge of his nose is broken, but that'll heal." He kept his voice low, trying not to wake his boyfriend. "He also had the tendons in his wrist torn up and had to have stitches in the back of his head. Otherwise he's fine."

She sighed through the cell. "That's a relief. Did he take your sorry ass back, or did he tell you to jump off a cliff?"

"I'm happy to say he's sleeping next to me right now." He resisted the urge to caress the sleeping man's body, though he desperately wanted to. He had over a week of separation to make up for.

Emily's voice splashed cold water on his thoughts. "Well don't screw it up this time."

He pursed his lips like he'd sucked an entire lemon. "Thank you for that wise piece of advice. I was actually calling to see if you wanted to come over for dinner tonight. Avocado salad with steak?"

"Sounds good. I'll bring the wine."

Jason raised an eyebrow. "Uh, I have plenty here." He winced at the memory of the last time she'd brought wine to dinner. It had smelled musty and tasted like vinegar. She'd bought it on sale from a distributor from Bulgaria liquidating his stock and going out of business.

"I have an excellent nose for wine," she snorted.

"Unfortunately, your eyes see the price tag and adjust accordingly," he shot back.

Her voice swelled in volume. "You shit. I'll show you how well I can pair. Steak and avocados? I'm on it. See you this evening, *Sweets*. Six o'clock?"

"That works." He grinned. "I'll have a reserve bottle standing by."

"Oh, I don't know why I put up with you," she said with a huff.

Jason chuckled. "It's my winning personality."

"Not touching that one." The cell beeped twice, and the call ended.

Placing the phone on the table, Jason eased himself out of the bed, slipped on a pair of blue running shorts, and padded downstairs to the kitchen. He'd let Mike sleep as long as he could and call him downstairs after he whipped up a quick lunch.

Upon opening the fridge door, his plans changed. A blast of rancid air met him, and he surveyed the remains of his shopping from two weeks ago. With a sigh, he cleaned out the offending items, dumping them into the compost and trash.

He took stock of what was left. A bowl's worth of tomato and bean soup, a couple of limp carrots, and three bottles of microbrew. Not the makings of a dinner for his lover and his best friend.

Mike appeared at the doorway to the kitchen wearing Jason's white terrycloth robe. He stood sleepy-eyed and utterly adorable. "Hey there. You should have woken me."

With a shove at the fridge door, Jason closed the distance between them and embraced Mike. "You need all the rest you can get."

Mike's soft hair rested on his chest, and Jason moved a hand up to lace his fingers in the wavy locks, careful to avoid the shaved parts and the stitches. They stood on the cool tiles holding each other. Jason loved the feel of Mike in his arms and caught himself wishing he'd never have to let go.

He frowned, realizing both of Mike's arms hung at his sides. "Hey, where's your sling?"

"Don't worry. I'll put it on later." He snuggled closer to Jason.

Jason closed his arms around Mike. "Okay, just don't go too long without it."

A rumble from Mike's stomach made Jason lean back. "Sounds like it's time for lunch, and I don't have anything worth eating. Can I take you somewhere?"

Mike kissed between Jason's pecs and brought his green eyes up. "I'm good with anything."

"Emily will be here at six, so we probably have enough time to grab a bite at the pub then hit the market and get fixings for dinner and tomorrow's breakfast."

"Cool. It'll be nice to see her. I'd better get a quick shower then." Mike eased out of Jason's embrace and headed for the living room.

He watched Mike go, enjoying the way his lover's form moved in the robe. At the staircase, Mike turned and faced him, letting the robe fall open and, with a shrug of his shoulders, drop to the floor.

Desire and expectation shone in Mike's gaze. "Coming?"

Taking in his sexy, masculine lover, heat rippled through Jason's body. Mike turned away, flashing his perfect ass and climbed the stairs. The slapping of his feet on the wooden stairs beckoned to Jason like a siren to an ancient mariner. Heeding the call, Jason hurried across the hardwood floor and, after snatching up the discarded robe, chased Mike up the staircase.

AFTER LUNCH, MIKE and Jason made their way through the Co-op and bought the vegetables and steaks needed for dinner. Jason decided to grill the steaks instead of broiling and slicing them for the salad, so they bought three T-bones.

Though he'd just eaten, Mike salivated at the evening's menu. He'd intentionally ordered light at the pub – meat pie with *no* tater tots – so he'd be hungry again for the feast Jason had planned. He also looked forward to visiting with Emily. The last time he'd spoken to her had been the tearful ride home to West Seattle after Jason had turned him out.

He glanced at his boyfriend, whose brow furrowed in concentration while he chose a packet of bacon to buy for breakfast. He found in Jason a man highly attentive and sweetly romantic, much more than just a hunky cop who'd made a pass at him. Still, an ounce of doubt kept Mike from completely trusting the relationship would work out. If Jason could get spooked once, he could again.

Jason met his glance with a grin. "What do you think?

This one seems to have the least fat." He thrust a pack of bacon at him.

With a chuckle, Mike examined the meat through the clear, plastic wrapping and concurred. "Looks great." He paced the bacon into the basket Jason carried.

Jason swept his gaze around the aisle. "Okay, just need the gorgonzola from the cheese counter and we're set. Anything else you'd like?"

A sudden urge for chocolate and coconut gripped Mike. "What about a dessert?"

"Sure," Jason said with a nod. "What did you have in mind?"

"I have a craving for coconut cream pie with chocolate on top."

Jason chuckled. "Well, that's pretty specific. How about we stop at Shoo-Fly Pie Shop on the way home?"

Visions of butter crust danced through Mike's head. Shoo-Fly had the best pies in Seattle. "Perfect. I can already taste the goodness."

Jason laughed. "But you'll have to wait to enjoy it until after we have the healthy stuff."

A smirk inched across Mike's lips, and he wriggled his eyebrows. "Yes, Daddy."

"You're not *that* much younger than me," Jason said, his eyes narrowing.

"Oh, I know," Mike cooed. "It's just fun to say."

"Come on, let's get our cheese and go." Jason quirked his lips. "Before I spank you."

They ordered the gorgonzola from the cheese monger and then proceeded up the aisle and waited in line to pay at the register. Jason placed the basket on the checkout counter and glanced at Mike. "Oh shit, I forgot something. Can you wait here with the groceries? I'll just be a minute."

Mike shrugged. The cashier had only just started ringing up the lady in front of them. "Sure."

"Thanks." Jason hurried away and disappeared around the corner of an aisle.

After scanning the headlines of the gossip rags, Mike stepped forward when the lady in front of him gathered her bags. He glanced around wondering what was taking Jason so long.

"Good afternoon, sir. How's your day going?"

Mike turned his attention to the young man scanning the groceries. Tall, lanky, and thin, a curly mop of dark hair hung over his eyes. His nametag said Noah. "Great. We're having a friend over for dinner and we had to run and get something to make."

The cashier glanced at their items, continuing to ring them up. "Looks like steaks and salad."

With a nod, Mike glanced around for Jason. He was so focused on the far aisles that he jumped when his lover sidled up next to him.

"Hey there. Sorry to take so long."

A dozen red roses bundled in brown wrapping paper graced the conveyer.

Staring at the flowers, Mike found his voice. "Are those for me?"

Jason grinned. "You bet they are." He leaned forward and kissed Mike's cheek.

Heat flared across his face and down to his toes. With a self-conscious glance around him, he noted the wide smile on the lady's face behind him.

Passing the flowers over the reader, the cashier gave a

nod of approval. "I wish my boyfriend did things like that."

Mike's gaze went from the flowers to Jason. "Thank you, they're beautiful."

Jason took his hand and gave it a squeeze, then turned to the cashier and swiped his card through the reader.

The cashier finished the transaction and handed Jason the receipt. "Have a great day and enjoy dinner."

Gathering up the groceries, Jason nodded. "You, as well."

Mike made to follow, but the woman behind him tapped his shoulder. "You have a good one there. Hang on to him. Not many guys spontaneously give their partners flowers."

Mike grinned, some of his earlier doubt subsiding. "Thanks, I will." He left the store and jogged across the parking lot to catch up with his lover.

Jason placed the last of the bags in the bed of his truck. "What was that about?" His gaze trailed back to the store entrance.

He shrugged. "Just some advice from a nice lady."

Jason raised an eyebrow. "Oh, yeah?"

"Yup," Mike replied, schooling his features to keep a straight face "She said to run for the hills."

Cocking his head to the side, Jason scrunched his forehead. "What?"

With a laugh, Mike patted his shoulder. "Nah, she said you were a good guy."

Jason shook his head and scooted around the truck to hold open Mike's door and help him into the cab. "Naughty boy. Just wait until I get you home." He helped Mike with the seatbelt.

"And what do you have in mind?" A thrill of excitement surged through Mike. Jason's hands trailed across his crotch when he latched the belt closed. "You said something about spanking me for being bad."

"Making dinner." Jason replied and closed the door. He trotted around the front of the truck and opened his door, climbing inside. "We don't have time for the fun stuff until after Emily leaves."

Though slightly disappointed, Mike looked forward to sleeping over with Jason. He'd desperately missed being in his arms for the week they'd been apart, and now he couldn't get enough of Jason's touch.

Jason started up the truck. "Okay, pie shop and then home, unless you can think of anything else we need."

"Nope, let's go." Mike laid a hand on his leg. "We have dinner to hurry through."

After shifting into reverse, Jason backed out of the parking spot. "Why? What's the rush?"

He caressed the jeans-covered thigh. "It's your turn to be on top."

THE DOORBELL RANG as Jason turned the steaks over on the grill. Emily had perfect timing. Dinner would be ready in less than five minutes, and the smell coming from the meat cooking in front of him made his stomach rumble.

Emily strode out the back door on onto the deck to stand next to him. "Heya, Sweets." She gave him a kiss on the cheek. "I brought a great wine."

Jason eyed the green bottle in her hand skeptically. "What is it?"

"Now, now. Don't get your nightstick in a twist. I

asked the wine cellar owner, and she said this would go great with the steaks." She rolled the bottle until the label faced upward. "Syrah. Perfect for grilled, red meat."

With a smirk, Jason turned back to the grill. "I'm impressed. You might just make a decent sommelier yet."

Mike sauntered out the door and joined them. "Table is set, and the salad turned out really well."

"Thanks, beautiful. I'm almost ready." He checked the steaks and, satisfied they were cooked to just about medium, he turned off the gas and used a spatula to transfer the T-bones to the serving platter.

Emily grinned. "Those look delicious. I'll open the wine." She scurried into the kitchen, leaving Mike on the deck with Jason.

Mike leaned over the steaks and inhaled. "Mmm. Nice job on the steaks."

Setting the platter on the lid of the grill, Jason swept Mike into his arms. "If we were alone right now, I'd say we should skip dinner and head upstairs."

Mike leaned in, planting his lips onto Jason's and pressing his tongue to gain entry to Jason's mouth. His boyfriend returned the lip-lock with passion, but broke away, trying to regain control of his hardening cock. His lover's erection pressed against his leg.

"Uh, I think we'd better attend to our guest." He let Mike go and snatched the steaks from the grill. "Don't want these to get cold."

Emily appeared at the door holding a glass of dark red wine. "Are we eating, or are you two giving the neighbors a show?"

Jason glanced around. "Well, if we are, they're damned

lucky they get to see it for free."

With a laugh, Emily tugged at Mike's arm. "Come inside and tell me all the reasons why you decided to take this lug back."

"It's not a long list." Mike eyed him playfully. "He begged mostly."

Jason trailed behind the giggling and chattering pair. The shaved part of his lover's head with the stitches clearly visible reminded him of exactly why he threw himself on Mike's mercy.

Rounding the corner, his eyes strayed through the entryway of the living room and onto the mantel. The photo of Christoph stood smiling back at him. Jason noted the change in himself since he'd regained Mike's affection. The cloud of sadness which often engulfed him when he looked at the photo had dissipated. He no longer harbored the sting of guilt or the grief of loss.

He approached the mantle and nodded to the picture, to Christoph. "I'm moving on like you told me." Tracing his finger along the outline of Christoph's cheek, he sighed. "I hope you approve." Turning, he joined the still chattering Mike and the giggling Emily.

Glancing in his direction, Emily grinned. "What took you so long, slow poke?"

With a smile, Jason shrugged. "Just giving you two a chance to chat." He nodded at the table. "How about you pass my wine?"

Emily grabbed the glass and handed it over to him.

Lifting the goblet in front of him, Jason locked his gaze onto Mike. "Here's to good friends and second chances."

Mike's smile widened. "And to my rescuer. I might not be here if you hadn't chased after me."

Turning to face his best friend, he raised his glass to her. "Well, then, here's to Emily for talking some sense into me."

Emily clinked her glass against Jason's and then Mike's. "That's what best friends are for." She took a sip of wine and set the glass down. "Now that you two are sorted out, how about you find a man for me?"

Covering his mouth with his hand, Jason stifled a laugh and cleared his throat. "Who do we know, Mike?"

Mike tapped his fingernails against his glass. "Well, let me think." His eyes widened. "How about that hunky bartender at the pub with the meat pies?"

Considering Mike's suggestion, Jason sipped his wine. He'd never thought to take Emily to the pub. "Maybe we can all go there for dinner next week and see if there's a spark. What do you think, Emily?"

She shrugged. "Sure. I'm free. What's this guy like?"

Leaning in toward Emily with his elbow on the table, Mike's eyes widened in excitement. "He's tall and kind of built, with a handsome face and big hands. I didn't see a wedding ring on his finger, either."

Regarding his boyfriend, Jason lifted one eyebrow. "I had no idea you were so captivated with him."

With a laugh, Mike stood and kissed Jason's lips. "Don't worry, straight guys don't do it for me. He's got nothing on you at any rate."

Warmth flooded through Jason, and he slung his arm across Mike's shoulders, careful not to hurt him. "You know all the right things to say."

Mike wriggled his eyebrows. "And I mean it, too."

Emily cleared her throat. "Dial down the heat level, boys. You're not getting rid of me until we finish these steaks and I get a piece of that pie."

CHAPTER TWELVE

M IKE STRETCHED OUT his arm and rotated his wrist for Isaac. After three weeks of light duties, he no longer had any pain. "I think I'm healing up pretty good."

"I'm glad to hear it." His boss closed the door to the office and motioned for Mike to take a chair. "What can I do for you?"

A flare of anxiety swept through him. He'd been dreading this moment since he'd returned to work, but he knew the time had come. Craig and Alan had upped the pressure to move on and prepare for school, and he finally felt ready.

"You know my cousins freaked out big time when I was attacked," he began, keeping an eye on his boss's reactions.

Isaac nodded. "I was afraid I'd lose my friendship with Alan."

Keeping his gaze leveled at his boss, Mike continued. "They've encouraged me to relax and prepare for classes next month."

"So, you're thinking about doing that?" Isaac asked, his tone neutral.

Mike nodded. "I need to give you my notice."

Sinking back in the office chair, Isaac sighed. "I've been expecting this, though I'd hoped it wouldn't be for a while longer."

"I really like the job, and you're a great boss, but it's time I move on and go to school." He fidgeted in his chair, waiting for Isaac's response.

Isaac grinned. "I'm not going to try and talk you out of it because I've had this discussion already with Alan. We actually agree it's best for you, even though it sucks for me."

Raising an eyebrow, Mike flushed with annoyance. "Alan came to see you?"

"Nah, we met for our weekly lunch date and you came up in conversation. He's been talking for months about you going to school." Isaac leaned forward on the desk. "He's ecstatic you're finally doing it."

The weight of giving his resignation lifted, and he no longer needed to worry about Isaac's reaction. "Yeah, I know. He's taken me up to the college a couple of times to deal with my financial aid and help me sign up for classes."

"Do you know what you're taking yet?" His boss sat back in his chair, elbows on the rests.

Relief overtook his annoyance at his cousin. "I have some catch up to do in math, but I'll also be taking a writing course and a philosophy class."

Leaning back again, Isaac steepled his fingers together. "And what does Jason think of you going to school?"

"I think it's finally broken the ice between him and Alan." He smiled, thinking of several conversations between his boyfriend and his cousin. "Jason has been really supportive and offered to help me with the school work if I have trouble."

"That's cool. So, when do you want your last day to be?"

Mike stood and moved to a large calendar on the office wall. He scanned the dates. "It's about two and a half weeks until the end of the month, so how about I leave on the thirtieth?"

Isaac joined him. "That should work." He slid his finger down the schedule. "Veronica can take the shifts early next month, and I can see if we can get a replacement in before you leave. If not, I can take a few nights if we need it."

"Thanks." Mike moved toward the door.

"Hey," Isaac called before he could leave the room. "If you need a reference letter, I'm happy to write one up for you."

Turning, Mike grinned. "Thanks. That would be great."

"I'll have it ready for you before your last day."

JASON PULLED HIS truck up to the curb in front of the hotel and waited for Mike. He stepped out into the early morning air, giving a slight shiver at the crispness.

Two guys strode out the door of the hotel and almost bumped into him. The blond man stepped back. "Oh, sorry mate. Didn't see you there."

Jason grinned at the British accent. "No worries."

The man turned to his dark-haired companion. "Where are we off to again, luv?"

With a sigh, the other man took the blond's arm. "Breakfast and then we meet Conroy in Bellevue."

"Right, then." The blond man turned back to Jason. "Cheers, mate. We appear to be off."

Jason nodded. "Have a good one."

The men strolled down the street and turned at the corner. Jason watched after them, admiring the handsome pairing. They seemed like a long-time married couple.

Mike pushed the door open and approached Jason with a grin and tired eyes. "What's up?"

"I almost got run down by a blond Brit and his curly-haired partner," Jason said, chuckling.

"Oh, yeah. The dark-haired one checked in a couple of nights ago. They extended the reservation when the Brit showed up. Nice guys." Mike glanced at Jason's truck. "Thanks for coming to get me. Where to?"

Turning his attention away from the hotel guests, he focused on Mike. "Breakfast? I waited to eat until you got off."

"You're so sweet." Mike gave him a peck on the cheek. "How about that place we went when we first met?"

With a nod, Jason guided Mike to the truck. "You're reading my mind." Opening the door, it struck Jason where he'd seen the two hotel guests before. "Holy shit. Weren't those two guys here several weeks ago when we went with Emily to the Chinese place?"

Mike's face lit up in realization. "You're right. I've been wracking my brain trying to figure out where I'd seen them before."

"At least the dark-haired one looks a lot happier this time." Stepping back, Jason held the door open for Mike, biting his lower lip as he waited for his boyfriend to discover his surprise.

With a glance inside, Mike turned to him and grinned. "There's something on my seat."

Grinning himself, Jason stepped back and admired Mike's ass. "Looks mighty fine to me."

Mike laughed and lifted a dozen roses off the seat of the truck. "This seat, silly."

"Oooh, *that* one." He nodded at the blooms. "Just some flowers for this hot guy I'm picking up."

"Yeah? What's he like?"

"Extremely sexy." He patted Mike's ass. "He's giving his notice today, so I thought he'd like something as beautiful as he is to celebrate."

Mike's face blushed red. "Thank you. They're lovely."

With a chuckle, Jason held the door open. "Climb in and tell me how it went."

After Mike was settled in his seat, Jason shut the door and ran around to the driver's side. Once in, he started up the truck and secured his seatbelt. "So?"

"It went better than I expected. Isaac was really cool about me going to school." He glanced sideways at his partner. "My last day is the thirtieth."

"Perfect. That gives you just under a month before school. Any plans?" Jason navigated the streets toward the restaurant. They probably could have walked, but Jason had wanted Mike to find the flowers before breakfast.

Laying his hand on Jason's thigh, Mike replied. "I'd like to spend as much time with you as I can."

Jason met his gaze for a moment before returning his attention to the road. Warmth bubbled all over as a smile plastered itself across his face.

Finding a parking spot in front of the restaurant, Jason parallel parked the truck and switched off the ignition. He turned to Mike. "You really want to spend your vacation with me?"

Mike leaned in. "Sure do."

Jason met his gaze and reached out a hand to cup

Mike's cheek. He pressed a kiss lightly onto his boyfriend's lips, giving a slight shiver as a jolt of desire surged through him. He nibbled on Mike's bottom lip, then pressed his tongue into his lover's mouth.

With a muffled moan, Mike broke the lip-lock, kissed Jason's hand, and pulled back. "Let's go and eat. We can talk about what we're going to do inside."

Jason's stomach rumbled. After a long night on patrol, he was ready for some food. "Gladly." He jumped out of the truck and ran around to open the door for his lover. Mike left the roses on the seat and stepped onto the sidewalk.

After closing and locking the door, Jason took Mike's hand and gave it a squeeze. "Shall we?" They strolled to the entrance and Jason held open the door. Mike let go of his hand and stepped inside.

Sonja, the waitress from the first time they had breakfast together, bustled over to them. "Where have you been, Officer Lynch? I haven't seen you in a month or more."

"We've been having some challenges, but everything's good now." He took Mike's hand again.

She led them to a booth by the window. "Coffee for you, Jason?"

"Please." After letting go of Mike's hand, he wiped his tired eyes and sat on the bench seat. While ready to crash into bed, he wanted to spend some time with Mike.

"And hot chocolate for you?" she asked with a wink.

Mike's eyes widened. "How did you remember that?"

She tapped the pen to the side of her nose and smiled. "I always remember my favorite customers' drink orders. I also have a recollection you like pancakes."

Facing his boyfriend again, Mike grinned. "That's my

breakfast taken care of. What are you having?"

Sonja clicked her pen and pulled a pad from her apron. "I'll bet he's trying to decide between biscuits and gravy or steak and eggs."

"You are good, Sonja," Jason nodded in approval. "I'll have the biscuits and gravy. Stick an over-easy egg on top so I can pretend to balance out the carbs."

After writing out their order, she returned the pad to her apron and the pen to her blouse pocket. "Comin' right up." She hurried away from their table.

Jason focused his attention solely on Mike. "Do you still want to go to San Diego with me?"

Mike raised an eyebrow. "Yes, but you're not paying for the whole thing."

Crossing his arms, Jason settled back into the seat. "What makes you think I'd do that?"

"I believe this is the restaurant where my money isn't any good." Mike leaned forward. "I'd be uncomfortable with you putting out that kind of money on me."

With his plan out the window, Jason let his arms fall to his sides. "Mike, please. You need to save up some money for college. I'd feel bad if you couldn't afford your first quarter."

Mike shook his head. "Don't worry about it. My financial aid will pay for everything. My mom's income is non-existent, and I can still use her as the basis for my application." His brow furrowed. "The only thing I need to do is get her to sign the paperwork."

Feeling his concern justified, Jason leaned forward. "You think that might be a problem?"

"I don't know," Mike grumbled. "She's not too excited about me going to college. I haven't spoken to her in a few months, so it's hard to say how she'll take me calling out of the blue and asking her to provide a tax return for me to go to school."

Sonja returned to the table with a cup of coffee and a small bowl with a handle filled with hot chocolate and whipped cream. A drizzle of chocolate sauce adorned the peak of the cream.

Mike's eyes widening in delight, and he turned to Sonja. "Whoa. That's an intense cup of hot chocolate."

With a grin plastered on her face, she placed silverware wrapped in a cloth napkin in front of each of them. "You said it had been a rough time lately. I find chocolate cures the ills of the world."

Mike unfurled the silverware. "I like your philosophy and heartily agree."

Laughing, Sonja moved on to another table.

Jason nodded at Mike's drink. "Formidable." His boyfriend's excitement was adorable, and Jason again wanted to skip breakfast and head straight to bed.

"I've had bigger." Dipping the spoon into the whipped cream, he brought a heaping serving to his lips and licked, keeping his gaze locked on Jason.

Jason pursed his lips. "Oh, have you now?"

Mike swallowed the cream and placed the spoon on the table. "Actually, you're probably the biggest I've taken."

Giving him a wink, Jason brought the coffee to his lips and sipped. "I can definitely say the same about you." His cock stirred in his slacks. Quickly shifting gears, he fought to keep from getting fully hard in the restaurant. "Maybe we should change the subject until we get home."

Mike shifted on his seat with a smirk on his lips.

"What's the matter?"

A sock-covered foot slid along Jason's right calf, making him catch his breath.

His boyfriend licked a large portion of cream off his spoon. "Are you getting excited?"

The foot traveled farther up Jason's leg and along the inside of his thigh. Tingles of pleasure shot from Jason's feet to his crotch. "Oh, shit."

At the moment Mike's toes made contact with Jason's throbbing shaft, Sonja returned with their food. Jason scooted forward, pressing his stomach against the edge of the table, hoping she couldn't see what was going on.

"Okay, guys, here you go. Biscuits and gravy for the officer, and a pile of blueberry pancakes for the chocolate connoisseur." She set the plates in front of each of them.

With a wicked grin, Mike moved his foot along Jason's hard shaft, dipping under his balls, and pressed upward.

Turning to Sonja, Mike continued his toe torture with an innocent smile on his face. "This looks great. I can tell Jason's excited for his breakfast."

Sonja raised an eyebrow and glanced at Jason. "Anything else I can bring you?"

Jason shook his head, unable to say anything for fear he'd moan out the pleasure Mike's toes were generating.

When she turned to leave, Jason grabbed onto Mike's foot. Once she was out of earshot, he slid his thumb along the sock-covered sole. "You're lucky I love you so much."

Giggling, Mike tugged his leg away quickly, dislodging Jason's grip. "I seem to remember something similar happening to me."

Jason sat back, his cock still throbbing hard in his pants. "I have no idea what you're talking about." He removed the silverware from his napkin. "I'd *never* do that to you."

Mike rolled his eyes and cut into his stack of pancakes. "As you said at the time, just wait until I get you home."

Chapter Thirteen

J ASON KISSED THE top of Mike's head which rested on his chest as they snuggled in bed. "I want to get a picture of us."

Mike lifted his head to meet Jason's gaze. "Don't you have several on your phone?"

"Not *that* kind of picture." He trailed his fingers along Mike's bare arm, making his boyfriend sigh. "A professional picture. Just the two of us. We can give one to Emily and one to Craig and Alan."

Shifting onto his side, Mike propped his head on his hand. "You're serious about this."

"You bet I am." Jason wasn't sure what Mike felt about his request until his boyfriend's smile lit up the room.

"What did you have in mind?" Mike asked, cuddling closer. His hardness poked into Jason's thigh.

"Um, did you sneak my nightstick into our bed?" Jason's own cock stirred.

Laughing, Mike ground his body against Jason's. "I brought my own, but I'd happily grab yours, too."

Jason gasped when Mike's hand wrapped around his dick and slipped up and down his shaft. After a few strokes, he replaced his hand with his mouth. Pleasure exploded through Jason's body, and elicited a moan. Mike swirled his tongue around the head and along the shaft.

Clutching the sheets, Jason's legs stiffened. His boyfriend's attentions accelerated the tingling in his balls. "Jeez, babe, you've already got me close."

Mike sucked faster, and Jason's eyes rolled back, the pleasure taking control of his body. Balls tightening, the rush of orgasm surged through Jason.

"I'm about to shoot," he moaned and tugged at Mike's shoulder.

Refusing to relinquish his prize, Mike didn't miss a beat and brushed away Jason's hand. With a tremble, Jason arched his back and roared out his release, nearly passing out from the rush and intensity of his orgasm.

Mike continued to lick and slurp at the head, stimulating Jason until he couldn't stand the pins-and-needles sensation any longer. He brought his legs up and pulled his cock away from Mike's mischievous sucking. Cool air hit his shaft, and he sighed in relief when Mike sat back.

With a nudge from Mike, Jason rolled onto his stomach. Though still trying to regain his breath, Jason realized what his man wanted and hoped he could reciprocate the pleasure Mike had just given him.

Reaching over Jason, Mike retrieved a bottle of lube and a condom from the bedside table. He straddled Jason's hips, then squirted cold lube along the crevice of Jason's ass. The sudden cold made Jason squirm and suck in a breath.

"Shit, babe," Jason gasped.

Mike pressed his warm stiffness along the cool lube. "Sorry." From the mischievous tone in his voice, Jason doubted the sincerity of Mike's apology. "Ready for me to warm you up?"

"Go for it," Jason replied. He stretched out, spreading his legs and grabbing a pillow to rest his head on. With a backward glance, he watched Mike rip open the condom package and remove the rubber. Mike rolled the latex down his thick shaft, reminding Jason just what a monster of a cock Mike had.

With a smack across Jason's ass, Mike slid his covered dick against the pucker and nudged the head inside. Pain stabbed Jason, and he struggled to relax and accommodate the thickness moving into him. He took several deep breaths.

Mike leaned forward, resting his chest on Jason's back and nibbling on his ear. "Do you need me to stop?"

"No," Jason grunted, knowing he'd be able to accommodate his boyfriend's thickness if he concentrated on relaxing. "I want you inside me. Give me a minute." With the pain already subsiding, Jason was grateful for the reprieve. After a moment's rest, he pushed back against Mike's cock and more slid inside. Another burning wave broke over Jason, and he froze, letting out a little whimper.

Mike held still and let Jason set the pace. Every inch presented a challenge. Jason fought to take all Mike had to offer, and desire for his lover outweighed the discomfort of his girth.

With one final push, Jason took the rest of Mike's cock. Trimmed pubic hair poked into the cheeks of his ass, and Jason knew he had every inch. Another gasp left his lips when Mike stirred his dick gently inside Jason.

Finally, pleasure completely overtook the pain, and Jason relaxed. Taking the signal, Mike pulled partially out and then slid back all the way inside. He increased his speed over the next few minutes, and soon he was plowing

Jason deep and hard.

Waves of lust and pleasure crashed through Jason. He met Mike's thrusts, tightening his ass around the shaft. Both men grunted and moaned, thrashing around the bed.

Mike pulled completely out, eliciting a yelp at the sudden emptiness from Jason. He gave Jason's ass another slap. "Turn over," Mike commanded. "I want to see your face while I make love to you."

Not hesitating, Jason flipped over onto his back and pulled his legs apart, eager to give Mike easy access. Mike nudged his legs wider and lined up against the waiting hole. With a quick thrust, Mike slammed all the way inside.

"Oh, fuck!" Jason's head whipped back, a jolt of pure energy flying through him. He clutched his thighs, spreading them back and apart. Mike hammered hard, angling to hit his prostate. Jason repeatedly moaned and cried out.

Mike's rhythm faltered, and he thrust deeper. Another orgasm built within Jason, and his balls rose. Releasing his legs and wrapping them around Mike's waist, Jason clutched his erection and stroked in time to his lover's thrusts.

"I'm coming!" Mike hollered and rammed deep.

Jason stroked faster, just on the edge of orgasm. The final thrust rammed his prostate again and sent him over the edge. Shot after shot painted Jason's chest and stomach as Mike unloaded inside him.

Pulling Mike down onto his heaving chest, Jason held his lover close while they both came down from their orgasms. Mike returned the tightness of the embrace, his hands wrapped under Jason's neck.

The rhythm of their breathing returned to normal. The now soft cock slipped from Jason's hole, and the younger man rested heavily on top of Jason. Savoring the connection, Jason massaged his fingers into Mike's back. His lover moaned and relaxed further, his body limp against Jason's.

With a deep breath, Mike rolled to the side and nestled his chin onto Jason's shoulder. "Thank you."

Jason took Mike's hand and brought it to his lips. "Thank *you*."

Concern creased Mike's brow. "I didn't hurt you, did I?"

Though the entrance of his ass throbbed, Jason shook his head. "Just a little ache. You got me to come twice." He kissed Mike's hand again and brought it to rest on his thigh. "Not something I can usually do."

Mike kissed his neck. "What made you this time?"

"Your battering ram hitting my prostate probably had something to do with it. That, and I'm crazy in love with you." Jason rolled onto his side to face Mike. Staring into his boyfriend's eyes, he grinned. "So, how about that picture?"

THE PHOTOGRAPHER BUZZED around the portrait studio checking lights and setting levels. Mike watched the slight woman with long black hair and dark-brown eyes, as she worked.

She snagged her camera from one of the shelves lining the wall and hurried over to them. "Okay, I'm ready. Let's have Jason sitting first, and we'll go from there."

Jason stepped to the chair and settled his muscular

frame on the seat. The navy-blue suit accentuated the V of his back and his blond hair. They'd both gotten fresh haircuts and had shaved especially for the portraits. Mike couldn't help but stare at how handsome his lover looked.

He cocked his head to the side and met Mike's gaze. "You okay?"

Mike nodded. "Just admiring how hunky you are."

With a lop-sided grin, Jason shrugged. "I guess I clean up okay."

"I'll say." Mike joined Jason at the chair. He stood behind his boyfriend and, laying his hands on Jason's shoulders, kissed his neck.

Sucking in air, Jason squirmed on his seat. "Behave yourself. I don't want to get a hard-on for our photo."

Mike nibbled on his ear before standing up straight. "I wouldn't be averse to that."

With a shake of his head, Jason settled back. "Maybe for a different kind of photoshoot, but not for our families."

Keeping his hand on Jason's shoulder, Mike faced Danielle and her camera. "Spoilsport."

She grinned and stared at the screen on her camera. "You two are adorable. I've already got a couple of good shots."

Mike squeezed Jason's shoulder. "Those'll be for the private album."

"I should say so," Jason chuckled.

Aiming her camera at the two men, Danielle peered through the lens. "Okay, you two. Give me the serious pose."

Mike kept his face as neutral as he could, fighting the urge to grin. The muscles under his fingertips kept his desire for his boyfriend heightened, especially with how sexy he presented himself in his suit.

Danielle clicked away. "Now the smiles. Look like you enjoy being together."

Mike grinned. "That's not difficult at all."

With a chuckle, Jason brought his hand up to grasp Mike's. "It better not be."

Warmth flushed through Mike as he laced his fingers with Jason's. "Don't worry. I'm crazy about you, and I'm sure it'll show in the pictures."

Clicking away, Danielle moved in closer. "It does. Keep smiling." She took a few more pictures, then lowered her camera. "I think I've got the portraits you wanted. Anything else?"

Mike's eyes widened in surprise when Jason pulled him into his lap. Wrapping his arms around Mike, Jason winked at Danielle. "Maybe a few just for us."

She raised her camera and resumed capturing images. "Just tell me when to stop. I've got plenty of memory on this card."

Facing Mike, Jason grinned. "You're so sexy in that jacket and tie. I could take you right now." Mike ground his ass onto Jason's lap, feeling his boyfriend's erection pressing against his slacks.

Jason leaned forward and, bringing a hand to the back of Mike's head, pulled him close to kiss him. Mike returned the fervor of the kiss, amazed at Jason's willingness to have their intimacy photographed.

Breaking the lip-lock, Jason pressed kisses and small bites down Mike's neck while he grabbed the red tie. Mike leaned his head back, giving Jason more access.

Danielle buzzed around them, not seeming embarrassed in the slightest by their escalating display of affection.

Jason nibbled around the collar of Mike's dress shirt then licked his way back up to his ear. "I love you," he murmured.

A rush of desire gripped Mike, and he gasped at his boyfriend's intimacy. "These pictures are going to be amazing," he choked out.

With fingers fumbling around Mike's collar, Jason released the top three buttons of the dress shirt but kept the tie around Mike's neck. One arm stayed wrapped around his lover's back to keep his balance while Jason pulled open the shirt. He tugged on the tie and kissed down, past the knot, and onto Mike's chest.

Mike glanced at Danielle, unsure if she was okay with them basically making love in front of her. Her grin while she clicked away reassured him she had no problem with their actions.

Relaxing into the moment, Mike closed his eyes and let the pleasure Jason generated fully wash over him. Jason massaged his pec while he leaned Mike further back. Moving his arms to support Mike, he lifted him and stood. Mike wrapped his arms around Jason's shoulders.

As Jason held him under his knees and across his back, Mike leaned forward and kissed him again. He placed a hand on Jason's cheek, massaging his thumb across the soft skin while their lips crushed together.

Mike broke the kiss and leaned back in Jason's arms grinning. "You okay holding me?"

With a smile, Jason nodded. "Wrap your legs around my waist."

Mike complied with the request, locking his legs

around his boyfriend's body then winking at Jason. "Hold onto me. I'm going to lean back."

Jason raised an eyebrow but held on.

Mike leaned backward and brought his hands to touch the floor, knowing full well the tightening in his slacks would show clearly in the photo.

Laughing, Jason kept a hold of Mike's back. "Silly boy."

With a laugh, Mike stared at the camera. "I know."

After Danielle took a few shots, Mike released his hold on Jason's waist and somersaulted forward. Standing, he rejoined a chuckling Jason. Mike reveled in the sparkling amusement dancing in Jason's eyes and brought his arms to embrace his well-dressed boyfriend.

Jason returned the embrace, touching his forehead to Mike's and grinning. "I so want to take you home right now."

Keeping his forehead in contact with Jason's, Mike brought his attention to Danielle. "Any more poses you want?"

"Jason, face me like Mike is, but keep your heads together." She kept her camera ready.

Jason turned his head.

"This'll be a close-up of your faces, so give me a big smile."

A mischievous thought popped into Mike's head. He slid his hand down Jason's back and under his suit jacket.

Jason stiffened. "What's going on?"

"Oh, nothing." Mike's fingertips lightly tickled Jason's ribs.

"If you think that's going make me giggle like a little schoolgirl, you've–" With a sharp intake of breath, Jason bit his lip trying not to laugh.

Mike tugged Jason's shirt from his waist and tickled his fingers along the smooth skin of Jason's side. Jason howled with laughter, and Mike joined him.

Releasing Jason from his torture, Mike attempted to move away, but Jason pulled him close and kissed him.

"You're in so much trouble," he growled.

Danielle lowered her camera and grinned. "You guys are adorable. I got some great shots."

Returning their attention to the photographer, Mike stepped out of Jason's embrace, though Jason kept his hand on Mike's shoulder. Danielle moved to her laptop and attached a cable to her camera. Her fingers flew over the keyboard and clicked the mouse a few times. She scrolled through the pictures, settled on an image, and double-clicked the icon.

The photo filled the screen. In mid laugh, Jason held onto an upside-down Mike.

The hand on Mike's shoulder traveled down his back and wrapped around his waist as Jason pulled him close to his body. "What a great picture. It captures Mike perfectly."

Mike swung to stare into Jason's gaze. "How so?"

"Fun-loving and adorable," Jason replied and kissed his nose.

Flushing with embarrassment, Mike returned his attention to Danielle. "So, what's next?"

She clicked through images and settled on the serious portrait at the beginning of the photoshoot. "I'll do some editing and send you a CD with the files. You review them and let me know which you want printed. I have a photo printer, so I'd prefer to process them here. Though I cost a little more than the big box stores, you'll be happier with the quality."

Jason nodded. "We'll look forward to it." Then to Mike, "How about some lunch?"

Mike's eyes lit up. "Or better yet, let's see if Emily's free and take her to meet the bartender."

THE DOOR TO the pub yielded to Mike's excited push. Jason held the door open for Emily and Mike to enter, then followed, surveying the room. Alex and Sarah Templeton were engrossed in conversation with his fellow officers Paul Tomlinson and Fred Collier around one of the pool tables. Alex spied them by the door and waved, making the others focus their attention toward them.

Fred hurried up. "Mike, thank goodness. We need you to settle a dispute."

Mike's eyebrow shot up. "A dispute? Between police officers? No thanks."

"Aw, come on. We're off duty," Fred pleaded.

With a chuckle, Jason patted Mike's arm. His boyfriend was now quite popular with every pool shark on the force. "Go on, Mike. These amateurs need an expert opinion."

"Amateurs," Fred blustered. "You're just sad you can't handle a stick." He winked at Emily who snorted back her laughter.

Mike waved his finger at Fred. "Now, now, Officer Collier. I won't tolerate such slander. Jason can handle a stick just fine. And he really knows how to rack a set of balls."

Unable to hold back any longer, Emily giggled.

"That's what I've heard."

With a roll of his eyes, Fred gestured toward his companions. "Seriously, we need a ruling."

Amusement danced in his lover's eyes. Taking Emily's arm in his, Jason nodded in the direction of the pool table. "Go on, Mike. I'll get Operation Drink-Squirter started."

Fred's brow shot up. "Operation what?"

Shaking her head, Emily tightened her grip on Jason's arm. "They're trying to set me up with the bartender."

"Seb?" Fred shook his head. "I think you're barking up the wrong tree."

Mike and Jason swung their gaze to the hunky man tending to the customers around the ornate bar. Nothing about his movements or behavior set off Jason's gaydar, but of course, he was out of practice.

Eyeing his boyfriend, Jason tilted his head toward the bar. "What do you think?"

With a shake of his head, Mike turned to Fred. "You guys should concentrate on pool. There's no way that he's gay."

Fred chuckled. "In all the times I've been here I've *never* seen him hit on any of the ladies."

Emily's face lit up. "Well, that may just mean he's not a womanizing Neanderthal."

Throwing up his hands, Fred moved toward the others. "Good luck, then." Mike followed, laughing.

Jason frowned, trying to size up Seb. "What do you think, Emily?"

Her face, moments ago full of laughter, turned serious. "I'm not sure, Sweets. I mean, if he doesn't flirt with his patrons, how am I supposed to get a date out of this?"

A smirk slipped across his lips. "This is you we're

talking about. He'll be begging for your number before you're finished with your first tater tot."

"If he's straight," she said, though he noticed her face changed, regarding her prey with a slightly tilted head and an upturn of her lips.

"You heard Mike. Besides, I've been coming here over two years, and he has never struck me as playing for my team." With a glance toward the bar, Jason spied three empty stools just past the curve of the counter. "Let's grab those seats before someone else gets them. Should have a good view of him making drinks."

With each step they took weaving their way around tables, Jason's anxiety heightened. The last thing Emily needed was another gay buddy instead of a hot date. They reached the stools and took a seat. He shrugged off his jacket and placed it over the stool next to him to save it for Mike.

Jason turned in time to see Mike break at the pool table. Two balls shot into the pockets. With a grin, he returned his attention to Emily. When the bartender faced them, Emily's eyes widened, and the man's mouth dropped slightly before quickly recovering and assuming his professional demeanor.

Relieved, Jason kept quiet, letting Emily take the lead.

"How's your evening, folks?" Though his words seemed meant for both of them, Seb's attention centered fully on Emily.

With a swift shift in her body language, Emily abandoned her nervousness and ratcheted up the flirting. "Hi." Her eyes lit up and she leaned her elbow onto the bar. With a little shake of her hair, she grinned. "And what's your name?"

"Sebastien Gunn, but you can call me Seb." He returned her grin, showing a row of straight teeth. "What's your pleasure?"

She wriggled her eyebrows. "Something strong and wild. What do you suggest?"

"I'm sure I can think of something to fit the bill." Realizing that Jason was sitting there, he ripped his attention away from Emily. "Nice to see you again." He glanced at the empty stool covered with Jason's coat. "Expecting another person?"

"He'll be here in a minute." Jason tilted his head back. "He's just wiping the table with my friends."

They all turned toward the pool table. Fred had a huge, toothy grin while Paul stood with his mouth dropped open and Alex shook his head with a deep frown on his face. Mike sunk the eight ball into the side pocket and handed his cue to Fred.

Jason swung back around and addressed Seb. "There we go. He'll have a ginger beer, and I'll take a Lucille."

"I remember him." Seb laughed. "Alex and Sarah went on and on about his fin going up after the innocent *I don't know how to play* act." He turned away, grabbing a couple of bottles from the bar.

"See, Emily? You haven't even gotten your drink yet, and you've moved in for the kill." He watched Seb mix a drink and slide it down the bar to another of the patrons. He poured Jason's beer and the gingery drink for Mike.

His lover returned triumphant, hopping up on the stool. "Thanks for saving me a seat. What did I miss?"

Wrapping an arm around Mike's waist, Jason leaned in and gave him a peck on the cheek. "Emily's working her magic on the decidedly straight bartender," he murmured.

Seb returned, setting the two pints in front of the guys and a tumbler with a light pink drink fizzing merrily. "Here you go. Strong and wild. Let me know if you don't like it, and I'll try again."

Batting her eyes, Emily raised the glass. "I'm sure I'll love it." She sipped the drink and gave out a little *whoop*. "Tasty."

"Success." With a grin, Seb laid out three menus in front of them. "Are you thinking about some food?"

She returned his grin with a lift of her eyebrow. "Among other things."

CHAPTER FOURTEEN

MIKE'S TRUCK RUMBLED along the roadway over the West Seattle Bridge, and he shifted into second gear as he approached the hill climb by the old steel mill. Several Audis and BMWs flew by him, their drivers swerving around him and making no attempt to slow down.

One of the drivers going particularly fast flipped him the bird, cutting Mike off and surging up the hill. Mike rolled his eyes. "Spoilt little rich kid," he spat with a frown.

He'd finished his last night at the hotel, and the entire crew came in on their day off to throw him a party after the end of his final shift. Though sorry to leave the majority of his co-workers, his growing excitement about starting college outweighed the bittersweet emotions at leaving his job. While his excitement grew, his anxiety blossomed as well.

He navigated the truck onto Dakota Street and chugged up the hill. Nearing the crest, a loud bang echoed around him and jarred the entire truck with the passenger-side back wheel suddenly sinking.

Pulling up to the curb, Mike shut off the ignition and jumped out of the cab. Rubber from his tire lay in shards all over both the road and the grassy strip next to the sidewalk. He surveyed the damage and stared in amazement.

The rubber of the tire was completely gone from the wheel. Bare metal rested on the concrete roadway. Large, rusty chunks of the wheel well also lay on the side of the road. The explosion of the tire damaged the already weakened structure of the truck.

Kicking himself because he didn't have a spare tire to at least get him the five blocks to the house, he scurried around the road collecting the pieces of rubber and debated what to do next. After dumping the debris in the bed of his truck, he strode to the door and sat inside.

"Screw it." He started the truck's engine and shifted into gear. The familiar rumble shook the truck when he stepped on the gas. He slowly drove the rest of the way to the house. Instead of parking in front as he usually did, he opted to drive through the alley and hoped both of his cousins had their vehicles out of the small parking strip at the back.

Luck was with him. He found the small, paved hill empty of cars. He pulled up to the drive and stepped on the gas, giving the truck a final surge to reach the top. Stomping on the emergency brake, he turned off the ignition and the truck shuddered to a halt.

Mike slammed the door after exiting the cab and hurried around the back end of the truck to have another look at the damage. This time, he could clearly see the truck was beyond reasonable repair. The axle was bent, with the wheel well pretty much gone. Pulling his phone from his pocket, Mike snapped a couple of pictures and texted them to Jason.

A touch of melancholy hit him as he moved through

the back yard and along the path to the breezeway. His truck had been with him through the thick and thin of his hellish high school years and carried him away from the horrendous situation he'd been in before coming to Alan and Craig's home.

His cell buzzed with an incoming call. Jason's face filled the screen. Accepting the call, Mike touched the screen and held the phone to his ear.

"Hey, baby, what happened to your truck?" Jason asked, worry in his voice. "Are you okay?"

Mike smiled, comforted by Jason's concern. "I'm fine. The tire blew up and took part of the frame with it. I had to drive a few blocks on the bare wheel."

"Uh oh."

Turning the key in the lock, Mike pushed open the back door. He smiled at the familiar tinkle of the bell.

"Mike, is that you?" Craig's voice called from the kitchen.

Holding the phone away from his ear, Mike responded. "Yeah. I'm on the phone with Jason." He returned the cell to his ear. "Sorry."

"No worries," Jason chuckled. "You just got home, I take it."

"Yup," Mike said and sat on the wooden steps going into the kitchen. "The last day on the job was great. I got a party."

"Cool." Jason's tone changed, and the concern returned to his voice. "You're sure you didn't get hurt when the tire exploded?"

"No, I'm okay, but the truck's not. I think it's totaled." He glanced out the back door, though the garage was in the way and he couldn't see his truck. "Not sure I want to put any more money or time into it."

"Probably just as well. You won't need a vehicle for school. Alan was telling me the bus is half a block from your place and goes straight to the college."

Mike sighed. "I know. I just really loved that truck."

"Believe me, I get it." He paused. "But I think it was a little past its prime."

With a laugh, Mike nodded. "I suppose. Alan will be overjoyed."

Craig entered the kitchen carrying a small plate. "Hey." He noticed Mike still on the phone. "Sorry, I'll be in the living room." He set the dirty dish on the counter and scurried out of the kitchen.

While resuming his conversation with Jason, Mike stood and climbed the five steps to the kitchen. He opened the refrigerator door and foraged for a bite to eat. "I'm not sure what to do with it now. I doubt I'll get much for scrap."

"Donate it. At least you could write it off on your taxes."

Mike reached for a platter of left-over hamburger patties. "It's not like I make that much."

"Like you said, you wouldn't get much if anything for parts, so at least you can feel good about yourself donating it to a charity."

Mike bumped the fridge door closed with his hip and set the plate on the countertop. "Like the policeman's retirement fund?"

Jason laughed. "A very worthy cause, though I'm slightly biased."

Finding a bag of buns on the top of the refrigerator, Mike held the phone with his shoulder to his ear and snagged the plastic bag. He fished one out for his burger. "You want to get together tonight?"

"Want to? Yes. Able to? No. I'm on patrol." Disappointment came clearly through the cell's speakers.

Mike sighed. "Oh, yeah." He knew this was one of Jason's nights working. He set the burger on a plate and stuck it in the microwave, pressing the auto-minute button.

"Are you sleeping today or going to try to stay awake?"

Yawning, Mike knew the answer. "I'm at least going to take a nap. This might be a slow process getting my clock reset to be awake during daylight hours." The excitement of his last day at the hotel and the blowout of his tire was waning.

"How about you hit the sack, and I'll do the same. Might be a good afternoon for you to spend with Craig and Alan. I'll see you in the morning. It'll be the start of my weekend."

Revived a little by the thought of a full two days with Jason, Mike strode to his room. "Okay, have a good sleep. I'll see you tomorrow morning. Should I come down to the precinct or meet you at your place?"

"Come on to the house," Jason replied without hesitation. "I'll be home about eight."

"It's a date." He dragged the curtains closed, plunging the room into darkness.

"I love you."

Hearing those words from Jason continued to bring a smile to Mike's face and a warmth to his heart. He knew Jason meant it, too, judging by the number of flowers he'd been receiving.

He clicked on the light by the bed and sat on the

comforter. "I love you, too." The connection ended, and he sprang up. *Oh, shit. My burger.*

JASON ENDED THE call and set his cell on the bedside table. Stripping off his clothes, he hung up his uniform and placed his shoes in the closet. He stepped into the bathroom and turned on the shower. Hot water flowed from the showerhead. Stepping inside, he let the warmth soak into his tired frame.

Steam enveloped him, and he soaped his body, scrubbing off the sweaty grime generated by patrolling alleys all night. Thankfully he hadn't needed to bust any druggies the prior evening, so he wasn't as tired as he might be. Still, bed called to him with a siren song promising restful sleep.

His thoughts drifted to Mike and his boyfriend's impending birthday. A mere three days away, Jason didn't know what sort of gift to get. His lover was adamant about paying his part of their upcoming vacation, so just giving him the trip was out. With Mike's truck now permanently out of commission, maybe a bus pass would fit the bill. The college likely would provide a discount for his transportation, but at least Jason could buy it for him.

After rinsing off the suds from his head, he turned off the water and opened the door. Leaning out of the stall, he snagged a towel off the rack and ran it over his dripping skin.

The ringtone on his cell lilted into the room, so he dropped the towel and strode back into the bedroom. He read the unfamiliar number on the screen. Normally he wouldn't answer, but since he was already there, he decided to risk it.

"Hello, this is Jason."

The familiar voice of Mike's cousin greeted him. "Hey, it's Alan."

Jason moved to the closet and grabbed his robe from the door. "Oh, hi, Alan. I've been meaning to get your and Craig's numbers for my cell."

"I can text you Craig's. Did you work last night?"

"Yeah. I was about to hit the hay." Concern for Mike suddenly hit him. Alan had never called him before. "Everything okay?"

"We're all good. I'm at work. Just had a few things to do here this morning."

Relieved, Jason padded to the bed and sat on the edge. "What's up?"

"I was wondering if you had plans for Mike's birthday? We're thinking of making dinner or taking him out, but I didn't want to trample on any arrangements you might have already made. You, of course, are absolutely welcome to join us if you're free."

"I was just giving that some thought," he said, returning his thoughts to gift ideas. "We don't have plans yet, but I'd also like to do something special for him. With his truck out of action, I'm thinking of getting him a bus pass."

"Whoa, what? His truck's not working?" The tone of Alan's question felt hopeful.

Jason's silently cursed, realizing he'd let the cat out of the bag. "Oh, crap. You're not at home."

"This is my office phone," Alan replied. "I'll act surprised. What happened?"

Sighing, he couldn't keep the news from Alan. "The

back tire blew out a few blocks from your place, and he drove home on the bare wheel. Guess it damaged the frame and the axle. He's going to get rid of it."

The joy in Alan's voice was unmistakable. "How tragic."

Jason couldn't help but chuckle. "Now, Alan, be kind to him. He's got a lot of emotion tied up in that junker."

"That is an apt description. I promise I'll be supportive – especially if he *junks* the junker."

Jason could imagine the scene at Mike's place later this evening and was glad to let the cousins duke it out over the demise of Mike's truck. Definitely another bouquet of flowers for his boyfriend tomorrow. "Back to the main topic. I'd be happy to join you for whatever you and Craig have in mind. Mike and I can have our own celebration another time. Maybe on our trip."

Jason's thoughts again wandered to their upcoming vacation. Warm water lapping the sand as they lay out on the beach. Mike naked in the bright sunshine while Jason's hands oiled his beautiful skin.

Alan's voice brought him back to the conversation. "Okay, great. Let's plan on having dinner at our place on Mike's birthday. We'll have his favorites."

A smirk nudged at the corners of Jason's mouth. "We have to have something *other* than mashed potatoes."

Alan's laugh boomed through the cell. "Actually, he's asked Craig for a turkey dinner. We did the same for him last year, and he loved it. Now it's a tradition, I guess."

"Can I help with anything?"

"We're having turkey, corn, mashed potatoes and gravy, and green bean casserole. I know Craig wants to prepare those. He uses Mike's grandmother's recipes."

Mulling over the menu, Jason considered what else would go well with the meal. "How about dressing? Or do you stuff the bird?"

"He doesn't like it, so we save that for Thanksgiving."

"A salad, then?"

"Perfect," Alan replied. "I'll let Craig know."

The drowsiness Jason experienced earlier returned with a vengeance. "What time should I come over?" he asked with a yawn.

"We'll eat at four, but come any time before that. Say, I'd better let you go. You must be exhausted."

"Yeah, it was a long shift, and I'm back in the cruiser again tonight." Jason scratched an itch on his scalp. "Thanks for the invitation."

"Of course. You're pretty much family now," Alan replied. "See you at dinner. Stay safe out there."

Surprise cut through Jason's weariness. "Bye." With two beeps, the call ended. Jason lowered the cell from his ear, staring across the room at the wall. *I'm pretty much family now? Holy shit.* He never expected those words to fall out of Alan's mouth.

The conversation set Jason's mind to work about his relationship with Mike. They'd survived a major crisis and grew stronger from it. He loved Mike and missed him when they weren't together. Perhaps it was time to take the next step.

But what *was* the next step? Did it make sense to ask Mike to move in when he was starting school at South Seattle College? Queen Anne would be a long commute, and while a bus connection wasn't *that* difficult, it would add time, especially if he had early morning or late-night classes. From Craig and Alan's, the commute would only be one bus and virtually door to door service.

Jason removed his robe, letting it fall to the floor and then stretched his body, lifting his arms over his head as he yawned. Climbing under the sheets, he pondered some more. San Diego. That would be the deciding factor. If they had as wonderful of a time as he anticipated, he'd ask Mike to move in.

He rested his head on the pillow and closed his eyes. With sleep not far away, he imaged beaches and crashing waves. *Yeah, after the trip I'll ask him.*

Chapter Fifteen

"**D**AMN IT, BRIDGETTE Schillerman, why are you making this so difficult?"

Ripping him from his sleep, Mike's eyes flew open at the mention of his mother's name. Alan's voice thundered through the closed door, and the conversation in progress didn't sound good. The old rotary phone in the hallway was both an advantage and a disadvantage, being right outside Mike's door. His cousins didn't use it much, but it was the primary way they communicated with family.

"He's your son." Alan's voice rose in pitch and intensity. "All you have to do is sign a piece of paper and his school is paid for."

Sitting up in the bed, Mike pushed aside the comforter. He considered opening the door and taking the phone from Alan but thought better of it. He'd learned long ago not to get in the middle of an argument between the two cousins, especially when he was the topic of the conversation. He certainly had no desire to speak to her after she'd been treated to Alan's fury.

Clearly trying to calm his temper, Alan spoke again. "Look, I'll pay you to sign that form if it's the only way you'll do it."

Shock washed over Mike, and a deep anger stirred inside him. The only way she'd do right by him was money? "Unbelievable," he muttered, swinging his legs off the bed.

A sharp bang and the clanging of the old phone's bell accompanied the stomping of feet away from Mike's door. "Fucking bitch," Alan spat.

With a sigh, Mike slipped on his jeans and threw on a t-shirt. Tentatively, he inched the door to his bedroom open and peeked out. The hallway was empty, but he heard rustling coming from the kitchen.

Stepping through the doorway, he entered the hall and sauntered into the kitchen to find Alan fuming at the table while leafing through some paperwork in his work backpack.

He took a seat at the small table. "Hey, what's going on?"

Alan looked up, anger still burning in his eyes. "I had a…conversation…with your mother."

"I'm sorry. What was it about?"

"Believe it or not, she actually had the gall to call the house." Alan's face flushed bright red from his anger. "I asked her about the paperwork you'd sent, and she said there was no way in hell she'd sign it."

Mike's stomach turned. "Why?"

"As you know, she doesn't believe in education." He slammed his fist onto the table. "I swear, our aunt must be rolling in her grave."

Closing the gap between them, Mike placed his hand on Alan's shoulder. "Calm down. There must be something we can do."

"Well, I hung up on her in mid rant, so I doubt she's going to want to speak to me again." He hung his head. "I failed you."

An idea sparked in Mike's mind. "Actually, maybe I should give her a quick call."

Alan's head snapped up. "No, you'd better not. You don't want to deal with her when she's all fired up."

With a smirk, Mike winked at his cousin and stood. "She's forgotten that I know where all the bodies are buried." He strode to the old black phone hanging from the wall and recalled his mother's phone number. The old mechanism sawed through the numbers as he dialed. Though he hadn't called it in a couple years, the number was seared into his memory.

"What do you want now, Alan?" His mother's sharp voice sizzled through the receiver.

Mike ground his teeth, then steeled himself for the onslaught. "It's not Alan. This is your son speaking."

A short silence hung on the other end of the line.

Taking this as a sign of shock, Mike dove straight in. "I understand you won't sign my financial aid forms."

His mother regained her voice, haughty ignorance dripping from her every word. "You're damned right I won't. I ain't sending no son of mine to get brainwashed by any of that Communist Hippy crap."

He'd expected this behavior, but it still frosted him to actually hear the words. "I don't give a shit about your opinions of college. I'm going whether you like it or not."

"Well, you're not getting any help from me." He could see in his mind her mop of curly hair bobbing as she swung her head and spat out each word. All attitude with no idea of what she was talking about.

"I know you never cared about me." He remembered the last time he'd seen her. She'd slammed the door in his face. "You even told me so when you kicked me out, so I don't feel bad about making this threat."

Another short pause. "What threat?"

His brow furrowed, and the smirk returned to his lips. "I remember a ring your aunt had."

A gasp sounded from the other end of the phone and her voice trembled. "I don't know what you're talking about."

Alan strode into the hallway, his face even redder.

Mike nodded at him. "Yes, you do. I'm almost *positive* it was gold with a family crest engraved on one side and the initials MB on the other. It had a large blue stone."

"How do you know about that ring?" Her voice quaked with fear.

"I found it one day and took a picture of it. I can text it to you if you want." He knew he'd hit his mark. Alan made a move to take the receiver from his hand, but Mike batted him away. "So, here's the deal. You sign those papers and send them back to me, or I'll send that picture to the *entire* family telling them you stole it and where you hid it."

Her rage blazed. "You rotten, ungrateful—"

"Ungrateful? Really?" Now his own anger rose to the surface. "You were the worst mother ever. My brother tried to kill me several times over and you did nothing. *Nothing!* Now you won't do the one small thing I need to make sure I have a real future, and you're calling *me* ungrateful?"

"How dare you threaten me." Her voice had lost its fury, but the venom remained.

Mike took a deep breath and blinked. "You have three days. If I don't have those signed documents by Friday, your ass is grass with this family. I'll start with Grandma. I think she'll want to know you stole her mother's ring from her dying sister, especially since she's bankrolling you right now." He slammed the receiver onto the cradle and turned to his fuming cousin. "Mission accomplished."

Alan's voice trembled with rage. "*She's* the one who stole that ring from Aunt Geraldine?"

"Yup." Mike kept his voice as even as he could, though the fight with his mother, and yet another example of her attempts to sabotage his life, threatened to break through his façade of indifference. He pointed a finger into Alan's chest. "And *you're* not going to say a word about it." His cousin spluttered his protest, but Mike held up a hand. "If you go spilling this to the family, she'll never sign those papers. I'm sorry this is the way you found out about her thievery, but it was the only way to make her sign."

Shaking his head, Alan turned and stumbled into the kitchen. "I get it. I'm not *happy* about it, but I won't say anything."

Mike followed him, taking a chair at the table. "Thanks. I understand you're angry. I was too when I realized what she'd done."

He fixed Mike in his gaze. "Then why didn't you say anything?"

With a sigh, he sat in the chair next to his cousin. "First, she's my mother. No matter what shitty things she's done to me, and continues to do, I have to respect that."

Alan's jaw dropped. "You're kidding me with this. She's been absolutely vile to you. Loyalty is your reason?"

"Somewhat. But you just heard the main reason. Leverage." A slight pang of guilt hit him when Alan shook his head. "I'm sorry I didn't tell you. I know you treasure things like that and get really upset when someone in the family does this kind of shit."

Alan nodded.

"But just think of it this way." He winked. "She's probably scared shitless that you now know what she's done, and I guarantee your future conversations with her are going to go a lot differently. She'll have those papers signed and in the mail today."

The skepticism in his cousin's stare was hard to miss. "I'll believe it when it happens."

Mike laughed. "Hopefully you won't have a reason to speak with her too quickly."

Easing back into the chair, Alan also chuckled. "Yeah, I've had my fill of your mother for a while." He cocked an eyebrow. "On another subject, care to fill me in on your truck? I noticed an obliterated wheel barely clinging to a bent axle."

A sudden sadness crept into Mike. "The tire pretty much exploded a few blocks from home, and I drove the rest of the way on the bare wheel."

"I'm sorry to hear that." Though Alan tried to suppress the smirk, he failed.

Mike could easily read his cousin, and sorrow was certainly not what he was exuding. Mike pursed his lips and narrowed his eyes. "I'm sure you are."

His eyes widening, Alan spread his arms wide. "Hey, I'm trying to show some compassion here."

"Uh huh…" The truck had been a bone of contention for a long time. Mike considered torturing his cousin with the notion of having it repaired, but he did need some advice on how to get rid of it.

Not waiting to be asked, Alan crossed his arms. "If you want *my* opinion, you should have dumped that rig a long time ago. Donate it and take the write-off on your taxes."

And there it was. Lecture mode. Mike rolled his eyes. "Donate it, eh?"

"Yeah. You can check online whether your favorite charity takes donations of junker trucks." He grinned. "I'll bet you could easily offload it."

His ire rising, Mike rose from the table and pushed in the chair. "Thank you for your input. I'll consider it." The thought of *offloading* the prized possession he'd put so much money and energy into depressed him. "See you later."

Without another word to his cousin, he hurried out the back door, slamming it shut, and trotted around the garage to his truck. Opening the door, he settled into the driver's seat and inhaled a deep breath. The scent of motor oil and axle grease filled his nostrils. This truck had provided escape from some horrible situations, and was the one thing that was all his, bought with his own money.

"Damn it," he yelled, slapping the steering wheel. A chunk of plastic dropped into his lap.

A rap of knuckles on the passenger window caught his attention.

Reaching across the bench seat with torn upholstery, Mike flipped the lock up and stared at his cousin through the dirty glass.

Alan pulled opened the creaking door. "Can I join you?" His demeanor had changed, seeming more respectful and conciliatory.

"Up to you," Mike said, examining the piece of detached steering wheel.

Settling onto the seat, Alan nodded at the broken plastic. "What's that?"

With a sigh, Mike handed it over. "Proof that you're right."

Alan took the fragment and looked it over. "This just came off?"

"Yeah." Mike's shoulders sagged.

After placing the chunk of plastic onto the cracked dashboard, Alan settled an arm across Mike's shoulder. "I'm sorry. I didn't mean to be such a dick about your truck, especially after the fight with your mom."

Mike leaned against his cousin. "Thanks." He took in the state of his vehicle. Tears and cracks went from windshield to dashboard to seats. The floor carpet barely existed, and what little remained was stained with oil and dirt. It would cost much more money than it was worth to fix his truck, and without a job, he couldn't afford the parts, let alone have time to do the work.

Alan hugged him closer. "Do you remember the red pickup I had when you were little? I think I drove it over to your mom's a few times."

"Yeah. You used to take me for rides in the country-side." He'd lived for those rides with his older cousin. They were an escape from the hell of his mother's house.

Alan stared forward out of the windshield. "I was driving the truck to work one day, and it made some very strange noises and became sluggish. I was working on the Eastside then, and barely made it to Eastgate. There was a mechanic walking-distance from my building, so I dropped it off and waited all day for the verdict."

Curiosity at the point of this story canceled out Mike's depression for a moment. "What happened?"

"Oil in the radiator and water in the cracked engine block. Total write off. I opted to drive it back to the house and somehow got it home." Alan fixed Mike with a stare. "I made the mistake of being home to watch the tow truck come to take my truck away for the last time. So, you see, I understand what you're going through with this silly truck of yours."

He'd never heard Alan speak of the demise of his little red pickup before. Meeting his cousin's gaze, he nodded. "I'd appreciate some help sending it off."

"Sure. How about you set up to have it taken away while you're in San Diego?"

Mike grinned. "You're so smart."

With a wink, Alan retracted his arm from Mike's shoulder. "I went to college."

"I'VE GOT A little present for you, birthday boy." Jason clutched the small box he'd wrapped that morning while Mike slept. He handed it to his lover, unsure how the gift would go over.

Mike's eyes sparkled with excitement, and he accepted the box. "What is it?"

Chuckling, Jason slipped back under the covers and laid his arm over Mike's bare chest. "Open it and see."

After tearing apart the wrapping, Mike opened the box and grinned. "An Orca card."

Jason chewed his lower lip. "I put a three-month pass on it."

"A practical gift. I love that about you." Mike kissed the top of Jason's head. "It's perfect. Thank you."

Tossing the box onto the floor, Jason moved on top of Mike. "I, of course, have something else to give you for your birthday."

Mike stared up at him, his grin widening. "And what's that?"

"Me." He leaned forward and touched his lips gently to Mike's. The kiss quickly intensified, and Jason ground his body against the muscular man beneath him. Mike pressed his full erection against Jason's stomach while encircling his back in an embrace. Wrapped in Mike's arms, a small shiver spread through his body, and he sank deeper into the lip-lock.

After a moment of gyrating against each other, Jason broke the kiss and shoved the covers back to reveal his naked lover's body. He savored the warmth and hardness beneath his fingertips as he rubbed into Mike's pecs. Pushing himself up to sitting, Jason ground his ass against Mike's erect shaft, trapping it in the crevice between his cheeks and flexing his glutes.

Mike groaned and pressed his cock against Jason's ass, the friction working Jason into such a frenzy that he almost forgot the proposition he had for his lover.

Jason placed his hand onto Mike's chest and stared into his eyes. "Babe, the other gift is me. *All* of me."

With a scrunch of his eyebrows, Mike stopped his grinding and returned Jason's gaze. "What do you mean?"

"I trust you more than anyone else." He paused, the subject difficult for him. "I haven't…given myself…to anyone since Christoph died."

Mike reached his hand to cup Jason's face, running a thumb against his cheek. "I know you haven't, and I stopped playing around with anyone else when we met."

Clutching Mike's hand in his, Jason kissed the fingers and returned his gaze to Mike. "I want you inside me. Without a condom."

Emerald eyes widened, and his lover's lips parted. "You want me to bareback you?"

"Yes." Jason laced his fingers with Mike's, working through the butterflies fluttering in his stomach. "I haven't been with anyone else in a really long time, and I tested free and clear of anything last January."

Mike's surprise turned into a grin. "I messed around with a couple guys before we met, but I got a clean bill of health at my physical in April." He stared hard at Jason. "I've never barebacked. The possibility of catching something was too scary." He released his fingers, and the caress down Jason's flank sent ripples of pleasure coursing through his body.

Anxious to feel his lover take him, Jason gyrated his hips. The hardness beneath him shifted, plowing across the pucker of his ass. "So, what do you think?"

Mike wriggled his eyebrows. "I think you are the sexiest man I've ever seen." He nudged his legs toward his chest, lifting Jason onto his thighs. The head of Mike's dick pressed against his hole. "If you're serious, and you're up to taking me, I want to make love to you." He thrust against Jason, prying for access.

Flexing his legs, Jason lifted himself off Mike. "I'll get the lube." Like an acrobat, he kept one knee on the mattress and leaned across the bed, opening the drawer to the nightstand. Retrieving his prize, he squirted a few dollops of the clear liquid onto his hand and reached back, slicking Mike's erection. The thickness pulsed, and he continued to stroke the lube up and down the shaft.

Mike squirmed beneath him. "I want you so bad."

"I'm yours." Jason gave one more squeeze around his shaft and released, squirting more lube into his hand and sliding his fingers against the tight entrance to his ass. He slicked the entrance and tossed the bottle aside. Grabbing hold of his cock, Mike positioned the tip against Jason's pucker and pressed upward.

A jolt of pain stabbed Jason, and he winced. "Easy. Gotta take this slow."

Mike dropped his hand to the sheet, concern washing over his face. "You set the pace. I don't want to hurt you."

Closing his eyes, Jason willed his body to relax. He pressed down, and more of Mike slid inside. Another jolt of pain made him squeeze his eyes tight and halt his descent.

"Are you sure you want to do this?" Mike's voice dripped with concern. "Last time was painful for you."

"You also made me shoot twice. Let's try a little more lube." Jason lifted himself off of the rigid pole and squirted more lubricant into his hand. Slathering it over the shaft and head, he resumed his position and eased the tip into his pucker. Relieved that the shaft slid inside him more easily, Jason slowly but steadily sank down until he reached his lover's pelvis.

Mike's hands rested on Jason's thighs, and he gently thrust his hips upward. The feeling of fullness and the prodding of his prostate kept Jason's cock straining.

Taking control, Jason ground his ass against Mike, taking all of the thick shaft inside as he locked his gaze onto the pools of green staring up at him. He set a moderate pace, careful not to bring his boyfriend over the edge too quickly. On each upward movement, he squeezed the muscles of his ass, tightening his hold on Mike's cock.

Mike's grip tightened around the muscles of Jason's legs, and his dick felt thicker and harder. "Baby, you're getting me close."

Jason stood slowly, easing the erection from inside him, and lay on his stomach. Taking the hint, Mike climbed on top of him and squirted more of the lube along the crevice between Jason's cheeks. Rubbing his shaft along the slick liquid, Mike eased back inside.

The thickness of Mike's bare dick drilling inside him made Jason's own cock throb. His lover's pace quickened, and soon Jason clutched the sheets while Mike plowed quickly toward climax. The friction of the sheet against his aching hardness brought him close to his own release.

"I'm there, baby. Oh, fuck!" Mike thrust hard and howled as his cock pulsed deep inside Jason.

With a few squeezes of his ass, Jason milked the man writhing on top of him. Close to blowing, Jason thrust up. Mike's body shook and pressed down, burying his still rock-hard shaft all the way in and sending a final jolt of pleasure to trip Jason's orgasm.

"Yeah!" Jason's back arched while Mike lay against him, and he shot onto the sheet beneath him.

Coming down from his release, Jason eased his body back down and rolled them both onto their sides. Though softening, Mike remained firmly planted inside Jason, and he brought an arm around to hug him.

Laying a kiss between Jason's shoulders, Mike nuzzled his nose against Jason's neck. "Thank you for my birthday presents."

"You're welcome, baby. Happy birthday."

With a sigh, Mike gave Jason a squeeze. "I suppose we should get up. We have dinner with Craig and Alan, and I want to get in some time downtown."

CHAPTER SIXTEEN

THE WEEK SLIPPED away quickly. As Mike had suspected, the financial aid documents arrived fully signed by his mother. Relieved to have school registration taken care of, he could enjoy the vacation with his boyfriend. Mike stood in Old Towne San Diego. The adobe buildings framed a large square with a covered, wooden boardwalk connecting them.

Jason beckoned him into a leather shop, holding up a belt and a wallet. "Do you like these?"

Following him inside, Mike marveled at all the different wares. Belts, chaps, handbags, pretty much anything one could want made out of leather. A large saddle hung from a wall lined with cowboy boots.

He sidled up to Jason. "Cool belt. I like the pattern." The strip of leather had a large metal buckle with a steam train surrounded by mountains. Along the belt, railroad tracks spanned the entire length.

His lover nodded. "Try it on."

Mike wrapped the belt around his waist and tightened it, clasping the buckle into place. "A perfect fit."

"I want to get it for you." Jason moved toward a display of hats and plucked a medium brown one with a wide brim from the pile. A leather band with a plain metal buckle sporting a short red and black feather circled the hat. "Try this, too."

Chuckling, he let his boyfriend set the hat onto his head. "How do I look?"

Jason whistled. "Like a sexy cowhand. Should we get you a pair of chaps?"

Shaking his head, Mike's chuckle turned into a laugh. "I think we're good with the hat and belt."

With a wriggle of his eyebrows, he took Mike's hand and led him over to the racks in the corner. "Chaps would set off the bulge in your jeans."

"I'd probably only wear them when we're alone. Not much call for chaps in Seattle."

The gleam in Jason's eyes when he pulled Mike close and held up a pair of black chaps left no illusion to his intent. "Try them on, baby. For me."

"Okay, okay. Hand them over." Mike slipped the chaps over his jeans and pulled them up. The crotch of his jeans jutted from the opening in the rawhide pants. "What do you think?"

Nodding, Jason licked his lips and raked his gaze over the leather and denim. "I think I want to get them and take you back to the hotel."

Mike held up a finger and assumed his best country accent. "Hold on a gosh darn minute, partner. I reckon we need some vittles first."

With a slight frown, Jason adjusted the front of his own jeans. "Are you sure?"

"Gotta get our strength up for the wild ride later." Mike winked, pulling off the chaps and the belt. "We might not make it out again this evening if the roundup goes well."

Jason's eyebrows shot up. "Round up? How many are

you expecting?"

Shrugging, Mike placed the cowboy hat onto the pile of leather objects in his hand. "Just you." He glanced around ensuring no one was looking at them then groped the hardness pushing against the crotch of Jason's jeans. "And your friend here."

"Okay, but no beans," Jason said, eyeing him closely. "I don't want any blowouts before we get down to business."

Mike dropped his hand and faked an innocent smile. "Don't worry. I'll be sure to stand clear of the campfire."

Jason leaned back with a full belly laugh. "You are too much."

Grinning, Mike gave him a quick peck on the cheek and leaned in to murmur in his ear. "You'll certainly think so if I fill up on beans."

THEY FOUND A small fusion restaurant just outside the main area of Old Towne. Tucked into a small house, the restaurant advertised Middle East inspired tapas. Olives and hummus were the starter, and they agreed to split a large lamb paella.

Jason sipped his watermelon *agua fresca* and leaned back against his chair. "We've got your outfit for the evening. What else would you like to do today?" He imagined his lover wearing only the chaps, regretting they hadn't picked up a vest as well.

"Old Towne was the main thing. Maybe we could hit the beach later today or tomorrow." Mike dipped a piece of tortilla into the tapenade in front of them. "I should also find something for Alan and Craig while we're here."

"Maybe send them a postcard." His mind wandered to Mike's cousins and wondered what the two men would want from San Diego. Neither struck him as the collecting-stuff type.

"Yeah, Alan would definitely like that. Memories are more important to him than things. Unless, of course, that thing is a family heirloom. What about Emily?"

"She loves silver things, so be on the lookout for something moderately tasteful with a hint of gaudy." The last time he traveled, he brought her back a silver statue of Atlas holding up a round, blue lace agate. Though beautiful, he'd never have it in his home. She adored it.

He still wanted to find something for Mike. The practicality of the young man made him difficult to buy for. The leather shop was fun, but he hoped to find something a little more special.

"School starts soon," Mike stated, glancing out the window. "I'm mostly ready."

Jason perked up. "Mostly?"

"Yeah. I need a couple of things, but I'm not sure I can quite swing them until the financial aid arrives." Mike returned his gaze to the table and took a sip of his water.

"Oh, like what?" All ears, Jason leaned forward.

"A book satchel. I know a lot of the material will be online, but some of the classes still use thick text books." He furrowed his brow. "The books are expensive. Alan and I checked out the student store when we turned in the paperwork my mom sent."

"I bet that was a relief, getting her signature. You never said how you got her to sign." Jason leaned back in his chair. He'd seen the perfect bag at the leather shop, and he only needed to figure out how to get back there and sneak the gift into Mike's suitcase for him to find later.

Mike smirked. "I can't. Suffice it to say, she'd be severely embarrassed, and potentially cut off by my grandmother, if what I threatened her with got out into the family."

Raising his eyebrow, Jason surveyed his lover. "So, basically, blackmail."

With a shrug, Mike wiped his fingers on the paper napkin in his lap. "Let's just say I encouraged her to do the right thing for her son with a gentle reminder of her wrongdoing."

"I'll be careful what secrets I tell you."

Mike smirked again. "Don't worry, officer. I'd never use anything you say or do against you."

The waitress arrived with their paella and set it onto the middle of the table. "Anything else?"

The aroma rising from the dish made Jason's stomach grumble. "No, I think this looks great."

WITH THE NEW leather satchel his boyfriend left in his suitcase from San Diego slung over his shoulder, Mike boarded the number 128 bus to South Seattle College.

Nearly shaking with nerves for his first day, he settled into a seat at the very back of the bus. The words of his mother and his aunt questioning his ability to hack college haunted his thoughts and rattled his confidence. With a shake of his head, he forced his gaze out of the window, watching the familiar buildings of West Seattle go by as the bus rumbled along California Avenue.

At a stop about a mile along the route, a dark-haired girl about his age stepped onto the bus and made her way to the back. She plopped down next to him, surveyed his satchel, and spread her lips into a wide grin.

"Hi, I'm Kelly. Are you studying at South?"

Taken aback by her forward introduction, Mike fumbled out a response. "Uh, yeah. It's my first quarter."

"Cool. I just returned from a two-year study abroad program." She slipped her backpack off her shoulders and unzipped the top.

"Oh yeah?" Mike's interest ignited. Travel was foremost on his mind after the trip to San Diego. He'd contemplated signing up for studying in Europe, but never thought he'd be able to afford it. Besides, the last thing he wanted was to be separated from Jason.

"Yeah," Kelly continued, fishing around in her backpack. "I signed up for a program with South three years ago and got accepted. It was a work study program in Berlin."

"Wow. What did you do there?"

"Mostly worked in a scarf shop." She fished a large journal out of her bag and flipped through about half way. Three photos slid onto her lap as the bus lurched over a bump, and she scrambled to catch them before they hit the floor. "Here's the shop," she said, pointing to one of the pictures. She flipped the second to the top of the stack. "And this is me inside."

Kelly showed the third photo, a picture of the Brandenburg Gate. "And the last one is about a five-minute walk from the shop."

"You were there two years?" he asked in a mixture of awe and jealousy.

"Yup. Studying philosophy and architecture." She slipped the pictures back into her journal and replaced the book in her backpack. "What are you going to school for?"

Mike shrugged. "I don't know yet. My counsellor said I needed to get a bunch of the basic classes out of the way."

She grinned. "Even with all the credits I did in Berlin, I have some of the basics to do to get the distribution requirements finished before I can transfer to the UW. What are you taking this quarter?"

Pulling out his phone, Mike opened his calendar and scanned the schedule. "English 100 at nine. Math 089 at ten, and Piano 101 at twelve-thirty. I was going to do philosophy but decided to switch it out for the music credit."

"We have English together. What's your name?" She stuck out her hand.

"Mike." He grasped her hand. "Mike Bryant."

"Kelly Jennings." She shook his hand enthusiastically. "So, Mike, are you dating anyone?"

"Uh, I'm gay." The last thing he wanted was a girl coming onto him the first day of school. If this had been Wisconsin, the scene would turn ugly quite quickly.

Thankfully, it was Seattle.

She laughed. "Oh, cutie, I'm not interested in you. I can see you're not on my team. I just have this friend who should be with someone. If you're single, I'll hook you up." She winked. "He's really hot."

His shoulders relaxing, Mike breathed a sigh of relief. "Thanks, but I have a boyfriend. He's a cop with the SPD."

"Well, that trumps Jeremy," she laughed. "You should still meet him, though. He's a riot. How long have you two been together?"

The bus flew over another bump in the road, and Mike and Kelly bounced on the seat. He clutched his belongings to keep them from flying across the aisle.

He shook his head. "The rough roads are the only part of riding the bus I don't like. Especially when the driver is going too fast in a construction zone." He stuffed his calculator deeper into his satchel after he retrieved it from the seat next to him. "It's been a few months since I met Jason."

"Jason the policeman. Nice." She raised an eyebrow. "Does he have a brother?"

"HEY, LYNCH. THE Chief wants to see you." Fred Collier stepped through the doorframe and into the locker room.

With the warmth drained from his face, Jason's stomach tightened. "Oh, shit. Was she pissed?"

Collier shook his head. "Nah, she seems pretty happy today. For her, of course."

Jason fished in his locker for his shirt. "Any idea what it's about?"

"Nope. Just said to come and get you." He opened the door of his locker and unbuttoned his shirt. "What are you and Mike up to this weekend?"

"Not much," Jason replied, his mind preoccupied with what he might have done wrong to gain the Chief's notice. "Probably stay at home."

"Haven't seen much of you since you got back from San Diego. Everything go okay?" Collier slipped off his shirt and placed it on the hook.

Jason finished buttoning his shirt and stuffed the shirttails into his uniform pants. "It was an amazing trip.

We had a lot of fun exploring."

With a smirk, Fred unclasped the top of his slacks. "Each other."

Chuckling, Jason placed his hat on his head. "We saw a lot of the city and hung out at the beach."

"Well, when you get hitched, I want to be in the wedding party."

Jason froze before he could close his locker door, not sure if he'd heard his partner right. "You do?"

Collier turned toward him, a crooked smile on his lips. "Of course. That is if you've got a spot for me."

"I don't know what to say." It didn't occur to him that any of the guys on the force would be interested in coming to a gay wedding, let alone want to be part of the wedding party. Collier treated Mike well when they were at the pub, but Jason suspected admiration for Mike's pool abilities as opposed to acceptance of his relationship status.

Shaking his head, the smile faded from Collier's lips, and he returned his attention to his locker. "Come on, Jason. Do you really have no clue how the officers here feel about you?"

His defenses kicked in. All his worst fears about dating someone while a police officer came to the surface. "I don't care what they think." The team in Spokane had been fine with him on the force, with the exception of Christoph coming to any of the off-duty events. Both of them would get the cold shoulder, and Christoph finally refused to come to any function related to his work. When his partner had died, the Spokane officers said nice things, but not one of them showed up to the funeral.

"Man, anyone here would take a bullet for you," Collier stated, annoyance tinging his words. "Kawaguchi saw how much it broke you up to see Mike lying unconscious on those steps. He said he wished someone cared about him like that." A sly grin parted his lips. "And Sarah Templeton gushed over how she adored your boyfriend even after he wiped the pool table with them."

Jason reeled at Collier—at Fred's revelations. "No one from the force in Spokane gave a shit." Not willing to repeat the mistakes he'd made including his boyfriend in anything work-related, Jason had kept a professional distance from the other cops on the force. He tried to just do his job, maybe grab an after-work drink with a group of the guys, but he considered it enough that they knew he was gay.

"I've met some of those douches, and I can guess which of them gave you a hard time. Go talk to the Chief." Fred dropped his trousers and stepped out of them. "We can discuss this later over a beer. I'll get Paul and Alex to come along. We're all here for you if want to let us in."

After spinning the combination on his locker, Jason paused before he moved to the door. "Kawaguchi really said that?"

"Sure did." Fred slipped on his jeans. "I'll meet you at four-thirty at the pub in Wallingford. We need to sort things out here. I think you have the wrong idea about us."

THE SCENT OF pasta sauce met Mike when he opened the front door and stepped into the house. "Craig? Are you home?"

Alan poked his head around the corner of the kitchen.

"No, he's at the store getting a couple of ingredients for dinner."

Kicking off his shoes onto the red rug, Mike strode across the wood floor with thudding feet and met Alan at the entrance to the kitchen. "What are you doing here?"

"I live here." After giving Mike a quick hug, Alan turned back to the stove and stirred the sauce before covering it with a lid. "I took half a day off. We finished a large project at work, and I didn't feel like starting something new. I'm warming up some of the sauce from the other night. We're having *Braciole di Maiale* for dinner tonight. Is Jason coming over?"

Mike salivated at the dinner menu. "I have no idea what that is, but it sounds delicious. I'll text him." He pulled out his phone and sent Jason a message, taking a picture of the large pot of sauce on the range top.

Jason immediately messaged back: *My aunt used to make that. You bet I'll be over. Finishing up with Collier, Templeton, and Tomlinson. Tell Alan I'll bring wine.*

With a smile, he looked up at Alan. "Yes, he'll be here. He's bringing wine."

"Great." Alan lifted the wooden spoon and tasted the sauce, closing his eyes for a moment. "Craig makes great sauce."

Shaking his head at his cousin, Mike frowned. "Oh, God, I didn't need to know that."

Alan shot him a sideways glance and returned the spoon to the pot. "Brat."

With a laugh, Mike stepped into the dining room and dropped his backpack on the table.

Tapping the spoon against the lip of the pot, Alan called from the kitchen. "How was class?"

"Good," Mike said, pulling out two large textbooks. "I met a girl on the bus, and she's in one of my classes."

"A *girl?*" His cousin brought his hand up to his chest melodramatically. "You're not turning bi, are you?"

He spun to face Alan, rolling his eyes. "Seriously?"

His cousin wriggled his eyebrows. "Well, you did say once that you liked the occasional booby."

Mike shrugged. "I did, but Kelly isn't going to be my tit-fix. Besides, that craving has pretty much gone away."

Alan moved to the counter and pulled open a package of meat. "Alrighty, then. So, Kelly?"

"She's great. I think we're going to have a lot of fun." Flipping open his notebook, he skimmed through the pages for the homework assignments for his three classes. Twenty pages for the English class, a series of problems for his math class, and some scales on the piano. "Wow, do I have a lot of homework." He turned back to Alan. "How did you manage the workload during college?"

His cousin gave him a wink, then turned back to the flank steak in front of him. "I spent a lot of time at Gasworks Park."

Cocking his head, Mike tried to figure out how the park had anything to do with studying. "What?"

"I goofed off during the first couple of quarters, but then hunkered down." He rolled the steak and tied string around it. "Summer quarter was hardest. You don't need to kill yourself with the homework, but the trick is to stay ahead. If you have some extra time, don't spend it goofing off. Get a few chapters further in the reading, and you'll find it easier to deal with the workload later in the quarter."

With a sigh, Mike closed the notebook. The amount

of information just in the first day had been overwhelming. "I hope I can do this."

Alan carried the steak to the pot and dropped it into the sauce with a plop. He turned to Mike, fixing him with the stare he reserved for serious moments. "I *know* you can."

CHAPTER SEVENTEEN

THE FIRST TWO months of the quarter went well, and spring was definitely in the air. Mike marveled at the February tease Seattle regularly experienced. Alan often spoke this time of year about the first February he spent at the University of Washington when it reached eighty degrees.

This year, the tease got to seventy degrees for two days, then promptly returned to the low forties. Mike frowned, hugging his pea coat closed. He waited for the bus, the damp cold cutting through him. Thankfully, the 128 appeared over the rise in the hill.

The last slivers of blue sky succumbed to dark clouds pushing in from the south. The wind picked up, and the misty drizzle turned into a pelting sideways rain.

Splashing to the curb, the bus pulled up and the driver opened the door. "Morning."

"Hey." Mike hurried on, pushing moisture from his coat and wiping his wet hands onto his jeans. After tapping his pass against the reader, he strode to the back of the bus. To his surprise, Kelly sat in their usual spot grinning at him.

Plopping down next to her, Mike stowed his satchel under the seat. "What are you doing on the bus?"

"I walked over to the grocery store this morning before

the heavens opened up." She reached into her backpack and retrieved a package of sliced salami and some squares of yellow cheese. "Bite?"

"No, thanks. Alan made me breakfast this morning. I had a refreshing bowl of oatmeal." The warm and pleasant fullness in his stomach made any thought of eating unappealing.

Kelly rolled her eyes. "You and your oatmeal. Is that all you eat?"

Chuckling, Mike shook his head. "Potatoes."

"I wish I'd made time for breakfast." She popped a small morsel of meat and cheese into her mouth.

"You're having breakfast." The salami's scent appealed to him, and he plucked one of the pieces from the packet in her hand.

She cocked an eyebrow. "I thought you weren't hungry."

With a grin, he snagged a piece of cheese. "That was almost a *minute* ago."

She rolled her eyes and shook her head. "You're incorrigible."

He stopped chewing for a moment, the meaty goodness mixing with the cheese. "Huh?"

"Nothing." She perked up. "Is that your phone?"

The light chime of the ringtone he'd programed for Jason's number softly lilted from his satchel. Fumbling with the straps, he retrieved the cell before the last ring, flicked his finger over the screen, and lifted the cell to his ear.

"Good morning, beautiful." Jason's voice sounded through the small speaker. A light shakiness tinged his words.

"Hey baby. I'm on the bus heading to school." His mind wandered to their weekend plans. "I'm super stoked to head to the beach tomorrow."

"Me, too. Are you packed?"

Mike paused as his cheeks heated. "Uh…"

"Don't worry, sweet man, I'm not packed either." He chuckled. "I haven't seen you in two whole days. Not sure how much more of this I can stand."

"I'm confident the wait will make the weekend even more amazing. You're working, and I have class late today. We *could* go for dinner if you're really desperate." Though Mike really wanted to see Jason, he knew he'd be sunk come Monday if he went away and didn't have a couple more chapters for his math class completed. He had a date with Alan that evening to work through the problems.

"Nah, I'll check in with Emily, and you can get some homework done so we can have fun on our mini vacation." The disappointment in his voice was unmistakable, but Mike knew he was right.

"I'll be home tomorrow about four. We can get out before the traffic gets too horrible." He glanced at Kelly who had her English textbook open.

The bus turned off of Sixteenth and climbed the hill toward the bus stop at the college. "Hey, I'm almost at school, so I'll let you go. Love you, baby. Get some good rest today. You'll need it."

Kelly rolled her eyes. "God, I need a girlfriend."

Laughter rolled out of the cell. "You goofball. Love you, too. Have a good day at class."

"I will. Sleep well." With reluctance, he ended the call and gathered his things. The bus rolled to a halt, and the driver opened the doors. Mike waved to him from the back door, and he and Kelly stepped out and into the wind and pelting rain.

Mike turned to Kelly as they ducked under the entryway to the campus. "See you in a couple of hours."

She nodded and gave him a wave. "Until English do us part."

HURRICANE EMILY BLEW through Jason's front door and stormed into his living room holding her cell in front of her. "And just what do you think this is?"

Cocking an eyebrow, he let his head fall to one side as if examining the object before him. "Well, I *think* it's a phone." Then he shrugged. "But these days, who can tell."

"Oh, you're a shit. I meant the picture on it." She tossed him the mobile. The screen was filled with a photo of the ring he'd picked out for Mike sitting in a blue velvet box with his text asking Emily what she thought.

"I think you didn't answer my question." He stood and returned the phone to her. "Do you like it?"

"Beautiful. But why are you asking?" Her eyes widened, and she brought a hand to her lips. "Is it for Mike?"

Shaking his head, he crossed his arms in front of him. "You're slow today."

She sprang at him, flinging her arms around his body and squeezing. "Did he say yes?"

Chuckling, he hugged her back. "I haven't asked him yet."

"Wow. I thought you dating again was a huge step, but now you're looking to get engaged." She leaned back, still embracing him. "You sure you're ready for this?"

He'd asked himself the same question repeatedly in the

last week. Each time he had any hesitation, he looked into Mike's eyes, or thought constantly of him if they were apart.

"Definitely. I'm still as crazy about him as I was when we started dating. I think the trip to San Diego sealed the deal for me." Jason released her from their hug and stepped into the dining room. He plucked the small velvet box off the table and returned to Emily. "Want to see the real thing?"

She did a little dance when he opened the box. Reaching out, she plucked the ring from its perch and lifted it into the light. "You have good taste. This is exquisite. He's going to love it."

"I hope so." The nerves he'd been fighting most of the week resurfaced. "There's still one more hurdle before I can actually ask him."

She cocked an eyebrow. "And what's that?"

He exhaled a heavy sigh. "I need to ask his cousins for their blessing. If they don't approve, I don't see how I can expect Mike to leave them to be with me."

"Sweets, they're going to be thrilled." She moved her hands to her hips. "And if they're not, I'll go over there personally and talk some sense into them."

Chuckling again, he reclaimed the ring from her and replaced the band into its perch in the box. "Hopefully it won't come to that. I think you discussing anything sensitive with them would be like throwing a hand grenade into a fireworks factory."

"Well, I don't take any crap from anyone where you're concerned." She winked at him.

"You say the sweetest things." He placed the gift in his pocket. "I wanted you to see it before I had it wrapped.

We're heading out for the coast tomorrow, so my plan is to check in with Alan and Craig this evening about coming over early to talk to them."

"You working tonight?" She checked her watch. "Because I'd like to take you out for a drink to steel your courage."

"Let me guess," he smirked. "You want a meat pie to go with that drink."

She shrugged. "Maybe your impending proposal will rub off."

Now it was his turn to stare wide-eyed at her. "You're serious, aren't you?"

"Maybe a little. I love Seb, and he'd make a fine husband." She frowned. "You *do* think he's a good guy, don't you?"

"Of course, I do. We wouldn't have introduced you two otherwise. I'm just a little surprised at the timing. You've only been dating about three months." He cocked an eyebrow. "You're not jealous that I'm potentially getting hitched before you?"

"No, silly. I know I'll look much better walking down the aisle than you."

Jason shook his head, imagining the disastrous ensemble she'd likely pick. "Only because I'll be there to help you choose the dress. You'd probably buy something that makes your shelf look like two torpedoes aimed at your fiancé." He eyed her current selection. "Or you'll put your bridesmaids in neon orange and dye your hair to match."

"Ha. Ha. Ha." She batted at his arm. "So funny, mister fashionista."

"Well," he sniffed haughtily "I can't help it if I have impeccable taste and refinement."

She rolled her eyes. "Oh boy. I hope Mike truly understands what he's in for."

THE STORM FROM the prior day had dispelled overnight, and the day promised to be bright and freezing. Mike's morning piano class had gone well, his teacher impressed with the progress he'd made on his midterm piece.

Meeting up with Kelly, they'd walked across campus to their English class only to find the room dark and empty. The notice on the door of the classroom spelled out their weekend and made Mike rethink the intelligence of going away with Jason to the coast. Kelly stood next to him, jotting down the homework assignment.

She turned as she stuffed her notebook into her backpack. "Well, that takes care of my weekend. I'm not sure I'll have time to do anything but homework."

Mike shrugged. "It's not really that much, and we have until Tuesday." He eyed the list of readings and then her raised eyebrow. "Okay, it's a shit-ton of homework. At least *you* didn't plan to be away."

With a sigh, she linked her arm into his. "Lunch is in order since class is cancelled."

His stomach rumbled. "You're on."

They strolled down the hallway, passed rooms filled with students, and emerged into the cold afternoon. The trees lining the campus walkways stood bare and stark but promised wonderful shade for the coming summer sun.

The cafeteria building loomed before them with its large, tinted windows and pebble-covered walls. Kelly let go of his arm when they entered the building and pushed through the turnstile. She made a B-line for the salad bar while Mike moved over to the grill.

Connor, the hunky student chef, grinned as he approached the metal counter. "Heya, Mike. Your usual?"

"I'll splurge and have tater tots instead of fries, but yeah. Double bacon cheeseburger hold the tomatoes."

"Comin' right up." Connor turned and flipped a burger onto the grill. "Thought you had class right now."

"Not for the next couple of days, I guess. The instructor is suddenly out of town. She left us plenty of homework, though."

"So, your weekend is set."

Mike eyed the other offerings kept warm on the steamer table. While the tater tots looked good, the mashed potatoes called to him more. "I'm supposed to go to the coast with my boyfriend later today. Guess I'll find some time on Monday to do it all. Hey, can I change the tots to mashed potatoes?"

"No problem." Connor turned the hamburger over and laid a piece of cheddar on the patty. After covering the cooking meat with a lid, he turned back to the counter and prepared Mike's plate with a healthy portion of potatoes. "Gravy?"

With a grin, Mike nodded. "Please."

He ladled the brown gravy over the spuds and opened a toasted bun. Covering one side with lettuce and onions, he lifted the lid and scooped up the burger, then slid the meat patty off the spatula and onto the bun. Two pieces of bacon finished the order.

"Here you go. Have fun at the coast. I'm taking Aiden to a soccer game."

Mike cocked his head to the side after he lifted the plate from the counter. "I thought you were dating

Jolene."

He shrugged. "We broke it off. She doesn't understand bi guys."

"Ah, gotcha."

"Besides, Aiden's a hottie," Connor said, his eyes dancing with excitement. "We have a lot of fun together, and he doesn't mind if I need the occasional booby."

Laughing, Mike gave him a wave and turned toward the cash registers across the room.

Kelly approached with a mountain of salad on her plate. "Mashed potatoes and a *burger*?"

Connor waved from behind the counter. "Hey, Kelly. You're looking gorgeous today."

"What a flirt." She winked at the short order cooking student. "But thanks for the compliment."

Glad for the deflection, Mike nodded toward the soda dispenser. "I'm grabbing a root beer. Want anything?"

"No, thanks. I'm getting water." She sidled up to the ancient lady at the cash register and paid for her lunch.

Mike poured his soda and joined her after paying for his meal. "Connor's sure looking tasty these days."

Crinkling her nose, she poured her olive oil and balsamic vinegar dressing on top of the salad. "If you like that sort, I guess. You're not looking to replace that handsome man of yours, are you?"

A grin crept across Mike's lips. "Not for me. For you."

She stabbed her fork into a cherry tomato. "You seem to forget that I'm more inclined toward tits than dicks."

"But you like the occasional boy, right?" Mike lifted the burger to his mouth and took a bite, enjoying the flavors of the beef and cheese.

"I do confess to a certain satisfaction a guy can give,

but then they start *talking* and I lose interest." She sighed heavily. "Ruins the whole scene."

Finishing his first mouthful, he set the burger back on the plate. "Connor can cook, and he's bi."

She arched an eyebrow and stared across the room toward the kitchen. "Is he, now?"

Mike followed her gaze and caught the grin and wave from Connor.

After returning the gesture, she turned back to Mike. "Enough about my deficiency of available cock. How's things with you and your hunky lover?"

While scooping a large helping of mashed potatoes and gravy onto his spoon, Mike smiled. "Amazing. I'm really looking forward to the trip this weekend." He let the potato melt in his mouth and savored the salty flavor.

"Nice. Full points for effort." She leaned in. "But where is the relationship going? Is it fuck buddies, or are you in love."

With no hesitation, his smile widened. "Head over heels. He's really attentive, and he tells me he loves me all the time."

Settling back, she nodded. "Okay, but what do you want out of the relationship?"

"I'm happy where we're at right now. I mean, I wouldn't say no if a ring showed up, but I have school to get through." He took another bite of his burger, contemplating what he would actually do if Jason wanted to take the next step. Moving in? Marriage? He munched on the food and set the burger back onto the plate.

"A romantic getaway so soon after the big trip?" She cooed. "Was it his idea?"

Mike nodded and took a gulp of his soda.

"Well, *I'd* say be prepared. He has something other than screwing in mind for the weekend." Her mouth set into a smug smile. "And you better text me immediately if he does."

"We'll see. Your salad is getting cold." Mike sank his spoon into the mashed potatoes, wanting to finish up and get away from her prying questions. Besides, he had to pack for the trip.

She shook her head. "I hope Jason is the cook. My salad is *supposed* to be cold."

Once their plates were clean, Mike stood and shouldered his bag. "Okay, I'm heading out." He checked the time on his phone. "I have about five minutes to get to the bus."

"Have a great weekend with Jason, and I'll look forward to your text." She glanced again in the direction of the kitchen. "I'll let you know if anything happens with cocky Connor."

Grinning, Mike pushed in his chair. "Or with Connor's cock."

STANDING BEFORE ALAN and Craig's front door, nerves shook Jason. He didn't have a Plan B if they said no. Steeling himself, he pressed the button of the doorbell. Footsteps approached, and the door swung open.

Craig grinned. "Hi, Jason. Come on in."

"Hey, how's it going?" He stepped inside and shut the heavy, wooden door behind him. After kicking off his shoes and setting them on the small, red rug by the front window, Jason followed Craig into the living room.

"Have a seat," Craig waved toward the sofa and settled

onto the wooden rocker by the fireplace. Jason lowered himself onto the white couch, stomach tied in knots.

"Thanks." He glanced around. "Is Alan here?"

Alan rounded the corner form the hallway and strode into the room. "Sure am. Hi, Jason." He joined them, taking the overstuffed chair across from Craig. "Mike's at class."

"I know. That's why I came over now." He cleared his throat. "I have something I want to ask you guys."

Rocking backward, Craig cocked his head. "What's on your mind?"

After a deep breath, Jason attempted to calm his nervousness and shifted his gaze between the two men. "I know that Mike's dad is out of the picture, and his mom is…well…not exactly supportive of him."

With a snort, Alan crossed his arms over his chest. "That's putting it mildly."

"You guys are his close family. So, I figure you're the ones I should ask." He fidgeted on the couch, not exactly sure how to phrase his request.

Craig chuckled. "Jason, you look like you might either explode or burst into tears. Whatever it is, just spit it out."

"Okay then. Mike and I have been dating for over a year now, and I love him deeply." He shifted his attention to Alan. "I'd like your blessing to ask him to marry me."

The question hung in the air as Alan and Craig glanced at each other. He looked at each of the two men, gauging their reaction. Alan's face betrayed no clue to his thoughts.

Craig raised an eyebrow, staring at his husband. "Well? He's expecting an answer."

Focusing his attention completely on Alan, Jason

waited for Mike's cousin to respond.

Alan shifted his arms to rest his elbows on the armrests of the chair and leaned forward, settling his chin on his clasped hands. His face broke into a smug smile, still holding Craig's gaze. "I told you so."

"Yes, you did. You're so smart," Craig teased. "Now answer his question, *dear*."

Still betraying no decision one way or the other, Alan's assessing gaze locked on Jason. "I suppose this means you want our darling boy to move in with you."

Carefully considering the phrasing of his response, Jason met Alan's stare. "Yes, I want that very much."

Alan's eyes narrowed. "And what about school?"

"First priority, of course. I don't want him to lose his financial aid, so the timing would depend on his funding."

Lifting his head, Alan unclasped his hands and sat back in the chair. "And if you had to wait until he's twenty-six?"

"He's worth the wait." He shifted on the couch. "I know things didn't go well between us early on, but since our hiccup, our relationship has grown quite strong. I hate seeing him go when he comes back here to spend a night."

Alan's eyebrow cocked, and he frowned.

"No offense."

Clearing his throat, Craig leaned forward in the rocking chair with an equally disapproving frown for his husband. "None taken. Right, Alan?"

Suddenly laughing, Alan softened his gaze and grinned. "Don't worry, Jason. You said all the right things. You had our approval the minute you asked to speak with us."

The tension left Jason's body, and he sank back on the

couch. "Well, thank goodness for that."

Craig shook his head. "Alan likes to play with people, in case you haven't noticed."

Laughing again, Alan leaned forward. "You're a fine one to talk. Watch out for this one," he said, jerking his head toward Craig. "He likes nothing better than to wind people up and watch them spin. Most of the time, the victim has no idea they're being played."

"Now, Alan," Craig snapped. "Don't give away my secrets. I prefer to keep my reputation as the nice guy in our relationship."

Rolling his eyes, Alan stood. "See what you're letting yourself in for?" He stuck out his hand toward Jason. "Welcome to the family."

Jason pushed himself off the couch and clasped the offered hand, shaking it while he grinned. "I really appreciate your approval, and I'll make sure Mike is happy."

Craig joined them, giving Jason a hug. "We expect nothing less."

Just as they broke their embrace, the front door swung open, and Mike stepped over the threshold. "Hey guys, what's up?"

Stepping around Jason, Alan faced his cousin. "A threesome. Wanna join in?"

Mike's face scrunched as if he'd just bit into a lemon. "Um, ew."

With a shrug, Alan stepped to Craig's side. "Your loss."

Chuckling at the playful banter between the cousins, Jason checked his watch. "I wasn't expecting you for another couple hours."

Mike kicked off his shoes and let his backpack drop to the floor with a thud. "My English class got canceled. Something about the instructor had to take an unexpected trip because of her mother. I guess she'll be back on Tuesday. I've got plenty of homework to make up for the missing class time, though." He hurried around the couch and flung his arms around Jason.

Savoring the embrace, Jason gave him a squeeze and a kiss on his neck.

His lover leaned back, cocking his head to the side. "I'm a little surprised to see you here this early. I thought we were heading for the coast at five."

The nerves returned, and he glanced at Alan and Craig. "My shift ended, and I was at loose ends, so I thought I'd come chat with the guys here for a bit while I waited."

Mike's narrowed gaze swung toward Alan. "You were nice to him, weren't you?"

Lifting his hands in front of him, Alan took half a step back. "I was the epitome of kindness and hospitality."

"Oh, brother." Craig rolled his eyes.

With a laugh, Jason drew Mike closer and gave him a peck on the lips. "They were both quite sweet to let me barge in here and interrupt their afternoon."

Alan gave his own chuckle. "Come on, Craig. Let's leave the lovebirds alone." He grasped Craig's hand, and they strode from the room.

Keeping their embrace, Jason planted small kisses on Mike's neck. He nuzzled his nose into his lover's hair, pressing his lips next to his ear. "How about you grab your things, and we'll head out early. I doubt if the owners of the cabin will mind if we get there a couple of hours earlier than I told them." He trailed his hands down Mike's back and cupped his butt. "And I'm sure we'll find something to do once we're there."

As Mike stepped out of the hug, Jason noted the bulge tenting Mike's jeans. "I don't know if I can wait three hours."

Jason shrugged. "There might be opportunities along the way, but I guarantee you it'll be worth the wait."

Stepping around the couch, Mike hurried to the entrance to the hallway, turning to Jason and rubbing the outline of the hardness barely contained in his jeans. "I'll change, and we can go. You're welcome to come to my room and help me get ready."

Though the urge was strong to skip the drive to the coast and just ravage Mike in his own room, Jason controlled his desires and adjusted his own arousal. "If I come into that bedroom, we won't make it to the ocean."

With a laugh, Mike grinned. "Okay. I'll be right back." He moved into the hallway, and Jason heard the bedroom door open.

Resuming his seat, he fidgeted on the cushion, anxious to be on the road and execute the next phase of his plan.

Chapter Eighteen

MIKE MANAGED TO control his urges for the entire three and a half hours out to the coast, though he'd hoped Jason would have stopped off somewhere several times for a bit of relief and play. As the truck pulled into the parking lot of the lodge, he noted several small cabins scattered around the lush green lawns and clusters of ferns. Across the highway, a row of houses stood as the only obstacle between them and the shoreline.

After parking the truck, Jason shut off the engine and turned to him, placing a hand on his thigh. "Here we are. What do you think?"

"It's great. I'm looking forward to walking along the beach." He placed his hand over Jason's and gave it a squeeze. "But first things first. Let's get into our cabin and start the weekend off right."

With a grin, Jason pushed open the door. "I was hoping you'd say that." He climbed out and ran around to open the passenger door.

Mike took Jason's offered hand and stepped onto the asphalt. "Why, thank you, kind sir." He kept his hand in Jason's, using the other to push the door shut. They strolled into the large, wooden lodge.

A tall, slender woman smiled broadly as they entered. "Good evening, gentlemen. I'm guessing you're Jason and

Mike."

Nodding, Mike squeezed Jason's hand. "That's us."

They approached the desk while the woman typed on the computer next to her. As she checked them in, Mike swept his gaze around the high-ceilinged room. Large logs made up the beams supporting the roof. A fire blazed in the stone fireplace taking up one wall of the sitting area, with chaise lounges and plush chairs dotting the room. A painting of a clipper ship sailing a rough ocean dominated another of the walls, and a pair of French doors opened into a dining room.

Mike returned his attention to the desk clerk. She handed Jason two keys. "You gents are in cabin number seven. We have old fashioned keys instead of key-cards, so we ask that you drop them off with us before you leave the property. Sorry if it's a hassle, but it ensures we don't lose as many of them. The desk is manned twenty-four hours, so no worries if you come back late."

Releasing Mike's hand, Jason took the keys, handed one to Mike, and signed the paperwork the woman placed before him.

She pointed to the dining room. "The restaurant is open until ten this evening, and in the morning at eight. The cabins also have stoves and microwaves if you prefer to cook your own meals. If you need anything else, don't hesitate to ask."

"I had called ahead about some…" he glanced briefly at Mike, "preparations."

Smiling, she nodded. "All taken care of."

Mike moved his gaze from his lover to the desk clerk, but neither elaborated on these mysterious *preparations*.

After pocketing his key, Jason took Mike's hand.

"Thanks very much. I think we're going to enjoy our stay here."

"Have a great evening."

They left the warmth of the lodge and stepped outside into the cold sea air. Mike shivered. "I didn't realize how chilly it was out here."

"Let's grab our packs and hurry to the cabin. Hopefully, we'll have a fireplace of our own to snuggle by." Jason raked his gaze over Mike.

After returning to the truck, they retrieved their backpacks and hurried to the log structure with an ornate, cast-iron *seven* on the wooden door. Mike could hardly wait for his lover to get the door open. Jason turned his key in the lock, and they entered the cabin.

Not bothering to look around, Mike tugged Jason into the room and bumped the door shut with his hip. He pressed his lover against the wall and kissed him deeply, tearing at the zipper of his coat and then the buttons of his shirt.

Jason returned the fervor of Mike's passion, shrugging off his coat. Mike finished with the last button of Jason's shirt and parted the fabric, running his chilled hands over Jason's chest.

With a gasp, Jason pulled back from the kiss. "Whoa, your hands are cold."

"Sorry." Mike dropped his hands to his sides and planted his lips around the erect nipple standing on a pec covered in goosebumps. While swirling his tongue around the tight nub, Mike rubbed his hands together.

His lover's body stiffened when Mike nipped and sucked. Hoping his hands had warmed enough, he fumbled with the belt buckle at Jason's waist and yanked it open. The button and zipper yielded next, and he tugged the jeans away from Jason's hips. Mike gave the nipple one last kiss and slipped his hand inside the waistband of the straining briefs to wrap around a pulsing, stiff shaft.

Sinking to his knees, Mike yanked the briefs away and slid his lips over the leaking head of Jason's cock. He swirled his tongue around the slit and lapped at the salty liquid before completely engulfing the rigid shaft.

Jason moaned and leaned back against the wall. "Baby, you're going to make me collapse if you don't get me to the bed."

Releasing the hard dick from his mouth, Mike helped Jason out of his pants and underwear, and led the sock clad cop to the bed, whipping back the covers and pushing him onto the sheet.

Mike quickly stripped off his clothes, anxious to resume the lovemaking with his partner. Jason scooted back, making room for Mike to join him on the bed. Mike crawled on top of the muscled man and kissed him again. Jason's arms wrapped around him, pulling their bodies together in a tight embrace and grinding their cocks together.

A strangled moan from Jason broke the kiss. Mike pushed up onto his hands, and Jason slid his fingers down Mike's ribs to grasp his hips, leaving tingles and radiating warmth in their wake. Mike kissed his way down Jason's chest and abdomen, tracing his tongue along the contours of the defined muscles. He followed the treasure trail to his prize, again sucking down Jason's leaking dick.

After a few moments of pleasuring his lover, Mike jumped off the bed, unzipped his backpack, and retrieved the bottle of lube he'd brought along. He popped open the lid and slid a slick finger along his hole, dipping the lube inside.

He returned to the bed and squirted a small pool into his hand before snapping the lid shut and tossing the bottle onto the bed near Jason's shoulder. Impatient to feel Jason sliding inside him, Mike wrapped his lube-covered hand around the shaft and stroked Jason's cock slowly, paying attention to the head and rubbing his thumb over the slit.

Jason thrust his hips into Mike's hand with a moan. "Fuck that feels amazing. I love how you stroke me."

With a couple more swipes across the tip, Mike straddled Jason's hips and pressed the head against his pucker. "I want you." Staring into his lover's eyes, Mike paused.

Nodding, Jason caressed Mike's thigh, lightly running his hands over the hair on his legs. "I'm yours."

Lining up his ass over the hard shaft, Mike sank onto the pulsing dick, a slight burn accompanying the entry. "Ahh…"

"Go slow, baby," Jason murmured. "I'm not going anywhere."

He paused a moment, letting his ass stretch to accommodate the thickness partially inside him. Pushing out slightly, he resumed his descent, savoring the delicious burn and stretch. He filled himself with all Jason had to give. His lover continued to rub his legs, then moved his hands upward across Mike's abs to cup the pecs in his meaty hands.

Swiping his thumbs across the erect nubs, Jason stiffened and grinned at his lover. "Feels so good, baby."

Mike rose up then dropped back down, establishing a slow rocking motion and riding his lover. Jason's hands clamped onto Mike's legs and the speed increased. Each thrust hit all the pleasure spots inside Mike, and he cried out his passion.

After a few moments, Jason planted his feet on the bed and pushed upward, bringing his hands around Mike's back. Mike held on, keeping Jason firmly planted inside him, and rolled with Jason. The cool sheets pressed against Mike's back, and he let go of Jason and pulled his knees onto his chest. Jason pressed forward, the weight of his body holding Mike's legs in place. Circling his arms around Jason's shoulders, Mike brought them together for another kiss while his lover drove into him.

Thrusting harder and faster, Jason took Mike deep and strong, continually kissing him and holding him. The tingle started in his balls, amplified each time Jason pounded against his prostate. The muscles of his lover's stomach slid along Mike's shaft, and Mike struggled to hold back his impending release.

"You're getting me so close," Mike whispered between kisses.

Jason rose up, adjusting his rhythm by sliding in and out much slower but not stopping. "Don't come yet. I want you in me."

Wrapping his legs around Jason's waist, Mike reached up and pulled his lover into yet another kiss. Their tongues probed and dueled. Jason slowly eased out, and Mike whimpered against Jason's lips at the emptiness.

After a quick peck to Mike's nose, Jason lifted off Mike and rolled onto his back. "Lube me up good and take me."

Taking a moment to catch his breath, Mike rose shakily and snagged the bottle. His cock throbbed, and he ached to be inside his man. "I won't last very long," he warned.

"That's fine." Jason pulled his knees back, exposing his hole.

Mike stroked a dollop of lube along the head and shaft of his dick, snapped the lid back onto the bottle, and tossed it aside. He crawled to his lover and pressed his cock against the pucker. Leaning forward, he pressed his lips against Jason's.

Still holding the lip-lock, Mike pressed inside, the pucker giving way and warmth enveloping his shaft. Jason let out a whimper as Mike established a fast pounding rhythm.

Breaking the kiss and shifting back, he thrust against the hard nub of Jason's prostate. "Oh, Mike," Jason wailed, clutching the back of his knees.

Mike's own moans increased, and the tingles of his imminent release intensified. "I'm close."

"Keep going," Jason urged. "I want it inside me." A squeeze of Jason's ass gripped Mike's cock in an exquisite pressure.

His volume increased as the rush of orgasm barreled through his cock.

"That's it, baby," Jason cried out. "Fill me up."

Mike thrust deep and shot his load, his body stiffening as he held Jason's gaze.

"Oh, God, Mike, I'm there." Jason reared back his head, and several spurts of come shot across his chest and stomach, a couple hitting his chin.

Panting, Mike eased back, his softening cock slipping from a gasping Jason. He hung his head and closed his eyes, letting the afterglow wash over him. "That was amazing."

Jason's hand caressed his thigh. "For sure."

Mike opened his eyes, surveying his lover. "You've got something on your chin." Mike leaned forward and licked the salty sweet remnants of Jason's load from his lover's face. He planted his lips against Jason's and shared his prize, gently biting against Jason's lower lip.

Sliding alongside his partner, Mike rested his head on Jason's sweaty pec. A wave of drowsy contentment washed over him. "I could easily fall asleep right now."

"Maybe not quite yet."

SMALL TREMORS INTERMITTENTLY shook Jason's body while he lay on his back staring at the ceiling and mustering his courage. Mike's head rested on his chest, his soft hair caressing Jason's skin like silk. Jason ran his fingers though the dark locks and bent forward to kiss the top of his lover's head.

With a contented sigh, he wrapped his arm around Mike's back. "I love you."

Mike kissed his chest. "I love you, too."

"We had an amazing time in San Diego, didn't we?" Jason's voice trembled slightly, and he gave Mike a gentle squeeze, needing the reassurance of his warm body and affection.

"I loved it." Mike pushed himself up, resting on one arm while meeting Jason's gaze with his emerald eyes. "Is something wrong?"

Jason's shook his head. "I just have something I need to ask you."

Visibly relaxing, Mike nodded. "Should I be scared?"

With a chuckle, Jason shook his head again. "I don't think so. I'm the frightened one." The butterflies in his stomach shifted into overdrive.

Mike brought his hand to Jason's cheek, the warmth of his fingers making Jason close his eyes for a moment to savor the tenderness of the touch and to calm his nerves. He returned his gaze to Mike.

A smile played across his boyfriend's face. "I'm sure you have nothing to worry about. What's your question?" His eyes and grin widened with excitement. "Or is it a confession?"

"Well, I did the confession part already," Jason chuckled nervously. "I told you I love you."

Mike leaned forward and pressed a quick peck on the lips. "I hope my response was okay."

Now, it was Jason's turn to smile. "Definitely. I spoke to Alan and Craig, and they gave me permission to ask."

Furrowing his brow, Mike cocked his head to one side. "What would you need their permission for?"

"I didn't *need* it, but I wanted it. Kind of old-fashioned of me, I guess." Jason shifted on the bed. "It was more preferable to ask them than your mother."

"Ask her what?"

The moment of truth. "Hold on a second." Jason snapped on the bedside lamp and rolled off the bed. The cold of the room made him wish he'd lit a fire. He hurried to their luggage and unzipped the top compartment of his backpack. Reaching inside, his fingers closed around the small box the jeweler had wrapped in gold foil for him.

Bringing the box back to the bed, he handed it to Mike with trembling fingers. "Open it."

With one last unsure glance at Jason, Mike concentrated on carefully separating the tape from the wrapping. He extracted a white cardboard box.

Lifting the lid, his gaze snapped up. "Jason, what did you get me?" He turned the box upside down and a smaller blue, velvet box dropped into his hand.

"Open it and see." Jason held his breath.

Mike's fingers fumbled with the box. He snapped the lid open and gasped. "Oh my god. It's beautiful." He lifted the white gold ring from the box, and the inset gems sparkled in the lamplight.

With a puff of breath, Jason steeled his courage. "Which leads me to my question."

Mike's eyes shifted from the band to Jason.

Plucking the ring from Mike's grasp, he held it in front of the man he loved. "Will you marry me?"

MIKE'S MOUTH DROPPED open as he stared wide-eyed at the two emeralds and the diamond woven into a Celtic knot of white gold. His initial shock gave way to a welling of emotion. The final and definitive confirmation of Jason's love hovered in front of him. Joy surged through him, and he choked back a sob.

With a sniffle, Mike wiped away a tear rolling down his cheek. "Yes," he choked out.

Jason grasped Mike's hand and slipped the ring on his finger. He exhaled heavily, rolling Mike on top of him. "I am so happy right now."

Flinging his arms around Jason, Mike kissed him deeply and held on tight, a sob shaking him. He'd never let this man go again. Jason returned the fervor of his kiss and hugged him back.

The question Jason had asked the desk clerk when they checked in returned to Mike's mind. With a deep sniff, he broke the lip-lock and pushed himself up to stare into his lover's eyes. "Preparations?"

Jason grinned and nodded to the small refrigerator across the room. "Take a look inside."

Arching his eyebrow, Mike climbed off and padded across the cold floor. He spied two glasses and a small, black box with a white ribbon on the counter next to the microwave. He pulled open the refrigerator door and found a bottle of champagne with a white bow. A card dangled from a ribbon around the neck of the bottle reading *Congratulations to the Happy Couple* in block letters.

Mike lifted the bottle from the shelf as Jason trotted over to him. "This place is awesome." He nudged the door closed with his foot and moved to the counter. "I think you should open this." His hands trembled slightly, and he set the bottle next to the glasses.

After ripping away the foil, Jason unwound the metal holder and popped the cork. Vapor rose from the mouth of the bottle, but it didn't overflow. He poured two glasses and set the bottle on the counter.

"Hold on." Jason scurried to his discarded jeans and retrieved his phone. "We need a picture."

"But we're naked," Mike cautioned. "You aren't going to send this to anyone, are you?" Mike imagined Craig and Alan receiving a nude selfie from Jason.

Chuckling, Jason propped the cell against the bottle. "Don't worry, it'll just be our faces and the glasses." He adjusted the angle and picked up his glass. "Ready?"

"Yup." He plucked his own glass from the countertop

and stood next to Jason. "What do you want to do?"

"Let's touch the glasses together and smile. Make sure the ring is in the shot." Jason set the phone's camera timer and stepped back, holding out his arm.

Still reeling from the proposal, Mike took a breath and stepped into Jason's embrace. He lifted the glass, clinked with the other, and grinned at the camera.

"Baby," Jason said after the checking the picture. "I can hardly wait for you to move in. I miss you so much when you're not with me." He gave Mike a squeeze and sipped his bubbly.

Mike couldn't remember a time when he was happier than in this moment. With everything he'd endured through his childhood, his first true happiness occurred when he escaped Wisconsin to live with Alan and Craig. The elation of Jason's proposal dwarfed even that memory.

A chill washed over him, and his mood faded. "Oh, God."

Jason's brow furrowed as he set his drink down. "What's wrong?"

"We're going to have to invite my mother."

CHUCKLING AT MIKE'S apprehension, Jason embraced his fiancé. "Let's worry about that when we send out the invitations. We've got a lot to consider before that."

"Like what?" Mike sipped his champagne.

"How this impacts your financial aid for one. I don't want to screw that up for you." Jason grabbed his glass from the counter and led Mike to the bed, glad to see the smile return. "Besides, I think you moving out of Craig and Alan's might be a bit more traumatic than dealing with your mother."

"Did Alan take it well that you wanted me to leave their place?" Mike's warm hand rested on Jason's thigh once they'd settled onto the side of the bed, and Mike took another sip of champagne.

"Well, it certainly was one of his questions when I asked for your hand." The caress of Mike's fingers sent tingles of pleasure through his body. "And you're going to make me ravage you if you keep teasing my leg."

"Would that be such a terrible thing?" Mike leaned in and kissed his neck.

"Definitely not." He drank the last of the bubbly in his glass and took Mike's from him. "Hold that thought." Hurrying across the room, he deposited the glasses next to the half-empty bottle and returned to the bed, pushing Mike backward onto the comforter.

"Once I move in, we'll get to do this every day," Mike cooed.

Jason's dick hardened, pressing against the soft skin of his lover's legs. "I'm definitely looking forward to that." He kissed the center of Mike's chest. "So, the question is, should we go have dinner, or should I make slow, passionate love to you right now?"

Mike's stomach rumbled at the same moment he pushed his erection against Jason's abdomen. With a chuckle, he caressed Jason's back with the light touch of his fingertips. "I don't think my body can decide."

With another series of kisses along the ridge of Mike's pecs, Jason savored the tingles rippling up his back from his lover's caresses. "I think we should feed your hunger before we go for round two. We have all night—hell, all weekend—to be together."

Jason rose from the bed and pulled Mike to his feet. They moved across the cold floor to the bathroom, and Jason turned the knob on the shower. Waiting for the water to heat, he surveyed the spacious room. A tub, big enough for the two of them to fit comfortably, sat in the corner. A glance over the edge revealed jets and two built-in seats.

Once the water ran warm, Mike stepped into the stream. "So, what would you have done if I'd said no?"

Jason joined him under the spray, stepping close to Mike and nuzzling against his neck. "Begged," Jason murmured, placing kisses along the sensitive skin. "And it wouldn't have been pretty. I'm glad you spared me that messy scene."

Laughing, Mike reached for the soap. "We've got to send that picture to Craig and Alan."

"And Emily. Careful with that bar. You might delay dinner." Jason reached around his fiancé and hugged him close, his cock reacting to the contact with Mike's body.

With a grin, Mike held the soap in front of him and let go. The bar hit the floor with a thud and a splash. "Oops."

Jason arched an eyebrow and gave Mike's ass a wet slap. "Naughty boy."

MIKE'S EYES POPPED open at the steak and mashed potatoes the waiter placed in front of him. "Whoa." The grilled meat covered over half the plate, and the potatoes shared the remainder of the space with a mound of carrots covered in butter.

The server set another plate before Jason with a bed of

green beans covered with a halibut steak. "Anything else I can get you guys?"

"Don't think so. This looks amazing." Mike placed the napkin in his lap.

"Enjoy." The waiter moved to another table.

Jason surveyed his plate. "Want to try a bite of the halibut?"

"Sure," Mike said, eyeing the fish. "I'll see if it is a good as Craig's."

Cutting off a piece, Jason shook his head. "I doubt if it's *that* good, but I bet it's close."

Mike cut a piece of steak and stabbed it with his fork, handing the morsel across the table. "Try mine." They traded forks, and each took their bite. The buttery fish melted in his mouth. "You're going to love this."

After Jason swallowed, he nodded toward Mike's plate. "The steak is perfect."

"Did you send the picture to our family?" *Our family.* He loved the sound of those words.

Jason reached into his pocket for his cell. "Not yet. Do you think Emily will mix well with Craig and Alan?"

"I'm sure she will." Mike scooped up a spoonful of mashed potatoes. "Will she be your maid of honor?"

"Definitely. She's the person I'm closest to after you." Jason tapped on the screen of his cell. "I'll text this to you. Do you want to send it to your cousins, or should I?"

Retrieving his cell, he received the text and brought up the picture of their smiling faces and the champagne. "Go ahead. How about I send to Emily?"

"Great idea," Jason said, tapping at his screen. "She's waiting to hear your answer."

Mike grinned, typing out a message. "She'll love this. I

also have to send it to Kelly."

Jason stopped to stare at him. "Kelly?"

"A gal in one of my classes. We're study-buddies." He smirked, thinking about her comments at lunch, and her interest in Connor. "I think I got her interested in one of the guys in the culinary classes." He finished his message and tapped the SEND button. "There. It's away." He quickly repeated the message and sent the picture to Kelly.

Jason's phone buzzed. "That was quick." He glanced at his screen. "Two messages. Craig's consists of five exclamation points, and Alan says *Congratulations* with a smiley face."

A text flashed on the screen of Mike's cell. A meme of a cheering champagne bottle popping its cork filled the screen. Mike showed Jason his cell. "From Emily."

He turned the phone toward Mike, displaying the same meme. "She sent me one, too."

Mike read the message from Jason's best friend. *OMG!!! Yes, yes, YES!* Sitting back, Mike slipped his phone into his pocket. "I can't tell you how happy I am right now."

Jason also put away his phone and lifted his wine glass. "Here's to us. May we have many years together."

Raising his own and clinking it against Jason's, Mike gazed into his fiancé's eyes. "We definitely will. I love you."

"I love you, too." Once they drank, Jason summoned the waiter. "What would you recommend for a celebratory dessert?"

The waiter glanced at the table. "I'd say either chocolate hazelnut cake, or the lavender and strawberry cheesecake."

Mike salivated at the choices. "I'd take either."

With a nod, Jason turned to the waiter. "The chocolate hazelnut."

"It's pretty rich," the waiter cautioned. "Do you want one or two?"

Glancing at his empty plate, Mike contemplated his full stomach and the workout he hoped to have later that evening. "I'd be okay with one to share."

"Well, that's what the celebration is for," Jason said. "Sharing our lives."

The waiter's looked between the two men. "Are you guys getting married?"

Jason's face lit up with a huge smile. "We sure are."

"That's awesome. I'll get it for you right away." He picked up their plates and hurried toward the kitchen.

"So," Jason said, leaning forward. "Where would you like to go for our honeymoon?"

"Hmm." Thoughts of Europe filled his mind. Germany was high on his list as was England. "What's our budget?"

With a smile, Jason took a sip of his wine. "I think we could splurge. You want to travel abroad, right?"

"Definitely. I'm thinking London or Berlin." He surveyed Jason's expression, hoping he'd agree to one of the options.

Jason nodded. "How about both with a stop in Paris?"

"That sounds amazing." Mike paused. "But won't that be expensive?"

Reaching his hand across the table, Jason laced his fingers with Mike's. "Baby, don't worry about it. We'll manage. I've been saving up for an overseas excursion, and there are so many places I want us to explore together."

Mike fought his flaring pride. "I want to help pay for

the trip."

Jason shook his head. "I know, baby. Let's get through the wedding before we worry about the honeymoon costs."

The waiter returned with the large slice of cake. "Anything else I can get you guys? Coffee?"

He let go of Jason's hand as the waiter set the plate between them and placed two spoons on the table. "Not for me."

Jason nodded to his half-full glass of wine. "I'm good, thanks."

Reaching into his apron pocket, the waiter retrieved the bill and placed it on the table. "Take your time on this. The dessert's on me. Congratulations."

"Wow, thanks." Jason reached into his pocket and pulled out his wallet. "That's really kind of you." He handed his credit card to the waiter.

"My pleasure. I'll be right back with this. Enjoy."

As the server moved away, Mike plucked a spoon from the table and ignored that Jason paid the bill. He had to remind himself that this weekend was Jason's gift to him. "Let's finish up here and go for a stroll on the beach."

Jason grinned. "And then we can try out that whirlpool tub."

"Sounds perfect." As Mike scooped a piece from their slice of cake, his mind returned to his family. The only person he'd consider inviting was his first cousin Monique. He dreaded the call to his mom, but at least he wouldn't have to contact her until they actually set a date and started planning the wedding.

CHAPTER NINETEEN

WITH HIS NERVES frayed, Mike stood next to Alan staring at the black telephone mounted on the wall. "Should I really do this?" He'd put off the phone call to his mother for three and a half years. Now that he'd graduated with his bachelor's, he was financially free to follow through on his engagement to Jason.

Alan patted his shoulder. "You should at least give her the option to come. She's been pretty quiet since she signed the financial aid paperwork. And she did send you that present for your birthday."

The small box waiting on Alan and Craig's table had been a shock as they celebrated his twenty-seventh birthday a month ago. She'd sent him a mug from the coffee shop he'd been a regular at during his high school years and a bag of hot chocolate mix from the local creamery.

"Yeah, I'm not sure what that was about. The card was an even bigger shock." She'd obviously made the card and wrote the three words he'd never expected from her. *I love you.* He hadn't known what to make of it and couldn't bring himself to call for fear that it was some sort of attack.

With a squeeze of his hand, Alan shrugged. "Time and no contact may have given her space to reflect on what you said to her about never loving you. I think, in her own warped way, she does care."

He fought the anger rising in him. "But all those horrible things she let happen."

"You know, Mike, at some point you need to release yourself from the burden of those memories. I'm not telling you to forget or even to forgive. Just come to terms that it happened and you escaped." He smiled. "I was in brief contact with her after your birthday, and she knows you're happy."

Mike narrowed his gaze. "You called her?"

Alan didn't flinch or turn away. "Actually, she called and apologized for how she screamed at me."

With a shake of his head, he stared at his cousin. "Why didn't you tell me?"

"I don't like to upset you with family news. Since your grandmother died, I don't hear anything from over there." Alan gave him a quick hug. "Go on. I have a feeling this might go better than you think."

Taking a breath, Mike reached for the receiver. "Let's get it over with." The rotary mechanism sawed through the numbers as he dialed. He could have called her on his cell, but there was a comfort about the old phone that he needed to bolster his courage.

The line rang four times before she answered. "Hello?" The person on the other end was definitely his mother, but her voice sounded tired and sadder than he'd ever heard before.

"Hi, mom, uh, it's Mike."

She paused and then burst into tears. "Oh, Mike."

With a frown, he tilted the handset toward Alan, her sobs loud through the receiver.

Alan's shocked expression likely mirrored his own.

"Holy shit," his cousin mouthed.

Returning the speaker to his ear, he pressed forward. "Are you okay? What's wrong?"

"I never thought I'd hear from you again," she sobbed. "After the last time we talked, I thought you hated me."

"I don't hate you, and I really appreciated the gift you sent me for my birthday." How could this be the same woman who'd made his childhood such hell? Never had she shown the slightest remorse for her actions or really any affection toward him.

Her voice calmed somewhat, though he could tell she could resume crying at any moment. "How are you? Have you graduated from college yet?"

Another shock. "Yes. I finished in June and have a degree in communications."

"Good. I'm glad you saw it through. Your grandma would have been so proud of you." Another pause. "I have something to tell you." She choked back another sob.

Mike bit his bottom lip. "Yes?"

"Your brother was stabbed to death last week." Her tears resumed, long, choking sobs drumming into his ear.

The warmth drained from his face, and numbness settled over his body. Her words took a moment to sink in while her crying rang through the receiver. His tormentor was gone, a victim of the life he'd chosen. Though he'd lost his brother, a weight lifted from his shoulders.

"Mike?" Alan nudged him, his brow furrowed in concern. "What's wrong?"

Regaining his composure, he covered the receiver. "Tony was murdered."

"Oh my god." His cousin's eyes closed, pain etched on his face.

Returning to his mother, Mike lifted his hand. "I'm sorry, Mom. Can I do anything?"

"The funeral is on Friday. Can you come?" Through her crying he could hear hope in her voice.

"I think I should tell you something before you decide you want me there." He took a breath, steeling himself for her rejection. "I'm getting married."

Her sobs faded away, and the pause on the other end of the phone lingered.

"Are you still there, mom?" Mike glanced to Alan who shrugged.

"I'm here," she replied, her voice still shaky. "You're marrying a man, right?"

"Yes, mom. His name is Jason…and he's a cop." His stomach tightened, waiting for the onslaught. Being gay was bad enough. And with a college degree. But to marry a cop was considered a cardinal sin in his family.

"Does Alan like him?"

Swinging his gaze to his cousin, Mike's mouth dropped open. "Uh, I think so. They had a rocky start, but I think he likes Jason now." He chewed on his lower lip.

Alan's eyes widened.

"That's good enough for me. I know a funeral's not a good place to meet my new son-in-law, but if you both come, it would mean a lot." She paused again. "Am I invited to the wedding?"

He could hardly believe he was speaking to the same woman who'd tossed him to the wolves when he came out to her. Even in her grief at losing her favorite son, she made a huge effort to be a part of his life.

"I wasn't sure you'd *want* to come."

"Look, Mike, I can't undo what's been done. I've had

a lot of time to think about what happened between us, and I know most of it is my fault." She sniffled again. "But you're my child, and no matter what you think about me, I do care."

Stunned into silence, Mike stared at Alan, hardly believing what he was hearing. "Um…" he spluttered. "Of course, you're invited. That's mainly what I called to ask you about."

"I'll be there." Her voice cracked. "Can you come Friday?"

"Let me check with Jason, and I'll text you." A lightness settled over him, and he knew his lover would never believe what had happened. He really couldn't either.

"Okay. Your aunt's here, so I gotta go." She paused again. "Love you, Mikey."

"I love you, too." After she hung up, Mike slowly replaced the receiver into its metal cradle and turned to his cousin. "What the hell just happened?"

THE WEEK HAD rolled by quickly since Mike called about his brother. After the flight from Seattle and the drive from Minneapolis, Jason brought their rental car to a halt in front of a small white hovel of a house in Mike's hometown in rural Wisconsin. Mike, clad in black slacks and one of Alan's black dinner jackets, stepped out of the car and stood at the chain-link fence of his mother's yard. A beat-up orange truck sat parked in the small driveway next to a battered gray sedan. A blue mini-van and a nicer SUV were parked across the street.

Locking the car, Jason joined Mike at the small gate and rubbed his back hoping to give him some courage.

"Are you ready for this?"

With a deep breath, Mike nodded. "I doubt it, but let's see what happens. That rust-bucket truck is my Uncle Jim's. Don't take any of his crap. He's a narcissist with an ego a mile high."

Jason chuckled. "Don't worry about me. I'll be fine. If you want to leave, just come get me and we'll go. No reason to stay if things get nasty."

Mike checked his watch. "About an hour and a half before we have to leave for the funeral home." He glanced at the house. "Maybe we should have met everyone there."

"Better any fireworks happen here. If we'd gone to the services first, you'd be stuck making a scene at your brother's memorial." After patting his shoulder, Jason lifted the metal latch on the gate. "After you."

His fiancé shook, but stepped onto the small, wooden stoop and knocked on the front door. A man with a graying handlebar moustache, a balding head, and a large gut answered the door.

The man's eyes narrowed, and he made no move to let them into the house. "You actually showed up," he sneered.

"Where's my mom, Jim?" Mike spat, his face dropping into a frown. Jason watched the man, ready to intervene if Mike was insulted or threatened.

"Inside with the rest of the family." He crossed his arms.

A large woman with curly, black hair charged to the door and shoved Jim out of the way. This, Jason mused, could only be Mike's mother. She got right up into her brother's face, poking a long-nailed finger at his nose. "You fucker," she spat. "I warned you. Shut your fat mouth or get out of my house and don't come back."

"Jeez, Bridgette," Jim said with his hands up. "I was gonna let him in."

Fury burned in her eyes, and Jason edged closer to Mike, ready to protect his fiancé if things got out of hand. She grabbed a handful of Jim's plaid shirt. "I'm only gonna say this one more time. Mike is here because I asked him. He's giving me a second chance. You blow this for me, and I'll make your life a living hell." She brought her face inches from his, hissing the next words. "You know *exactly* what I mean."

The bluster from her brother quickly dwindled, and he shrank back, fear reflected behind his bushy eyebrows. Turning to Mike, his uncle stared at his shoes. "Sorry, Mike."

"Now get your sorry ass back on the couch, and don't you move it until we're ready to go." She released his shirt, and he slunk away like a beaten dog.

Bridgette gave her brother one more lingering glare and turned back to face them. "Mikey."

"Um, hi, Mom," Mike said, staying close to Jason.

She stepped across the stoop and enveloped him with her arms. "Thank you for coming. It means everything to me." She shuddered, and a sob overtook her.

Jason took a step back, allowing Mike and his mother to have their moment of reconciliation. Mike hesitated a moment, but then returned the hug. As they pulled apart, her attention turned to Jason.

"Are you Jason?"

"Yes, ma'am," Jason replied. "It's nice to meet you, though I wish the circumstances were better." He extended his hand.

With a shake of her head, she wrapped him in a hug. "I'm glad you came."

Jason returned the hug, shooting Mike a quick glance. He shrugged. "Thanks."

Stepping back, she waved them into the house. Jason followed his fiancé and his soon to be mother-in-law into the living room. Jim sat sulking on the couch, unwilling to make eye contact with any of them. A stylishly dressed woman in her mid-fifties stood next to a slightly older man with gray hair and a neatly trimmed moustache. Another woman close to Mike's age leaned against the doorway to the kitchen holding a baby boy wrapped in a blue blanket.

A girl in her late teens stepped around the corner of the hallway and hurried into the room. "Mike!" She flung her arms around him and hugged him tight.

Mike seemed as startled as Jason was. "Monique, what are you doing here?"

With a final squeeze, she released him. "Just helping your mom out." She turned to face Jason, her eyes raking over and assessing him. "And who's this?"

"My fiancé." Mike stated, pride in his response. Jason couldn't help the smile tugging at his lips.

Her eyes flew open wide, and she grinned from ear to ear. "You're getting married? I hope I'm invited." She rushed forward to Jason and grabbed his hand. "I'm Mike's cousin, Monique Fischer. We're actually second cousins. My grandpa and his grandma were brother and sister."

Jason chuckled at her rapid-fire introduction. "Nice to meet you."

Bridgette stepped between Jason and Mike, wrapping an arm around each of their waists. She swung her attention to Jason. "Let me introduce you to the rest of the family." She turned them toward the nicely dressed couple. "That's my sister, Jessica and her husband, Kevin." With a jerk of her head, she glared at the couch. "You already met my jackass brother, Jim."

Standing, Jim made for the door.

Jessica shook her head. "Always the definition of class, aren't you, Jim."

Without a word, he hurried through the door and slammed it shut behind him.

Frowning, Monique spared a quick glare at the door. "Asshole."

A loud rumble of an unmuffled engine filled the room, and a moment later, tires squealed as the rumbling moved away.

Jason stifled a chuckle. Bridgette turned them to face the woman with the child.

"This is my niece Renee and her new baby Russell." She gave Jason and Mike a squeeze. "This is Jason. He's gonna be my new son-in-law."

Assessing the room during the awkward pause, Jason felt the shift in attitude from Mike's aunt and uncle, and Renee. Frosty detachment gave way to curiosity.

Kevin stepped forward first, sticking out his hand to Jason. "Well, a pleasure to meet you, Jason. Could be better circumstances, but welcome." He leaned in, lowering his voice. "It's a wild ride in this family."

Bridgette let go of the two men, raising an eyebrow at her brother-in-law. "Now don't you go scaring him off, Kevin. You had a rocky start, too."

With a snort, Kevin nodded. "That's putting it mild-ly."

Curiosity piqued, Jason cocked his head. "Oh, yeah?"

"I decked Jim about a minute after I met him. He insulted Jessica, and I wasn't going to stand for it." He glanced at his wife who smiled as she approached. "It was embarrassing because their mother was standing right there when I did it."

Jason's eyes widened. "Whoa."

The disdain in Kevin's tone left no doubt in Jason's mind to his feelings for his brother-in-law. "We tolerate each other when we have to be in the same room."

Slipping her fingers into her husband's hand, Jessica smiled freely. "It's good he took my sister's hint and kept his mouth shut. You could probably do some serious damage."

With a glance at his fiancé, Jason frowned. "Not intentionally." Though Mike's uncle certainly pushed a few buttons, and Jason could easily see needing to defend Mike.

Eyebrow cocked, Jessica turned to her nephew. "You'll have to tell him some of the shit your uncle has done to you over the years. I'll bet that's why he bugged out so fast."

"One of the reasons," Bridgette muttered, exchanging a smug grin and a nod with her sister.

Mike stared at his aunt and mother. "What's going on?"

Lifting both eyebrows, Bridgette stared intently at her son. "I've got a few things over Jim that he doesn't want anyone to know about. Keeps him in line." She frowned slightly. "I'm sure you understand."

Lowering his head, Mike sighed. "Yeah, sorry."

Jason stared curiously at Mike, but he didn't raise his

gaze. He knew Mike had something over his mother but had declined to say the one and only time the subject had come up. Alan had also kept quiet at Mike's insistent stare. Jason had let the question drop, though he had no doubt that Alan would tell him if pressed.

She patted his shoulder. "Don't be."

Renee stepped forward. "Do you want to hold your new cousin, Mike?"

Turning away from his mom, Mike nodded and held out his hands. "Please."

Gently taking the baby into his arms, Jason felt as much as saw the glow emanating from Mike as he held the small bundle. The baby cooed and gave a little sneeze, and Mike laughed. "I think he likes me."

The baby giggled and reached a tiny hand to grip the end of Mike's nose.

Bridgette checked her watch and sighed. "It's time to go. I need to talk to the pastor about a couple of things."

Jason laid a hand on her shoulder. "Would you like to ride with us?"

"That's sweet of you, Jason." She nodded. "I'd like that."

After handing back the baby to Renee, Mike stood next to Jason. "Ready?"

AS THEY WOUND through the streets of the small town, Mike sighed at the flood of bad memories surging to the forefront of his thoughts. The corner where he'd run into the convenience store to escape his brother's gang. The park where he'd been forced to hide in the undergrowth while his brother hunted for him with a gun in his hand.

They passed the sprawling high school he'd attended. Paint peeled off the side of the main building, and weeds covered the front lawn. Bullet holes pock-marked the front façade of the gym. His brother's doing. Thankfully no one had been hurt, but shooting a gun on school property had sent Tony away for seven years, giving Mike a respite from the fear of constant attacks.

Jason patted his knee. "Doing okay?"

"Yeah." He turned to the back seat where his mother sat staring out the window, the occasional sob shaking her. "We're going to Schlessinger's, right?"

She nodded and dabbed away another tear streaking down her face. "Mike, I'm selling the house and going to live with Jessica and Kevin. If there's anything you want, you should take it now."

"It's probably a good idea for you to sell up," Mike agreed. Their neighborhood had degraded even more since he'd left, and without his brother to protect her, his mother would be a prime target of the gangs. Especially those with a beef against Tony Bryant. "What are you going to do in Menominee?" Though picturesque, the small town didn't offer much in the way of opportunity.

"I'm broke and can't pay the mortgage anymore. With mom and dad gone, and now Tony, there's nothing for me here." With a heavy sigh, she leaned back in the seat. "After the funeral, figure out what you want at the house and we can get it shipped to Seattle." She dug in her purse and handed him a small box tied with twine. "Give this to Alan when you get home."

Mike turned the box over. "What is it?"

"You'll see when he opens it. I'm sure he'll know what to do with it." She turned to the window, staring out.

Pocketing the box, he settled back in his seat and got his bearings. Not much farther. "Turn left at the next light," he directed Jason. "The funeral home will be two blocks down on the right."

AFTER THE SERVICE concluded, everyone stood, and Jason surveyed the room of mourners. Jim hurried out the door before anyone could interact with him. Jessica and Kevin, followed by the other members of Mike's family he'd met, approached the casket and stood, holding onto each other. Mike helped his mother to view the body of his brother. She nearly collapsed and burst into tears. Mike and Kevin helped her move away and sit in the first pew.

Several of the other attendees were obviously gang members. They held back, showing a surprising amount of respect for the family. Though he didn't have his body armor on, Jason had taken the precaution of carrying his service revolver in his jacket holster just in case.

The line of thugs and their girlfriends sauntered past the casket and out the door to the back, each mumbling some remorseful sentiment to Bridgette as she tried to pull herself together.

Though he wanted to comfort Mike, he thought it best to let his partner have his time with his family. The line to view the body dwindled, and once the last gang banger shuffled away, Jason stepped forward and looked into the coffin. Although the undertakers had done a good job of disguising some of the worst of the wounds, the disfigured face and pocked skin of Mike's brother told a tale of drug abuse and a rough life.

With a glance toward Mike, Jason marveled at the

difference between the brothers. Mike could easily have fallen into Tony's life. Instead, he defied his upbringing and the environment he'd been born into, escaping to the relative safety of Alan and Craig's home. Alan's protective stance made a lot more sense to him now that he'd met Mike's immediate family.

Joining him at the casket, Mike stared at his brother. "I'm really grateful you came with me. This would have been impossible to handle on my own."

"Things seem to be going pretty well," Jason commented. He resisted the urge to slip his arm around Mike's back. While the gathering at the house had gone well, he could easily see a gesture of gay affection in front of the casket not going over well.

Mike glanced back at his family. "They're on their best behavior, probably more for Mom than for me."

Giving in to his curiosity, Jason leaned in. "What do you think they have on your uncle?"

With a shrug, Mike stepped back from the casket. "Not a clue, but I've never seen him so scared shitless." They turned toward his mother. The pastor greeted her and, sitting next to her, held her hand.

Jason noticed Mike's body tense. "Do you get along with the pastor?"

Mike's brow furrowed, a flash of anger burning across his face. "Not in the slightest. Let's go outside."

"Mike," his mother beckoned. "Reverend McCauley wants to speak with you."

Continuing passed Bridgette, Mike spared the clergyman a hard stare. "He said all he needed to say to me eight years ago." His eyes narrowed. "In his private offices."

Jason stared between Mike's long strides toward the

back of the hall and the pastor. The preacher's face shifted from pasty white to bright red, and he turned away from the family. "I'll prepare for the graveside service," he said in his whiny voice. Standing, he motioned to the pallbearers waiting patiently at the back of the room.

The five men stepped forward, and Kevin joined them. The preacher lowered the lid of the casket while the men gathered around.

Hurrying to catch Mike, Jason quickly strode to the back of the room and out the door. He found Mike standing at the curb. "Baby, what was that about?"

"McCauley and I have some history," Mike murmured.

Crossing his arms, Jason stared hard at his partner. "What kind of history? From your reaction to him, I'm guessing something abusive."

Mike held his gaze. "He's one of those preaches-against-the-evils-of-gays-from-the-pulpit-but-gets-sucked-off-in-his-office kind of pastors."

Struggling to keep from shouting, Jason's words hissed through his teeth. "He made you suck him off?"

"He didn't make me. I was more than willing," Mike replied with a glance back inside. "He was definitely better looking ten years ago."

"Mike, that's statutory rape. What were you? Sixteen? Seventeen?" Jason's anger burned as he glared into the funeral home. The preacher caught Jason's eye and gawked, turning white. He paused in his instructions to the pallbearers but quickly recovered.

A hand on his arm brought Jason's gaze back to Mike.

"It was a decade ago, and like I said, I was willing." Mike stared hard at him. "It's not worth bringing up, especially today."

The pallbearers wheeled the casket out the door, passing them and heading to the hearse parked a few feet away. As the Reverend attempted to scoot by, Jason caught his arm and leaned in, whispering into his ear.

"I'm a police officer." He squeezed the man's arm tighter in his grip, making McCauley wince. "If I find out you've done to Mike what I *think* you've done, I'll take you down."

The preacher gasped, staring at Jason. After releasing the preacher's arm, Jason stood next to Mike and wrapped a protective arm around his fiancé while glaring at the Reverend. Practically running, the frightened man scurried around the hearse and joined the pallbearers at the back.

Jason steered Mike toward their rental car, struggling to control his fury. "I won't go after him right now, but I'll strike the fear of God in the bastard."

With a frown, Mike placed his hand on Jason's chest. "Just don't really strike him."

Glancing back at the hearse, Jason sized up the older man. "I'll promise you a lot of things, but not that one."

THE GRAVESIDE SERVICE was mercifully short. None of the gang members showed up, much to Mike's relief. The last thing he wanted to deal with were Tony's scummy associates. His mother insisted Jason sit with the family up at the front, but Jason compromised with her, standing behind Mike and resting a reassuring hand on his shoulder.

During the middle of the ceremony, Mike glanced at his fiancé. After a quick wink, Jason hardened his gaze at the preacher, causing the man to fumble over his words. Mike bit his lip and bowed his head to keep from laughing. His mother, misunderstanding his movements, patted his knee, making his urge to laugh even more difficult to quell.

At the conclusion of the service, McCauley moved to his mother and took her hand. "He's in the arms of the Lord, now."

Sobbing, Bridgette nodded. "He had such a difficult life."

With a cringe, Mike made no effort to comfort his mother. The Reverend moved to stand in front of Mike but locked his gaze on Jason. "It was good of you to come to comfort Mike and his mother in their time of grief."

Jason brought his other hand to Mike's shoulder. "I'm *always* here for Mike," he said through gritted teeth and a forced smile.

With barely a glance to Mike, McCauley moved away. "I'm sorry for your loss."

Bridgette rose, dabbing at her eyes with a tissue. "Mikey, come stand by the casket with me."

They stepped forward to the raised coffin draped in a large spray of lilies and roses, and his mother took his hand. "I hoped Alan and Craig would've come."

"Neither of them was able to take the time off of work, but they send their sympathies." He turned his attention to the casket, in many ways still not quite believing his brother lay inside.

Bridgette placed a red rose at the top of the casket and released Mike's hand, turning away. "Let's go. The family is going to the Barbeque Pit for lunch." She shot him a sideways glance. "You didn't go vegetarian or something in

Seattle, did you?"

With a chuckle, Mike shook his head. "I still love ribs."

Nodding, she gave him a hug. "Good."

Jason joined them, and Mike and his mother made their way among the raised stones. A large, grey obelisk rose from the ground in front of them with an engraved S near the top.

Mike paused, reading the inscription. *Here lies Deloris Rae Hobbs, wife of Marcus Schillerman, aged 92 years, 3 months, 14 days. Beloved mother and grandmother.* Painful emotion welled up in Mike for his grandmother. Her loss was much harder to come to terms with than his brother's.

"She didn't suffer. Just died in her sleep." Bridgette touched her hand to the stone. "She liked to get your calls, and she understood why you didn't come back."

Unsure what he should say, Mike stared at the monument.

Jessica and Kevin joined them, nodding at the stone. "We really appreciated how Alan and Craig put in for the funeral. Mom adored them."

"It's really nice." Mike slipped his phone from his pocket and snapped a picture of it, texting the image to his cousin.

"They sent us most of the money to pay for it, so I thought we should get a standing monument instead of the flat one we got dad." She stared at the grave of her father. "I'm sure you don't remember him, Mike, but he was a real shit."

"Alan's told me a few stories." Mike had been shocked at story after story of selfish lies and the daughter who'd come to light after his death. Alan made no attempt to sugar-coat the tales or hide his disdain for his uncle.

The sisters stared at each other before Bridgette looked at her son. "He doesn't know even half of what went on."

Jessica cleared her throat. "Well, let's go get some lunch. You can tell us all about your life in Seattle, and we can have a chance to get to know Jason."

CHAPTER TWENTY

A LAN WAVED WHEN they strode through the security door at SeaTac Airport. Jason hung back, allowing Mike to hurry to his cousin and gave him a hug. Chuckling, he watched Mike dig into his carry-on and hand Alan the box his mother had given to him at the funeral.

Joining his lover, Jason rolled his eyes. "He's been dying to know what's in that box since his mother gave it to him."

With a shrug, Mike grinned. "She was so mysterious about it."

"Do you have any other luggage?" Alan scanned the box, turning it over in his hand.

"No, just what we have with us." Mike glanced at Jason. "Though you'll be receiving several deliveries in about a week."

Looking up from the box, Alan met his gaze. "Oh?"

"Mom moved in with Jessica and Kevin, and I had to take what I wanted from the house." Mike gave a sheepish frown to his cousin. "Hope you don't mind."

Alan shrugged. "Not at all, unless you left behind any family stuff."

Mike patted his shoulder. "Don't worry. I made sure I got what she was willing to give me. Are you going to open the box?"

"Okay, mister impatient." Alan pulled away the twine and opened the box. A small, gold locket and a ring were wrapped in a folded piece of paper. "Holy shit, it's Great Grandma's ring."

Looking between the gaping cousins, Jason frowned. "What's the significance?"

Wide-eyed, Mike ripped his gaze from the pieces of jewelry. "Mom stole the ring. What's the locket?"

Alan shrugged and unfolded the paper. "Whoa."

Trying to see the writing, Mike crowded against his cousin. "What?"

With a shake of his head, Alan pocketed the two pieces of jewelry. "Um, let's head to the garage. Want to get something to eat?"

Mike nodded and craned his neck to see the loopy scrawl on the note. "Sure, but what's the locket?"

"When we get to the restaurant." After handing the paper to Jason, Alan led the way across the sky bridge and into the parking garage. He paid for the parking and continued to the silver sedan on the fifth level.

Jason had a good idea that Alan was torturing his younger cousin by not telling him about the two family heirlooms. Several times before they left Wisconsin, he had to admonish Mike to leave the package wrapped. Now, he had a good chuckle at Mike's expense.

They stood outside the car, and Alan unlocked the trunk. "What sounds good for dinner?"

Mike hefted his backpack into the car. "Let's get a burger at the pub."

Grinning, Jason deposited his bag next to his fiancé's. "Didn't you get enough fries in Wisconsin?"

With a sharp turn of his head, Mike stared at Jason.

"Are there *ever* enough fries?"

Alan pulled open the car door. "Not for you. The pub sounds good to me. Jason?"

"Sure. A burger would hit the spot." He winked at Alan. "And so would a beer."

They piled into Alan's car, and he drove out of the parking garage. "So, what did you think of Mike's family?"

With a glance over his shoulder to the back seat, Jason met Mike's gaze before answering. "Certainly an interesting experience. I didn't sock his Uncle Jim on the nose, but then he didn't come anywhere near us after Bridgette threatened him."

Chuckling, Alan glanced in the rearview mirror at Mike. "Threatened him?"

Mike grabbed the backs of the seats and pulled himself forward. "Yeah, I was going to ask you about that. Any idea what mom has over Uncle Jim?"

Frowning, Alan stared at the road. "Could be any number of things. Cousin Jim is a real shit, nearly as bad as his dad. When he met Jessica's husband, Kevin broke his nose. Laid him out flat." A small grin played across his lips. "I think that's the main reason she married him."

With a laugh, Mike released the seats and settled back. "What did he say? I can't imagine Uncle Kevin hitting anyone."

"Kevin has an engineering degree and, as you found out, your family doesn't really value education. I'm not sure Jessica was really all that hot on him." Alan maneuvered the car along the exit from I-5 and onto the West Seattle Bridge then continued. "Jim made some comment about his sister never marrying some college sissy."

"Wow." Jason shook his head. "What a dope."

"I don't really know what Bridgette has on him, but you can bet Jessica is in on it, too." They descended from the high rise of the bridge and curved up the small hill next to the steel mill.

Mike chuckled. "Yeah, they were thick as thieves over whatever it was, and Jim sat like an obedient dog on the couch until he couldn't take anymore."

With a full laugh, Alan turned briefly to Jason. "I'm glad you got to see that."

Jason smiled, but said nothing. His thoughts returned to Reverend McCauley and the bombshell Mike dropped about the pastor's abusive ways toward his young parishioners. He'd honored Mike's request not to take the bastard down during the funeral, but he wasn't ready to drop the matter.

The pub came into view, and Jason pulled his attention back to his fiancé and Alan. Mike shot out of the car as soon as Alan parked, and he headed to the front door of the restaurant. Jason strolled along the sidewalk with Alan and handed him the piece of paper from Bridgette's surprise gift.

"Thanks," Alan said. "I'll read it to both of you after we order."

They entered the pub and found Mike waving from one of the far booths. The wooden floor squeaked under Jason's feet as they passed several tables full of chatting couples and trios. Jason slid in next to Mike, giving his leg a squeeze while Alan took the seat across from them.

One of the waitresses approached the table with an iced tea and a lemonade. "Hi guys. I assume Mike is up for his usual." She placed the lemonade in front of Mike. "Tea, Alan?"

He nodded. "Sure, sounds good, Vicky."

She set the glass onto the table and turned to Jason. "Can I get you something to drink, hun?"

Jason scanned the beer list. "Yeah, I'll take a Manny's with a slice of lemon."

"Coming right up." She hurried away.

Alan spread the note open. "Ready to hear what your mother wrote?"

Mike sat straight and folded his hands on the table. "Go for it."

Alan read from the paper.

"*Dear Alan, I know you found out about Great Grandma's ring, and I've had a long time to think about taking it. I don't want any of the family here to have it, so I'm giving it to you. You'll know who to give it to. Just please don't say where it came from.*"
Alan glanced at Mike. "At least she came clean."

"Keep going," Mike pressed.

Placing a hand on Mike's leg, Jason could feel the tense muscles. He rubbed along the denim, trying to calm his fiancé. "Doing okay, baby?"

"I'm fine," Mike replied, still tense and on the edge of his seat.

Alan continued to read.

"*The locket belonged to old Granny Astor, great grandpa's grandmother. Auntie Geraldine gave it to me (I swear), and I don't think anyone here would care for it like you would.*"

Digging into his pocket, Alan retrieved the locket and

clicked open the clasp. A simple gold ring dropped out and rolled across the table. Jason snagged it before it bounced onto the floor.

Mike nodded at Jason's hand. "Nice catch."

>*"Inside is a ring. Geraldine told me it was Granny's wedding ring from her first husband. Must be from the 1870's."*

"Wow, what a treasure." Jason carefully handed the ring back to Alan. "Nice of her to give it to you."

Alan frowned. "I suppose the move got her thinking about things. At least Jim's girl didn't get it. The locket and both rings would be at the nearest pawn shop."

Reaching out his hand, Mike took the locket from Alan and turned it over. Jason wrapped an arm around Mike and examined the antique. Gold leaves interlaced around the outside while two painted portraits stared out at him.

Mike glanced up at his cousin. "Who are they?"

Alan leaned across the table. "That's a young Granny Astor and her husband John Taylor. He died in 1885, and they were married in 1873, so I would guess this was a wedding gift."

With a grin, Mike handed the locket back. "I can't believe you remember all those dates."

Shrugging, Alan sipped his iced tea. "I've been working on the family history a long time."

"Who are you going to give this to?" Mike pressed.

Alan folded the note and slipped it into his pocket. "Probably one of our Astor cousins in California. They didn't get anything when Great Grandma died. I'm surprised these two things didn't end up in Oklahoma with my aunt." He frowned as he lifted the menu. "She raided the family heirlooms and walked away with most of them before anyone else had a chance."

Mike frowned, and Jason saw the utter disdain in his expression. "Too bad you couldn't stop her."

Peering over his menu, Alan's brow furrowed. "I was still cooking inside Mom's tummy. Great Grandma died six months before I was born." He peered across the menu at Mike and Jason. "None of her kids or grandkids care squat about the family, so I'll probably end up with everything anyway."

Jason's thoughts turned to his mother and all the stories she'd told about their family heirlooms going up in flames. "You're lucky to have this stuff. Everything was destroyed in my family when the Allies bombed Hamburg. My grandma and her parents barely got out of the house before the bomb exploded. My great grandfather had just pulled the door to the shelter shut."

Returning with Jason's beer, Vicky slid the glass in front of him and pulled out her pad. "What's for dinner, boys?"

"Double Trouble Burger with no lettuce, onions, or tomatoes." Mike handed her the menu.

"Your standing order. Fries and extra tartar sauce." With a grin she turned to Jason. "How about you?"

Jason took a final glance at the menu. "Italian club, with a salad."

"Dressing?"

"Vinegar and olive oil if you got it."

She nodded. "Yup. Alan?"

"I'll do the smoked turkey, bacon, and Swiss sandwich, and I'll also take the salad instead of fries." He also handed her the menu, and she hurried away.

Alan folded his hands on the table. "So, a month before the big day."

Warmth flooded Jason as Mike snuggled against him. "Hard to believe it's coming so soon."

Mike craned his neck to stare at Jason. "So soon? I've been waiting for three years."

Slinging an arm around his waist, Jason gave Mike a squeeze. "And worth every minute." He gave his fiancé a kiss on the top of his head. Joy filled him as he held Mike close.

With a roll of his eyes, Alan settled back against the wall of the booth. "That's so sweet I could get a toothache."

Laughing, Mike rested his head against Jason's shoulder. "Just like you and Craig did to me when I moved here. Not that I minded. It was cute that you didn't want to kiss in front of me."

Jason raised an eyebrow. "Were you afraid of corrupting him?"

Snorting, Alan took a sip of his tea. "Hardly. We were more worried about the commentary. Technique pointers, grading the intensity." His gaze narrowed at his cousin. "And the incessant ooo-ing and aw-ing."

"I was offering encouragement," Mike proclaimed. "Besides, you got back at me." He shuddered. "All that tickling."

A smile played across Jason's lips. He clamped Mike against his body and used his other hand to lightly play across his ribs. Mike stiffened in his arms, squeaking in protest while he struggled against the onslaught.

"Like this?" Jason stared at Alan while he continued

his torture.

Alan leaned forward. "Nah, there's a spot…"

Mike wrenched himself free of Jason's restraining arm. "No, Alan! Don't you dare tell him."

With a single lunge, Jason wrapped his arms around Mike again, kissing his neck. "I already know where." Jason zeroed in on the sensitive spot where the collarbone met the neck. "Could it be *here*?"

Mike stiffened when Jason dug a finger into the depression of the skin and wiggled. Sinking into the seat and squealing like a little girl, Mike slid along the bench. Jason caught him before he could slide off and released his lover from his torture.

Gasping for air, Mike leveled a glare at his cousin. "Traitor."

Alan exploded into laughter. "My lips were sealed. He found the spot on his own."

With a shake of his head, Jason pulled Mike next to him. "It's okay, baby. If you're good, maybe I'll let you in on some of my more sensitive spots."

"Don't tell me," Mike huffed. "I want to find them for myself."

"HOW ARE YOU doing on the old saying?" Kelly buzzed around Mike, styling his hair.

Attempting to quell his nerves, he recounted the list. "Something old, Granny Astor's locket around my neck. Something new, the pin on my kilt." He fingered the small, pewter sword with the thistle ring. "Borrowed, the sporran."

"And something blue?" She snipped at his eyebrows.

"My class ring. Might as well get some use out of it." The large fake sapphire nestled into a white gold setting, the insignia of his high school etched into a small coat of arms in the center of the stone.

She brushed away the excess hair and whipped the yellow plastic cape from his body. "You're finished. Now get the rest of your kilt on before Jason gets here."

He stood on shaking legs and clutched the kilt pin. "I don't know why I'm so nervous."

The door burst open, and his mother bustled into the room. "How are you doing, honey?"

Scrambling to the small sofa, he lifted the kilt to shield his underwear. "Mom! You could have knocked. For goodness sake, shut the door."

"Oh, sorry, Mikey." She kicked the door with her stiletto heel and barreled past Kelly. Plopping on the seat next to him, she wrapped her arms around him and pulled him to her breast. "I'm so proud you're marrying that wonderful man."

Mike pulled away, standing again to get away from her smothering grip. "Thanks, mom." He wrapped the woolen kilt around his waist and shoved the leather belt through the small slit in the fabric and into the buckle.

With a whistle, his mother lifted the kilt. "Good, you keep that underwear on until you get the ring."

Kelly exploded into laughter. "That's what I keep telling him."

Mike batted her hands away and strode to the mirror where his jacket hung. He buttoned the cufflinks at his wrists and slipped into the black dress jacket with several metal buttons, each with a thistle etched into the center.

Turning to face them, Mike spread his hands. "Well,

how do I look?"

Both women nodded their approval.

The room filled with a Latin beat, and Bridgette fumbled for her phone. "It's your aunt." She flipped open the phone and pressed a button. "Hello?" She listened intently for a moment, and her face fell. "Holy shit."

"Looking good, Sweets." Emily buzzed around Jason, tugging at his uniform jacket and helping him with the brass buttons. "You ready for this?"

"Of course, he is." Fred Collier grinned from a chair in the corner, his dress uniform freshly cleaned and buttons shiny. "Make sure the cording hangs correctly. Can't have him looking like a slob."

Jason stood in front of the mirror and adjusted the gold cords over his shoulder. "Better?"

"Much." Fred shook his head with a grin. "I can't believe this day is finally here. What's it been? Three years?"

"Yeah, about that." Jason donned his hat and turned to face them. "I'm ready."

The door opened, and Mike stood at the threshold with a furrowed brow and an angry glare. "I need to have a word with you."

Emily and Fred glanced at each other.

"Alone, if you two don't mind." Though Mike made a good attempt to keep his tone even, Jason could tell Mike wasn't happy. The warmth drained from his face, and he struggled to think of what he might have done to infuriate his partner on their wedding day.

Fred stood and patted Jason on the shoulder. "Good

luck." He took another look at Mike. "Call Tomlinson if you need backup."

Emily and Fred left the room.

Mike stepped inside and closed the door. "When were you going to tell me?"

He wracked his brain to figure out what Mike could possibly mean. "Tell you what?"

Pulling his cell from the sporran at his waist, Mike tapped angrily at the glass and held the phone for Jason to see. A picture of Reverend McCauley filled the screen, the preacher's face drawn and tired. Two Wisconsin State Troopers led him away from the front of his church.

Large block letters blared the headline above the photo: *Wisconsin Preacher Arrested for Child Abuse and Pornography*.

"Oh." Jason faced his soon-to-be husband, wishing the news had broken even a day later. "I couldn't let it go. He's a pedophile. Maybe you were willing, but I bet he forced himself on a lot of kids."

Mike threw the phone back into his sporran. "I trusted you to respect my wishes and not go after him. You even *said* you wouldn't." Mike's temper built, and his face turned red. "Jason, what the hell were you thinking? My mom's freaking out right now. She demanded to know if I was one of the kids he fucked around with."

He hadn't considered Bridgette's reaction when he'd set the Reverend's downfall in motion. Keeping his voice calm, he led Mike to the chair Fred had vacated. After Mike sat, Jason knelt in front of him and took his hand.

"I had no intention of hurting you or your family. I didn't say anything about you when I had Paul call the Wisconsin AG's office." He held his lover's gaze. "I had a responsibility to stop him."

Anger blazed in Mike's eyes. "That's not the point. This is about trust. You did this behind my back, and it directly affected me and my family. The absolute last thing I wanted at our wedding was my mother's drama. She put two and two together from my reaction at the funeral home, and I had to fess up that the bastard and I had messed around."

He gripped Mike's hand tighter, terrified he'd messed up their relationship again. "I'm sorry. I didn't realize how this would hit you." Panic welled up at the fear of losing Mike. "How can I make this up to you?"

Mike took a breath and closed his eyes for a moment. With a heavy sigh, he returned his gaze to Jason. "You'll never keep things from me. If our relationship is going to work—if our *marriage* is going to work—you need to be completely honest and open."

"I promise this won't happen again." He kissed Mike's hands and held them to the side of his face.

"We're marrying for life," Mike continued, his tone stern. "I don't believe in divorce, so I have to be sure things will work out." His voice softened, and his hands cupped Jason's cheeks. "I need to be able to tell you my deepest, darkest secrets and trust you to keep them and not act on them if I ask you not to."

Jason frowned. "There's not more like this are there?"

With a shake of his head, Mike retracted his hand. "No, but if there were, you'd need to respect how I deal with my problems."

"Is your mom angry with me?" The thought of Bridgette exploding at him in front of everyone turned his stomach into knots.

"Not at you. I doubt she realized who outed the preacher. She's ready to rip his balls off." Mike shook his head. "I'm the only one who figured it out."

"I understand." Jason stood shakily, holding out his hand. "Do you still want to go through with this, or do you want to postpone?"

Mike took the hand and pulled himself up. "I still want to marry you."

Jason's shoulders relaxed, and he embraced his fiancé. "Thank goodness. I'll never give you reason to doubt me again."

The floorboards creaked outside the room, making both men whip their heads to stare at the door. Mike held a finger to his lips and crept to the door. He grabbed the handle and yanked it open.

Five startled people leapt back. Alan and Bridgette bumped into each other while Emily, Kelly, and Fred stared with wide eyes into the room.

Kelly bit her lip. "Uh, we were just…"

"Listening in. I know." Mike stood with his arms crossed.

Alan tentatively stepped forward. "Is everything okay?"

With a smile at Jason, Mike nodded. "Yeah, we're all right."

Bridgette held a hand to her forehead. "Thank God."

Frowning, Mike shook his head. "Not at the moment, thank you."

ANXIETY CLAWED AT Mike as he followed the row of police officers led by Emily, each escorting Kelly, Isaac, and Craig.

Alan stepped alongside him and murmured in his ear. "Last chance to turn and run."

With a chuckle, Mike continued forward. "Not on your life."

Jason stood at the front of the small chapel. The afternoon sun shone through the stained glass, casting color throughout the room. The dashing officer stood at attention, his nerves on clear display.

Behind Mike, a bagpiper dressed in full Highland regalia played a wedding march. Fred and Paul peeled off from the procession to form a line next to Jason and Emily while the other officers took their seats in the front row. Kelly, Isaac, and Craig stood at the other side of the altar, leaving a space. Alan led Mike to the step.

The officiant smiled, her red hair falling around her shoulders. "Who gives this man?"

Stepping forward, Bridgette dabbed her eyes and joined Mike and Alan. With a wink, his cousin grinned. "His mother and I do."

The wedding party chuckled, and Bridgette sobbed. "I'm so happy for you." She gave him a quick hug and hurried back to her seat.

Mike stepped to Jason's side and grasped his hand. Alan stood in his place next to Craig in the line of groomsmen and shot him a grin.

The minister continued. "Dearly beloved, we are gathered here to join Jason and Michael together in the bond of marriage." She turned to Jason. "Do you take Michael to be your husband, in good times and bad, to have and hold, in sickness and in health, until death parts you?"

Without hesitation, Jason replied in a clear and calm voice. "Yes, I do."

The gaze of the minister turned to Mike. "And Michael, do you take Jason to be your husband, in good times and bad, to have and hold, in sickness and health, until death parts you?"

He stared into Jason's eyes. "I do."

Jason's face lit up in a huge smile. He squeezed Mike's hand and he mouthed the words *I love you.*

"Michael asked to be first to say his vows."

His hand shook as he reached into the inside pocket of his jacket, retrieving the notecard he'd written out the night before. He fought down his nerves, meeting Jason's gaze for a moment and finding reassurance in the happy smile and warmth in his fiancé's eyes.

"Jason, our meeting was a total accident, pure serendipity. In the last four years, we've had our ups and downs, but I've grown to love you so much I can't imagine a day without you. I'm looking forward to our life together."

Kelly stepped forward and handed him the ring they'd chosen for Jason. The gold and diamonds glittered in the light of the chapel.

Mike placed the ring on Jason's finger. "I give you this ring, the symbol of my love and devotion to you for the rest of my life." His nerves calmed, and he returned the notecard to his pocket.

Turning to Emily, Jason accepted the ring from her and took Mike's hand. "Being with you has shown me how much I could love someone. I promise to make our life together as happy as possible and pledge to support and protect you until the day I die."

Blinking through tears of happiness and love, Mike held Jason's gaze.

Jason placed the ring on Mike's finger. "I give you this

ring as the symbol of my undying love and devotion." Once the ring was in place, Jason intertwined his fingers with Mike's, and they turned to face the minister.

Mike sniffled, a tear running down his cheek.

By the authority of the State of Washington and in the presence of these witnesses, I now pronounce you married." She winked at Jason. "Give him a kiss."

The witnesses chuckled as the two men faced each other. Before Mike knew what happened, Jason grabbed him and pressed their lips together, dipping him. Mike wrapped his arms around his new husband, savoring their connection.

The room erupted into cheers and applause. Jason gave Mike a little tug to get him to standing again. Warmth rushed to Mike's face, but a grin plastered itself onto his lips.

With a glance at his husband, Mike nodded. They stepped off the landing and down to the main floor. The bagpiper played *Scotland the Brave*, leading them down the aisle and out of the chapel into the bright sunshine.

Rice rained onto them as they ran for the limo parked in front of the chapel. Jason held the door while Mike climbed in, placing a hand under the plaits of his kilt. The cool of the upholstery on the seats felt a good contrast to the warm chapel and the hot day outside.

Jason scampered into the limo and slammed the door shut. After the driver pulled away, he slung an arm around Mike. "We're finally married."

Grinning, Mike rested his head on Jason's shoulder. "At last."

"I got you a wedding present."

Mike shifted to gaze at Jason, excitement filling him.

"Oh? What is it?"

Slipping his hand into his uniform jacket pocket, Jason fished out a pair of keys. "We met because someone stole your truck, so I bought you a new one."

"Really?" Mike stared at the keys.

"Yup. You're driving us home tonight." He glanced down Mike's legs with a leer. "You can drive in that kilt, right?"

"Damned right I can." Mike grinned and inched his kilt up his leg. "You might even get a show now that we we're married. The underwear is coming off when we get to the reception."

Jason's hand slid up his thigh and under the plaited wool. "Why wait?"

Mike brought his legs together and lifted his butt while Jason inched the briefs down. His fingers tickled along the hairs on the inside of his thigh. Giggling, Mike lifted his feet from the floor, and Jason maneuvered the fabric over his shoes.

Holding the underwear in front of him, Jason wriggled his eyebrows at Mike. "Mission accomplished. I can't wait to have you in your new rig."

The limo pulled up to the reception hall. Parked out front, a small, blue truck, similar to his old one but without all the rust, glistened in the late afternoon sun. A massive white bow adorned the top with ribbon running into the cab. *Just Married* in white letters covered the rear window.

Jason hurried around the limo to Mike's door and opened it. He led him to the driver's side of the truck and opened the door. Inside, a card sat on the seat. Mike used the key to open the envelope.

My dearest Mike,

May this truck drive many miles.

With all my love as we start our life together.

Jason

Mike threw his arms around Jason. "Thank you so much. Let's take a road trip after our honeymoon."

Epilogue

Ten years later.

MIKE PULLED INTO the driveway of their Queen Anne house, shifting his truck into park and turning off the engine. Grabbing the bouquet of roses from the passenger seat, he jumped out and slammed the door.

As he approached the house, Jason opened the front door. "Hey, baby, how was your day?"

Thrusting the flowers at his husband, Mike grinned. "It just got a whole lot better seeing you. Happy anniversary."

"Aw, thanks." Jason took the flowers and grabbed Mike around the waist, pulling him in for a kiss.

After lingering a moment in their embrace, Mike pulled back and looked into Jason's eyes. "Can I take you to dinner?"

With an arm still wrapped around Mike, Jason led him into the house. "As nice as that sounds, I cooked us an anniversary supper. Hope that's okay with you."

The scent of steak and potatoes filled the house as they moved down the hallway. Mike grinned, staring at the table. His grandmother's china adorned the table with the silver his aunt had given them as a wedding present. A crystal wine goblet from the set Emily and Seb had given them five years ago sat at both place settings while an open bottle of red wine stood next to a lit candelabra.

Taking in the table, Mike filled with warmth at the efforts Jason had gone to for their anniversary dinner. "Wow, the table looks beautiful."

Jason guided Mike to his chair and pulled it out for him. "May I invite you to sit down, sir?" He pushed in the chair as Mike sat and unfolded a napkin, draping the cloth over Mike's lap. After a quick kiss on the cheek, Jason hurried into the kitchen with the roses.

A ding from his cell caught his attention, and he pulled the phone from his pocket. The message from his mother lit up the screen. *Happy Anniversary to my wonderful sons.*

Jason returned, placing a crystal vase holding the roses on the sideboard and a large serving platter with two steaks in the center of the table.

Turning the cell toward his husband, Mike showed him the text. "Nice of her to remember."

"Alan and Craig each sent me a note today." He hurried back into the kitchen and returned a moment later with the mashed potatoes, gravy boat, and a plate of steamed broccoli.

Eyeing all the food, Mike shook his head. "Who else did you invite?"

With a chuckle, Jason took his seat at the table. "Like you couldn't eat the whole bowl of mashed potatoes yourself."

"True." He shoveled a huge spoonful of potatoes onto his plate and snagged one of the steaks. "This looks delicious."

Jason poured a glass of wine for Mike. "How did your

day go?"

"Busy. I was trying to finish up before our trip. My boss said she's green with envy and asked why she couldn't go along in one of our suitcases." Envisioning his six-foot boss cramming herself into a backpack made Mike laugh. "I'm not sure how we'd explain that to customs."

"It's bad enough we can't take Ethan," Jason said, lifting the other steak onto his plate.

"Where is he by the way?" Their son had come along five years into their marriage. Kelly had agreed to have a kid for them, and so Mike now had a son.

"Aunt Craig and Uncle Alan's." Jason wriggled his eyebrows with a smirk. "All night."

"That Alan always knows the perfect gift to give." He cut into his steak and took a bite. The warm beef nearly melted in his mouth. "You are such an excellent chef."

"Maybe that can be part of my next career." Jason poured gravy onto his potatoes. "Speaking of which, I know we discussed me retiring from SPD and trying something else."

Mike set his fork and knife down and lifted his wine glass. "Have you made a decision about what you'd want to do?" He took a sip, enjoying how the tannins interacted with the flavor of the steak.

"I was thinking of taking classes at South Seattle," Jason replied, swirling the deep purple liquid in his goblet. "Their wine program looks like a lot of fun."

With a grin, Mike nodded. "I like the idea of you making your own wine instead of being out on patrol."

Jason shrugged. "I'm getting a little old to be pounding the pavement. Better to pound grapes."

Rolling his eyes, Mike took another sip of his wine.

"Forty-six isn't old. I have more gray hair than you."

"So says the thirty-eight-year-old. Do you think I should sign up for classes after we get back from Reykjavik?" Jason took a bite of his steak.

"Definitely." Mike raised his wine glass toward his husband. "Here's to new beginnings."

Jason clinked their glasses together, and they both took a sip.

After returning the glass to the table, Jason dug in his pocket and produced a small box. He handed it across to Mike. "Happy anniversary."

Mike filled with excitement as he took the gift. "What is it?"

Chuckling, Jason shook his head. "You always ask that when I give you something."

"And you never tell me." Mike lifted the lid and pulled away a layer of cotton. Four small studs and two large cufflinks caught the light and sparkled. Each was inset with a mermaid holding a diamond.

"I know you often wear a tuxedo for the formal fundraisers at your job, and I thought these would be perfect." Jason nibbled the corner of his lip. "I had them made for you."

Mike examined the carving closer. The mermaids were male. "Mermen."

"Actually, they're male sirens. You always call to me, whether we're together or apart." He grinned. "But unlike the sirens in the stories, you never steer me toward the rocks." Reaching across the table, he took Mike's hand. "I love you more each day and can hardly believe we've already been married a decade."

"I love you, too." Mike rubbed his thumb along the

palm of Jason's hand. "Let's hurry and finish this wonderful dinner. Then I'll give you your present and call you upstairs for a night of wild lovemaking since we have the place all to ourselves."

With a final squeeze, Jason released his hand and raised his glass. "To ten more years of passionate lovemaking."

Mike laughed. "I'll drink to that."

Did you enjoy *The Officer's Siren*?
If so, check out *Past Secrets Present Danger*,
Book Two of the Rain City Tales.

Also by Brent Archer

Rain City Tales
The Officer's Siren (Book 1)
Past Secrets Present Danger (Book 2)
I'm Yours (Book 3)
The Wedding Weekend (Book 4)
Mitch's Men (Book 4.5)
Saving Parker (Book 5)
Song of Salvation (Book 6)
Memories of Coromandel (Book 7)
Blaze of Cortez (Book 8) – Coming in 2024

Black Rock Cult Series
Rediscovering Todd (Book 1)
Hiding Hayden (Book 2) – Coming in 2024
Dragging Marshall (Book 3) – Coming in 2025

Stand-Alone Stories
Throuple Honey

ABOUT THE AUTHOR

Brent Archer was born in Spokane, Washington, and lived there most of his adolescent life. At 18, he left for Seattle to attend the University of Washington for Electrical Engineering. Quickly, it became apparent that he wasn't wired for the required science and differential equation classes, and so he switched his major to International Studies with a minor in History. After graduation, he pursued an acting career in musical theater and dance. Once thirty hit, however, he decided to focus on numbers, getting a certificate in accounting, and became the Financial Controller of a non-profit arts and music organization.

Though writing most of his life, he never thought to submit his work for publication. In 2012, he visited his cousin Delilah Devlin in Arkansas, and she prodded him to write a story and submit it. So, he did, and it sold right away. With the encouragement of Delilah, his other writing cousin Elle James, and his husband, Brent embarked on a writing career. He's loving the journey, finding inspiration and a story everywhere he goes, whether it be the local coffee shop, driving through each of the United States, or riding the train to explore the world.